Love *and*
BASKETBALL

J. L. Rose

Good2Go Publishing

UF
Rose

Love and Basketball
Written by J. L. Rose
Cover Design: Davida Baldwin
Typesetter: Mychea
ISBN: 9781947340220
Copyright © 2018 Good2Go Publishing
Published 2018 by Good2Go Publishing
7311 W. Glass Lane • Laveen, AZ 85339
www.good2gopublishing.com
https://twitter.com/good2gobooks
G2G@good2gopublishing.com
www.facebook.com/good2gopublishing
www.instagram.com/good2gopublishing

Acknowledgments

To my heavenly Father first. I gotta show my love to You because You first loved me! Also, to my boy Jerrod Adams. Good looking out on the information when I needed it. We Dade County 4 Life, my dude!

If I didn't mention you, look for it in the next book coming real soon. It's all love! Peace!

Dedications

To my fans—and the loyalty and love each and every one of you keeps showing. One love!

Prologue

Anthony hung up the phone after finding out that one of the four other guys on the team he put together to play in this year's Bigfoot Hoops Tournament was no longer playing. He drove home and wondered what the hell he was going to do to fill the open spot on the team before it was time to leave for the tournament.

After hearing his cell phone begin to ring in his lap, Anthony started to ignore it, but he went ahead and answered it after seeing his sister was calling.

"Yeah, Steffaine! What's up?"

"What's good, Cuzo?"

Anthony was confused for a brief moment but smiled after recognizing the voice.

"Sean, that you, nigga?" he asked.

"There's only one me, fam! What's really good?"

"Oh shit!" Anthony yelled, laughing after realizing who was on the phone. "Yo, where the fuck you at, Cuz?"

"He at the house, Anthony!" Steffaine spoke up,

also on the line.

"Wait!" Anthony said in confusion. "Sean, you at my momma's house or at—?"

"I'm in Brooklyn at my mom's house, Cuzo!" TaSean interrupted. "Me and my pops's new wife wasn't getting along, so I went back to my mom's just until I get my paper up and find a spot of my own!"

"Yo, we may be able to help each other, Cuz!" Anthony told TaSean. "You still doing ya thang on the b-ball court, right?"

"No doubt! That's what I do, Cuzo! But you already know that!"

"Perfect!" Anthony stated, smirking even harder.

He first explained to his cousin about the tournament in Orlando that was starting in two weeks. But he then got into telling TaSean about one of his guys on the team suddenly quitting.

"So, basically, you need a fill-in, and you're asking me to take the spot for you, right?" TaSean inquired once his cousin was finished explaining.

"The winning team gets $25,000 and is crowned

the Bigfoot Hoops champions," Anthony explained to his cousin.

"You said twenty-five grand, huh?" TaSean repeated before he asked, "So, when we supposed to leave for Orlando?"

Chapter 1

Four days later . . .

TaSean found the address he was looking for ten minutes after arriving in Miami-Dade County. He slowed his 2016-model Cadillac Escalade in front of a royal-blue and white house that had a GMC Denali and a Cadillac CTS-V parked in front. He then turned the truck into a parking space.

After shutting off the engine, TaSean opened the driver's door, only to hear his name screamed out loud. He looked back into the truck and across to the passenger side window to see his cousin Steffaine take off from the porch while her brother, Anthony, stood on the porch with a big smile on his face.

TaSean got the driver's door shut and made it around to the front end of the Escalade, just as Steffaine jumped onto him and wrapped her arms around his neck. He had to catch his balance as he held his cousin mid-air against him.

"Oh my God!" Steffaine cried as she leaned back

to look at her cousin.

She stepped back once TaSean put her down and looked over his tall, lean, and muscular, toned body.

"Look at you, TaSean! You done got fine as hell, boy!"

"And you still look like road kill!" Anthony told his sister as he walked up.

"Shut up!" Steffaine told her brother after shoving him.

Anthony laughed as he and TaSean embraced each other. Anthony then stepped back and looked over his athletically built cousin who stood six foot five and weighed 220 pounds.

"I see you done put on some size since the last time I seen ya ass!"

"I was thinking the same thing about you!" TaSean told Anthony, seeing his cousin's six-foot-seven, 232-pound frame. He was even bigger muscle-wise than when he saw him a few years ago.

"What's up with Auntie Pat?" TaSean asked as he and his cousins started walking back to the porch. "Where she at?"

"She went somewhere with Eddie," Steffaine told him as she led the way into the house.

Once they were inside, and he dropped onto the sofa with Steffaine beside him, TaSean asked about Eddie. He wanted to know who he was.

"Dude's name is really Edward," Anthony said, sitting across from the two of them on a chair. "My mom's supposedly seeing homeboy."

"What good with him?" TaSean asked, sitting forward on the sofa and staring at Anthony. "Dude cool or what?"

"Boy, relax!" Steffaine said, grabbing TaSean's arm and pulling him back into the sofa. "Eddie's okay, TaSean. And he treats my momma good."

After hearing Steffaine's comments, TaSean looked over at Anthony for the okay. He relaxed when he saw his cousin nod in approval.

"So, what up, Ant?" TaSean asked his cousin. "What time we leaving?"

"Everybody's meeting here at 8:00 p.m., and we leaving from here!" Anthony told TaSean just as they heard a car horn being blown from outside.

Anthony and TaSean both stood up immediately.

"That's Momma and Eddie!" Steffaine announced, looking out the window.

TaSean followed Anthony outside and stepped onto the porch just as Anthony called out to his mother. TaSean jogged over to his Auntie Patricia as she was turning around.

"What in the—?" Patricia got out before she was snatched up off her feet.

She screamed at first, until she realized whose arms she was in.

"TaSean!" Patricia cried out happily, throwing her arms around her nephew's neck and hugging him tight.

"Hey, gorgeous!" TaSean said with a smile as he set his auntie back onto her feet.

"Oh my God!" Patricia said in complete surprise as she stepped back and looked over her extremely handsome nephew. "TaSean, look at you, boy! You're almost as tall as Anthony, and what's those things in your ears, boy? When you start wearing earrings, TaSean?"

"It's been about two years now!" he answered, but then looked past his auntie to the muscular, dark brown guy who stood behind her. "Who's that, Auntie?"

Patricia looked behind her at Edward and then back at TaSean. She could see the protective look in his handsome eyes.

She smiled and said, "TaSean, calm down, baby. That's my friend Edward."

Patricia turned back to Edward and introduced the two men to one another.

"Eddie's what I go by," Edward told TaSean, holding out his hand to the young man.

Patricia waited and watched TaSean stand there, until she nudged him to shake Eddie's hand. "TaSean, please!"

Once he heard his auntie's plea, TaSean shook the older man's hand and said, "I'll be watching you, homeboy."

"Now I'll have two more sets watching me since Anthony already promised to keep his eyes on me as well!" Edward told the young man, holding TaSean's strong stare, for some reason instantly liking the boy.

* * *

Once the groceries were taken from Edward's car into the house, TaSean talked with his auntie on the sofa while Steffaine put everything away.

"How's your daddy doing, TaSean?" Patricia asked him, still surprised at how tall and handsome he had gotten.

"Pops is still Pops, Auntie!" TaSean told her, but then said, "He went and married Lucifer's daughter though!"

Patricia burst out laughing before she could catch herself. She then looked over at Edward to see him laughing as well.

"TaSean, don't call that woman that, boy!"

"I'm serious, Auntie!" TaSean told her. "Pops is married to the Antichrist!"

"Oh my God!" Patricia cried as she burst out laughing again as she slapped TaSean on his arm. "Boy, you need to stop!"

TaSean continued talking with his auntie and keeping her and her friend laughing until Anthony appeared from the back room with two duffel bags in each hand.

"Cuzo, what's up?" TaSean asked him. "It's about that time?"

"My boy Tim just called!" Anthony said as he stopped in front of the front door. "Everybody should be here in ten minutes."

TaSean turned back to his auntie after Anthony stepped outside, and asked her if she was coming to the tournament to watch them play.

"Anthony says the tournament is a four-day event," Patricia stated. "I'm going to try to make it up there by this Friday and catch as many games as I can before I need to get back home, sweetheart."

"That'll work!" TaSean told her, kissing her cheek before standing up, nodding over to Edward, and then walking out the door behind his cousin.

Chapter 2

TaSean met Tim Johnson, since he was the first to arrive. TaSean stood out in front of his Escalade talking with his six-foot-ten big man, just as a Lincoln Navigator pulled up. He was then introduced to Kyle, who stood six six, and Howard Green, who was six eleven.

TaSean smirked when he saw what he had to work with. He loved the whole twin-tower combo with Tim and the bigger man, Howard, who was built like Dwight Howard. TaSean looked at his cousin nodding his head in approval at what he was seeing so far.

"A'ight, fellas!" Anthony spoke up, getting everyone's attention. "We got a two-hour drive ahead of us, and I've already called ahead and made sure the hotel we're staying in has our rooms. Is there anything we're forgetting?"

After not receiving an answer back, Anthony told his team it was time to go. He then turned and walked over to TaSean's truck.

"Whoa!" TaSean said, seeing Anthony climbing up into the passenger seat of his Escalade. "I guess you telling me I'm driving, huh?"

"It's your ride!" Anthony stated with a grin as he shut the truck's passenger door.

"Yo, TaSean!"

"Call me Sean!" he told Kyle. "What's good though, son?"

"You mind if I roll with you and Anthony?" Kyle asked. "I can't deal with Howard and Tim arguing about every fucking thing."

"Yeah!" TaSean answered with a little laugh. "Come on, playboy!"

Once they were inside the Escalade, TaSean started up the truck to have Beanie Sigel and Jay-Z's "It's On" come through the Escalade's sound system. TaSean leaned back and relaxed in his seat as he pulled off from in front of his Auntie Patricia's house.

* * *

They made the two-hour drive and stopped only once, to pick up food, once Howard waved them down and told them he and Tim wanted to get something to eat. After they got back on the road, TaSean used his truck's navigation system and a little help from his cousin and Kyle and found the Best Western Hotel where the five of them were supposedly staying while in Orlando.

"I'ma grab our keys," Anthony announced as he was climbing out of the truck.

Once Anthony left, TaSean dug out his phone and kept his word. He sent a quick text message to his mother.

"So, Anthony say you used to play ball!" Kyle stated as he sat forward between the two front seats. "He say you used to be a beast on the court before you stopped playing for awhile."

"I did a'ight!" TaSean answered before asking, "You play before?"

"One year in college and all through high school."

"What position?"

"Shooting guard."

TaSean nodded his head in approval of what he

was hearing. He then looked up to see Anthony, Howard, and Tim coming back. He opened the driver's door and shut off the truck as Anthony and the twin towers walked up.

"This for you, Cuz," Anthony said, handing TaSean a card key and telling him what room he was in. He then turned to Kyle as he walked up, and did the same with him.

TaSean broke off from the others and grabbed his two duffel bags and his backpack. He then tossed the truck keys to Anthony for him to lock up the truck. He walked off and headed toward the steps to the second floor of the hotel.

TaSean walked up the hallway and kept an eye on the numbers on the room doors. He found his room, used his key card to unlock it, and then stepped inside.

* * *

"Oh, Nina! Look, girl!" Vanessa cried out as soon as she spotted the four guys standing next to a diamond-white metallic Cadillac Escalade. "Bitch, they already showing up for this tournament, and they looking good too!"

"You ain't lyin'!" Shawna added from the back seat, staring out her window as Nina drove past.

Nina shook her head and listened to her girls as she parked her 2018-model Infiniti QX80 truck. She then looked over at Vanessa and saw her best friend looking at herself in the mirror as if she was about to go out on a date or to a club.

"You hookers is a trip!" Nina told both her girls as she opened the door and got out.

Nina grabbed her bags from the back seat, and then she left Vanessa and Shawna and went to get the key to her room.

"Nina, where you going?" Vanessa called out.

"Getting my room key!" Nina yelled back while walking past the four guys and ignoring the way they were all staring at her.

After getting her key card, Nina walked back around the side of the parking lot and wasn't surprised to see Vanessa and Shawna talking with the guys. She shook her head as she headed up the steps to the second level, finding her room a few moments later.

She let herself inside and locked the door behind her. She then tossed her bags at the foot of the bed and sat down on the surprisingly soft bed. She pulled out her cell phone and called her boyfriend.

"Yeah! Who this?"

Nina heard the loud music in the background once Derrick answered the phone. She had to yell his name four times until the noise finally faded out and Derrick's voice came in clearly over the line.

"Hey, what's up, Nina? Where you at?"

"You finally realized it was me, huh?" Nina asked with a slight attitude. "What are you doing?"

"The guys wanted to go out, so that's the noise you heard. Where you at?"

"I'm in Orlando, Derrick!" she told him, but then asked, "Where are you, and when am I going to see you?"

"Baby, let me see you in the morning after we sign up for—"

"Wait!" Nina yelled. "Nigga, you been up here for three days and you still ain't signed up for this tournament? What the hell you been doing all this time, Derrick?"

"Nina, let's talk about this tomorrow."

"Whatever, Derrick!"

After hanging up the phone in his face, she sat down and stared at the walls. She was already pissed off, and she had only been in Orlando a short time.

"I can't believe this shit!" Nina said aloud as she got up from the bed and headed to the bathroom to run herself a bath, since she was going to bed early.

Chapter 3

Nina awoke while it was still slightly dark outside, just before the sun started to rise. She got herself together to go for a jog. She put on her running tights and her sports bra and then stepped into her black-over-white lucky Air Max.

With her MP3, cell phone, and key card in her hand, Nina headed for the room door and then stepped outside, just as the door next to hers opened and a guy stepped outside. He was wearing Nike running sweatpants, a wifebeater, and matching Air Max that went with his pants.

"Morning!" TaSean said after noticing her staring.

"Ummm, good morning!" Nina got out after snapping out of her stare. She then started toward the steps the same time he did.

"After you!" TaSean said once he and the female reached the top of the stairs.

He then motioned for her to go first.

"Thank you!" Nina told the guy as she started

walking downstairs.

She could feel his stare and looked back, only to meet his eyes. She had expected him to be staring at her ass, only to receive a gorgeous, deep-dimpled smile.

Once she was downstairs, Nina began her stretch routine before she began her run.

"Excuse me!"

Nina paused in mid-stretch and looked to her left after hearing his smooth and deep voice.

"Did you say something?" she asked him.

"Actually, I wanted to ask you a question," TaSean told her as he walked over to stand in front of her.

"I'm listening!" Nina answered as she lifted her head just a little to look up at him.

"First, my name's TaSean."

"Nina!"

"Good meeting you, Nina," TaSean told her. "You're about to go for a run, right?"

"That's the plan."

"You mind if I run with you?"

TaSean saw the surprised look that appeared on Nina's face, so he quickly said, "I kind of feel some type of way about you being out by yourself this early in the morning when you're not from Orlando."

"How do you know I'm not from here?" she asked in surprise by his statement.

"Your accent gives you away."

Nina smiled at his reply and asked, "So, what part of New York are you from?"

"Brooklyn," TaSean answered with a light laugh, seeing she had caught on to his accent as well.

"I'm from Chicago," she admitted, surprising herself since she had only just met him.

They continued their talk as the two began stretching again. Nina found herself laughing at his humor that easily got her to relax a little since she loved to laugh.

"You ready, shorty?" TaSean asked once the two of them were finished stretching.

"Just keep up!" Nina told him, shooting TaSean a smile as she started to jog off with TaSean right behind her.

* * *

They ran longer than either one of them had planned. TaSean spotted a Waffle House and waved Nina to follow as he led the way across the street to the diner.

"Now we're going to eat after a run like that, huh?" Nina asked.

She was winded, but she followed TaSean into the Waffle House.

"We gotta eat, right?" TaSean stated, winking his eye at her and then smiling as the waitress showed up and escorted the two of them to a window seat.

Once they were seated and menus were placed in front of them, Nina spoke up first as she picked up her menu.

"So, let me guess. You're in Orlando for the tournament, aren't you?"

"Pretty much!" TaSean answered, lifting his eyes from his own menu and looking across the table to Nina. "Why'd you come to Orlando?"

"Truthfully," Nina began, with a loud sigh as she sat back in her seat, "me and two friends of mine came to see my boyfriend play in the tournament as well."

"Support team?"

"I guess."

TaSean set down his menu after hearing the way Nina replied to him and noticed her expression.

"If it's cool to ask, what's wrong? You sound like you really don't wanna be here."

"Truthfully, TaSean, it's not that I don't want to be here, because I don't mind the trip out here just to relax. It's just that dealing with my boyfriend first living in New Jersey and me in Chicago is hard enough, since I'm doing most of the traveling; and now I'm out here, and he's with his boys. I couldn't even see him last night because he went out with them, and I was left to sleep alone with my man being in the same city as I was."

"He didn't come to you?"

"You're sitting in front of me and not him, so that should answer your question!" she told TaSean just as the waitress reappeared.

The server took their orders, and the two of them

handed her their menus. Nina waited until she walked away, and then said, "TaSean, I'm sorry."

"About what?" TaSean asked, with a confused look on his face as he stared across the table at Nina.

"About what I just said!" Nina told him. "I don't want you to feel like I haven't enjoyed your company this morning because I really did. I was just expressing my feelings about my so-called boyfriend."

TaSean waved his hand dismissively and said, "Ma, relax! It's cool to express yourself, since I was the one that asked the question. Feel free to say whatever you feel, and I'm here to listen."

Nina smiled across the table at TaSean after listening to him, and then asked, "Where's your girlfriend at, TaSean? She actually trusted you to come down here without her?"

"I gotta have one for her to trust me, right?" TaSean told Nina with a small smile.

"Wait a minute!" Nina said in disbelief. "You serious, TaSean? You really don't have a girlfriend?"

"You sound like you don't believe me!"

"I don't!" she replied. "TaSean, look at you, boy! You're an extremely handsome guy, and you not having a girlfriend is hard to believe."

"Well, it's true," he admitted.

Nina shook her head and smiled as she stared across the table at him.

"You're amazing, TaSean."

"I'm glad you think so!" he told her, winking his eye at her and getting her to blush and lower her eyes.

* * *

After finishing their breakfast, TaSean paid the bill and the two of them left the Waffle House. Nina felt bad because she realized she hadn't brought any cash with her. When they made it back to the hotel, the two of them didn't notice the crowd outside in the hotel parking lot, since they were laughing with each other so much. TaSean looked up after hearing his name called, just as Nina's name was also called out. They both looked over and saw TaSean's cousin Anthony and the rest of the guys with two females.

"Here come my girls now!" Nina told TaSean when she saw Vanessa and Shawna headed their way.

"Well, good morning!" Vanessa said, stopping in front of Nina with a look on her face. "What have you been doing, Miss Thang?"

"Ummm, Nina!" TaSean spoke, drawing not only Nina's attention but her girls' as well. "I'ma see you later, shorty. I gotta get ready to go sign up for this tournament."

Nina hugged TaSean goodbye and watched him walk off and head over to his boys, who he had told her about when they were at breakfast.

"What is this?" Vanessa questioned as she stood watching her best friend.

"Girl, it looks like Miss Nina Ortiz is in love with Mr. Sexy!" Shawna added, smiling as she too stood watching her girl.

"You two hookers are crazy!" Nina told her girls as she started walking off, with Vanessa and Shawna right behind her.

Nina passed TaSean and his boys as she headed upstairs to her room.

"Nina!" Vanessa called, following her friend

down the hallway. "Bitch, I saw how you was looking at him."

Nina paused just inside the doorway of her hotel room after opening the door. She looked back at Vanessa and asked, "How do you know his name?"

"Anthony told me," Vanessa told her with a smile.

"So, you're already messing with his cousin, huh?" Nina asked as she stepped into the room.

"I see you and Mr. TaSean did a lot of talking!" Vanessa told her girl, following her into the room as Shawna closed the door behind them. "I wanna know everything, but you need to call Derrick first."

"Call Derrick for what?" Nina asked as she stared at Vanessa, pausing while looking for something to change into after her shower.

"Girl, he came by looking for you!" Vanessa told her. "He just left about ten minutes ago."

"Where'd he say he was going?" Nina asked her girl.

Vanessa shook her head when she saw the look on Nina's face.

"I don't know, Nina. He didn't say, which is why you need to call his ass!"

* * *

TaSean and the guys left the hotel and arrived twenty minutes later at the park where the tournament was being held. A crowd was already out and about. He parked his Escalade in an open space, and then he, Kyle, and Anthony stepped out of the truck.

"Damn, baby daddy! Come here, sexy!"

TaSean heard the comment and looked around to see the group of four girls a little ways off to his left. He simply smiled as he walked around the truck to where Anthony and Kyle stood waiting for him.

"Y'all see this shit?" Howard asked as he and Tim walked up and joined them. "They acting like the tournament starts today instead of Friday."

"You know how muthafuckers is!" Anthony stated as he too stood looking around. "This ain't nothing but some see-and-be-seen type shit going on out here!"

"Yo, TaSean!" Kyle said, tapping him on the arm

and then nodding toward the gathering crowd. "Ain't that the chick you was with this morning!"

TaSean turned his head and looked in the direction Kyle was nodding. TaSean first spotted the crowd, but then he smiled when he saw Nina.

"Y'all hold up a second!" he told his boys, walking off and heading in the direction where Nina was signing autographs.

* * *

Nina was smiling and taking pictures with fans, and signing pictures, magazines, and even her new calendar. She was taking the *Smooth Girl Magazine* from a female and had just finished signing it when the pen she was using was taken out of her hand.

"Excuse me!" Nina got out just as her hand was grabbed.

She realized at the last moment just who was in front of her as he finished writing in the palm of her hand.

"Now you're the first to have my autograph," TaSean told her with a smile.

Nina saw the boy actually sign his name and a

short message inside her hand. She then shook her head and laughed as she looked up at TaSean.

"Boy, you are so crazy, TaSean!" she laughed while signing another magazine. "How long you been out here?"

"Just got here," he replied, but then said, "So, you're a bigger-known model than you told me, huh?"

"I guess!" Nina stated as she handed the magazine back to the guy who had given it to her. She followed up her autograph with a big hug for her fan.

Getting Nina away from the crowd caused her to burst out laughing as TaSean threw up his arms and acted like her bodyguard, just to get her away for a bit.

"TaSean, you crazy!" Nina told him, still laughing.

"So, where ya girls at?" TaSean asked as he and Nina began walking through the crowd together.

"They're out here somewhere," she told him. "Where's your cousin and boys at?"

"Right there!" TaSean answered, nodding up ahead at Howard and the rest of the boys.

"Nina!"

When she heard her name, both she and TaSean looked back behind them to see Vanessa and Shawna rushing through the crowd to catch up to them.

"I'ma let you go!" TaSean told her. "Let me get over here and sign in. I guess I'ma see you later."

"Hopefully!" Nina replied as she reached up and gave TaSean a hug before turning and walking off to meet her girls.

TaSean watched Nina as she walked off, but he noticed a few guys stop and look back at her ass as she passed. TaSean found himself looking over her 34-26-45, five-foot-six, slim, firm, and curvaceous body. He couldn't help noticing the thick muscular thighs, curvy hips, and the high bubble butt the girl had fitted into some skin-tight jeans.

TaSean shook his head and smiled as he turned back around. He then started toward his cousin and the rest of the team, missing the look Nina made back over her shoulder, smiling as she stared at him.

Chapter 4

TaSean saw Nina again in passing over the next three days after seeing her with who he quickly realized was her boyfriend, after pulling up to the hotel and seeing her with some red-skinned guy he later found out was last year's champion. He watched Nina and homeboy hug it up and kiss.

TaSean spent his last three days preparing for the start of the five-on-five tournament. He was up early on Friday morning, which was the first day of the tournament. He was met out in the hall by Nina, who was also out for a run.

"Hey!" Nina spoke up, looking up at TaSean.

"What's good, ma?" he answered as the two of them started up the hallway.

"You know, TaSean, I was hoping you would tell me what's up," Nina said as they headed downstairs together.

"What you mean?" TaSean asked. "We got a problem or something, shorty?"

"That's what I want to know!" she told him.

"You haven't said nothing to me but a 'hi' or 'good morning' for the last three days. Why is that? Did I do something?"

TaSean smiled after hearing her concerns. He began stretching and then said, "Relax, ma! We good, and I was trying to keep it that way, shorty."

"How? By ignoring me?" Nina asked with an attitude. "I know we haven't known each other that long, but I thought we was friends."

TaSean grabbed her before he realized what he was doing. He had his arms wrapped around her and held her.

"Ma, relax! We are friends, but I've just been trying to respect the fact that you been kicking it with ya dude, so I gave ya space, that's all!"

Nina laid her head against TaSean's chest as she held her arms wrapped around him. She lifted her head to look up at him.

"Don't you ever do me like this again, TaSean! If you want to know something, ask it, and I'll do the same. You understand me?"

"Loud and clear, Your Majesty!" TaSean replied

with a smirk, getting a smile out of Nina before she pushed away from him laughing and shaking her head.

* * *

TaSean saw the fully crowded park once he pulled up. He slowly trailed behind the line of cars and SUVs that were trying to get into the entrance to the park. He finally pulled up to the front entrance and showed the attendant proof that he was playing in the tournament.

Once they were inside the parking lot and found an open spot, TaSean shut off the Escalade as Kyle and Anthony got out of the truck. He then got out just as Howard's truck was driving past.

"Yo, this shit is packed!" Kyle yelled, looking around as TaSean walked up.

"They even got cameras out here too!" TaSean added, nodding his head in the direction where he saw the ESPN vans parked, along with a few other sports news companies.

Anthony left the Escalade once Howard and Tim showed up. He then led the group toward the court and saw women and guys everywhere. There were even kids all over the place.

"Yo, TaSean!" Tim called. "There go your girl from the hotel!"

TaSean looked in the direction that Tim nodded, and he saw Vanessa and Shawna staring straight at him. TaSean then looked over and watched Vanessa nudge Nina and point at him.

TaSean saw the smile that lit up her face. He then noticed the boyfriend when Nina leaned over into him and whispered into his ear before walking off and heading in TeSean's direction with Vanessa and Shawna.

"Hey, you!" Nina cried happily as she threw her arms up and around TaSean's neck.

"What's good, ma?" TaSean said with a grin as he returned her hug.

"So, is Nina the only one you see, TaSean?" Vanessa asked as she stood beside Anthony with a smirk on her face while she stood watching him and Nina.

"You seem pretty busy with my cousin!" TaSean

told her, causing the others to laugh. "What's up though, cutie?"

Vanessa rolled her eyes at TaSean but smiled at the same time. She was just about to say something else when Nina's boyfriend, Derrick, and his boys walked up.

"Nina, what's up?" Derrick asked, hard-staring at her.

When Nina saw Derrick, she quickly introduced him to TaSean.

"What's good, son?" TaSean spoke up first, nodding to the boyfriend.

Derrick heard Nina introduce TaSean, but he ignored him. He simply told Nina that they were going to find their seats.

Nina shook her head at Derrick as she stared at him at how disrespectful he was being to TaSean. She then rolled her eyes at Derrick and turned to apologize to TaSean.

"It's cool, ma!" TaSean spoke up, stopping her before she could attempt to say anything. "It's not that serious. I'll just check you when you got time, shorty."

"Thank you!" Nina told TaSean in a lowered voice.

She received a nod and a small smile in return. She then turned and, without saying a thing to Derrick, walked off with Vanessa and Shawna right beside her.

* * *

TaSean signed the team in and received blue jerseys with the number 4 in white lettering on the front and back. He sat in the stands as the commissioner of the tournament explained the rules and regulations. The commissioner announced that the games would be a one-game elimination format. TaSean looked around and felt someone watching him, only to end up locking eyes with Nina as she sat in the left side of the stands watching him.

He winked his eye at her and caused her to smile and look away. TaSean focused back onto the commissioner when Anthony leaned over toward him.

"Be careful, Cuz!" Anthony told him, seeing the

exchange between TaSean and Nina.

TaSean heard his cousin, but he chose not to respond. He kept his attention on the commissioner and what was being said.

Once the commissioner finally finished, teams #2 and #7 were called for the first seven-minute game that was about to be played. TaSean sat back and watched the tip-off, when somebody sat down beside him.

"Hey, handsome!"

TaSean looked to his right into the light golden-brown eyes of a pretty white girl with shoulder-length, honey-blonde hair that matched perfectly with her eyes.

TaSean gave a light laugh and said, "You finally made ya way over here, huh?"

"So, you did see me watching you?" she teased him with a smile, showing the four golds on the bottom teeth inside the front of her mouth.

"How could I miss you?" he asked, looking back over to the white girl and remembering her curvaceous five-foot-six, 142-pound, 34C-24-40 body. "But what's really up, ma? You ain't come way over here just to have some casual conversation. What's on ya brain?"

"You!" she admitted truthfully with a smile.

* * *

"Nina, who is that white girl talking to TaSean?" Vanessa asked her best friend after noticing the bitch all up on him.

"Probably some thirsty female that saw him like the rest of these girls out here!" Nina stated, already watching TaSean with the white girl, who she had noticed when she first sat down beside TeSean.

Vanessa looked back at Nina and asked, "Girl, you want me to go over there and straighten that bitch?"

Nina laughed at Vanessa's question and responded, "Vanessa, TaSean is not my man, girl! We are just friends, and he can talk to whomever he wants to!"

"Whatever!" Vanessa said, waving her hand dismissively and then looking back over in the direction of TaSean and the girl.

Nina shook her head and smiled as she sat staring at her best friend. She then shifted her gaze back over to TaSean and saw him and the White girl laughing as the girl flirtatiously leaned into him. But Nina slowly lost her smile the longer she stared at TaSean with the girl.

"Here!" Derrick said as he sat back down alongside Nina and handed her the hot dog and soda she requested.

* * *

"Showtime, Cuz!" Anthony said, nudging TaSean after hearing their team number called after team #1 was called.

TaSean first looked over at Anthony and saw his cousin and the rest of the guys getting up and heading out to the court to play. TaSean then pulled off the T-shirt he was wearing and received a few screams from the women in the crowd who saw him. He handed the shirt to the white girl, who he now knew was named Alexus after they introduced themselves to each other. After a little more conversation, he also found out that she was a mixed race of white and black.

"Good luck, handsome!" Alexus told TaSean, holding his shirt and his towel as he put on his jersey.

TaSean winked his eye at Alexus before heading down the stands. He joined his cousin and the rest of the team, and they all showed love by bumping fists and embracing each other.

Team #1 made it out onto the court and received some yells and cheers from the crowd, since they were returning from last year's tournament. The referee called both teams out to center court for the tip-off.

"Here we go!" Tim yelled after catching the ball from Howard, who tipped it his way. He shot the pass to Anthony, who tossed it over to TaSean.

"It's game time!" Anthony told his cousin as he smiled at him when they all began jogging up the court.

TaSean nodded his head in response to his cousin while dribbling the ball. He then looked the floor over but shot the ball off left to Kyle. He then took off, shooting past his defender and calling for the ball back.

TaSean caught the pass back from Kyle and was driving to the basket; but with a no-look pass, he lobbed the ball up and a little behind him into the air, catching Howard up the baseline, who took flight. He caught the alley-oop and scored with a two-hand dunk.

"Good pass, my nigga!" Howard yelled as the five of them jogged back down the court.

* * *

"My rebound!" Tim called, snatching the missed shot out of the air before quickly shooting a pass to TaSean, who took off up the court on offense.

TaSean pushed the ball up the floor, crossing over right but swinging the ball back to the left from behind his back. He fucked the defender up, leaving homeboy stumbling in the opposite direction. TaSean then threw the bounce pass across the court to his right, catching Anthony on the run to the basket. He watched his cousin spin off a defender toward the left inside and pull up for a mid-range jump shot off the glass and score.

* * *

Even though their team ran through team #1, TaSean didn't score a point. Instead, he allowed Anthony, Tim, Kyle, and Big Howard to work the scoreboard, making all the points. TaSean pulled in the assists, rebounds, and even three steals. He smiled at the end of the seven minutes after they won their first game and received some cheers from the stands.

After leaving the court and heading back to the stands, TaSean looked over in Nina's direction to see her smiling and watching him. He winked at her and smiled.

"Damn, handsome!" Alexus cried as soon as TaSean made it back up to the spot in the stands where they were sitting. She smiled at him until he sat down. "You can actually play for real!" she told him, handing TaSean his towel.

"I do a lil' something!" TaSean stated just as Anthony sat down beside him.

"Yo, Cuz!" Anthony called, getting his attention.

"What's good?" TaSean answered.

"That's what I wanna know," Anthony responded. "What's up with all the passing? Don't get it twisted though. You did ya thing with the set-up with all them fly-ass passes, but why you ain't do no shooting? You ain't score no points at all, and that ain't like you! What's up?"

"This not my team, Cuzo!" TaSean told him. "I'm just here to help in winning."

"What?" Anthony yelled. "Yo! Fuck all that shit you talking about, nigga! This our team, so kill that bullshit you talking, nigga! You either with us all the way, or we done with this shit now! What you gonna do?"

TaSean laughed lightly after a moment as he sat down and stared at his cousin.

"Yeah, Cuzo. I'm here!"

"That's what the fuck I'm talking about!" Anthony said with a smile as he and TaSean dapped up with each other.

* * *

TaSean kicked it with Alexus for a bit until he noticed Nina's dude and his team walking out onto the court to play in game four against team #12. TaSean refocused his attention on the game that was about to start up. He also noticed that Alexus must have sensed that he wanted to pay attention since she sat back quietly beside him while the crowd went crazy for the returning champions.

Once the ball was up in the air for the tip-off, team #12 got the ball and put Derrick's team #8 on the defense. TaSean kept his eyes on the boy playing defense, but quickly noticed homeboy didn't have any defense after the player shot past him.

"Oh shit!" TaSean heard Anthony cry out after seeing Derrick's big man spin off his player and step off his right foot. He then leapt up into the air, just as homeboy with the ball went up for the lay-up, only to have his shit slapped away by Derrick's big man.

TaSean heard the crowd's reaction to what had just happened, but he wasn't impressed. He kept his eyes on Derrick as the boy quickly ran the offense, but TaSean also noticed that homeboy was a ball hog. He watched his dribbling through the whole defense before he made a seven-foot jump shot that he pulled up.

"You see that?"

TaSean heard the question and looked to his left at Anthony.

"I see him! I ain't impressed at all, Cuzo!" TaSean told him.

"I ain't either!" Anthony reiterated as he turned his attention back to the game.

Chapter 5

Nina got away from Derrick once the tournament let out for a ten-minute break after the first eight teams that lost were eliminated. Nina left her so-called boyfriend to his fans and wasn't surprised to find Vanessa and Shawna with Anthony and the rest of the guys, except for TaSean.

"You actually got away from Derrick, girl?" Vanessa asked playfully after noticing Nina.

"Whatever, hooker!" Nina said, rolling her eyes at her girl. "Where's TaSean at?"

"Right there, girl!" Vanessa answered, pointing to the crowd of six girls and two guys that were with TaSean and the white girl.

Nina saw TaSean but noticed the white girl who had been sitting with him through the tournament so far. Before she realized it, Nina then called out to him to get his attention. She watched him say something to the white girl, who then hugged him before he jogged off and headed toward her and the others. Nina stood waiting until he slowed to a stop in front of her.

"What's good, shorty?" TaSean asked as he hugged Nina. "You actually got free of ya man, huh?"

Nina looked over at Vanessa as she and the others began laughing at his question, since Vanessa had just asked the same thing. Nina rolled her eyes at her girl as she looked back at TaSean.

"So, who's the white girl?"

TaSean looked back over his shoulder at Alexus, only to find her watching him and smiling once they locked eyes.

TaSean looked back at Nina and answered, "Just this shorty I met. Her name's Alexus!"

"Alexus, huh?" Nina repeated. "So, what's up with you and Alexus?"

"Here she goes!" Vanessa said, causing the others to laugh again.

Nina shot a look at both Vanessa and Shawna before she turned back to TaSean, grabbed his hand, and pulled him away from the group.

"Come on, TaSean!" Nina stated as the two of

them walked away from the others. "Let's get something to eat!"

After finding a pizza stand that had a line in front of it, Nina and TaSean fell in at the back of the line.

"What's on ya brain, ma?" TaSean asked Nina as the two of them stood in line together.

He then dropped his arm across her shoulder as he stared at her as she slowly shook her head.

"I just want you to be careful, TaSean. You not from up this way, just like I'm not from here. Don't be so quick to fall for anything from out here!"

"You talking about Alexus, ain't you?" he asked.

"Her and any other one of these girls out here that you don't know," Nina expressed to him. "I don't want you to get hurt! You're a really good guy and my friend, and I'm just being a friend to you, TaSean."

TaSean got a hug from Nina as she wrapped her arms around him. He was just kissing her lightly on the forehead when he was pushed away from Nina from the back, causing him and Nina to stumble forward.

"What the fuck is this shit?" Derrick yelled angrily as he stood with his boys mean-mugging TaSean and Nina.

"Derrick, what the hell is wrong with you?" Nina asked, pissed off now at how his ass was acting. "Why the hell is you—?"

"What the fuck you doing over here hugged up with this nigga?" Derrick yelled, shooting TaSean a look.

"I'll call you later, TaSean!" Nina told him as he began walking off.

TaSean saw the crowd forming, and even a few cameras were pointed in their direction.

"Ma, look! I'ma get up with you later before shit gets out of hand and me and ya man get kicked out of this tournament," TaSean turned and said to Nina.

Nina looked angrily back at Derrick as he stood staring at TaSean, who wasn't paying him any attention at all.

* * *

TaSean was still heated about Nina's punk-ass boyfriend. He took his anger out on the next team he and his team played, once the tournament started back up for the second half.

Once his team—team #4—and team #13 were called out onto the court to play, TaSean wasted no time after their opponent won the tip-off. He got the ball first, quickly stealing it from the other team. He ended up shaking two defenders and pulling off a nine-foot fade-away jump shot, scoring the first point.

TaSean kept the pressure on homeboy from the opposite team that was controlling the ball. He then knocked the ball away and got past the guy to scoop up the ball, only to spin off one of the homeboy's teammates who was rushing for the ball.

TaSean took off up the floor on a fast break. He put on a show, taking flight as he stepped onto the free throw line, shooting into the air and doing a 360-style dunk that got the crowd on its feet and cheering him on.

TaSean started back up the floor but looked back in time to see the ball being thrown in. He spun back around and rushed the ball, catching the new player who was now controlling the ball off guard.

TaSean then ripped the ball from homeboy's hands and spun off, only to throw the no-look pass just out of the spin. He caught his cousin, Anthony, running down the middle of the court from the top of the key, catching the ball and taking flight as he stepped past the free throw line and tomahawk slammed the ball.

"Aaaghhhh!" Anthony yelled to the skies after the dunk, all while TaSean started back toward the stands right after the clock ran out and the referee blew the whistle to end the game.

TaSean saw and heard the crowded stands going stupid as he was met by Alexus. He then caught shorty when she threw her arms up around his neck and hugged him excitedly. He turned his head and looked to where Nina was sitting with her boyfriend. He locked eyes with Derrick, who sat smirking back at him

* * *

TaSean was happy to see that Derrick was still in the tournament after the next game he and his team played, beating team #10. That left teams #16 and #15 as well as teams #3 and #5 still to play. TaSean sat through the last two games, watching teams #15 and #5 winning those games.

TaSean's team returned to the court once more for the best of the last four teams that were supposed to play. After that, the last two teams would play in the championship game that was going to be played Saturday morning. TaSean and the rest of the team met up with team #15.

Howard set up for the tip-off and knocked the ball over to Kyle, who then shot the pass to TaSean. TaSean pushed the ball up the floor, looking the floor over as he got to the top of the key. He then faked the drive, getting the nervous defender out of position. He crossed the ball back to his left through his legs, but quickly shot the left-hand pass up the floor, catching Kyle on the cut across the floor and then watching his boy score with the finger roll.

Chapter 6

TaSean's team would face Derrick's team in Saturday's championship game after Derrick's team beat #5 for the lock in the finals. TaSean was leaving the stands with Anthony and the rest of the guys, with Alexus hugged around his waist, when he heard his and Anthony's names being called out.

"Yo, Anthony!" Howard yelled as he stood talking with a redbone who had stopped him. He got Anthony's attention and pointed across the court.

Anthony looked in the direction Howard was pointing and quickly spotted Steffaine running toward him. He then noticed his mother with Edward, his Auntie Yolanda, and TaSean's step-sister, Tiffany, all heading in their direction.

"Yo, Sean!" Anthony called out.

"I see, Cuzo!" TaSean said, smiling when he saw his family.

He then looked over at Alexus since she said she had to go, but promised to call him later.

He turned his attention back to his family after

she walked off. TaSean barely braced himself as his step-sister slammed into him, wrapping her arms around him in a hug.

"Oh my God!" Tiffany cried out happily. "TaSean, you were amazing, boy! I didn't know you played like that!"

"Oh, so he the only one you seen, huh?" Anthony asked his cousin as he stood with both his mother and sister with their arms around him.

"Boy, I see you too!" Tiffany told Anthony before she threw her arms back around TaSean. "But my step-brother showed the hell out there!"

"I agree!" another voice spoke up, drawing everybody's attention around to him.

"Who you?" Anthony asked as he stared over the dark-haired white guy. He looked to be in his mid-thirties as he walked up dressed in casual clothes.

TaSean looked from the white dude that walked up to them after feeling someone tap his arm. He then looked to his right to see Nina.

"What up, ma?"

"Hey you!" Nina said as she gave him a hug.

"Good playing that last game."

"Thanks!" TaSean said before he got his mother's attention and introduced her and Nina to each other.

"Hello, Mrs. Prince," Nina said as she shook Yolanda's hand.

"Actually, it's Jackson!" TaSean corrected Nina before he introduced his step-sister and then pointed to his auntie when Anthony called his name.

"Yeah!" TaSean answered, looking to his cousin.

"Cuz, you gotta hear this!" Anthony told him. "You hear who this guy says he is?"

"Naw!" TaSean replied, looking at the white guy. "Who are you?"

"As I just told your cousin, Mr. Prince, my name is Brian Adams," he introduced himself as he handed TaSean a business card that he took out of his pocket. "I'm with Pro Sports Agency, and I just witnessed both you and Mr. Brown's performances you put on out here today."

"So, what exactly is it that you're here to talk to us about?" TaSean asked the guy as he handed the business card over to Nina as she was reaching for it.

"I'll get straight to the point, Mr. Prince!" Brian told him while focusing back onto TaSean. "I'm interested in representing both you and Mr. Brown."

"Representing us how?" Anthony asked the guy.

"In the NBA, Mr. Brown!" Brian Adams answered, looking from Anthony back to TaSean. "Mr. Prince, you have an abnormally amazing ability on the basketball court, and I truthfully believe you're hiding your true ability."

"Wait a minute!" Anthony spoke up again. "How can you represent us in the NBA when we're not even in the NBA?"

Brian smiled at the question that was just asked.

"Because, Mr. Brown, I believe I can get both of you onto an NBA team once they've seen what the two of you can do!"

"What team?" TaSean asked Brian.

"I have a few friends on a few of the teams inside the NBA, Mr. Prince, and I may be—!"

"What team?" TaSean asked again.

"You have an accent from up North, so how

about the New York Knicks?" Brian asked a now-smirking TaSean.

"Not gonna work!" Anthony spoke up, drawing the agent's attention back to him. "I'm born and raised in Miami."

Brian remained quiet a moment and then spoke up.

"I may know somebody with the Miami Heat that can get you on to try out for their team. I'm going to have to speak with my friend in the Miami area with my company to represent you instead of myself. How does that sound?"

"Before we answer anything," TaSean spoke up before Anthony could say anything, "I understand we're trying out for these teams, but we need to make sure that—!"

"I already know what you're going to say, Mr. Prince," Brian stated, cutting off TaSean. "You or Mr. Brown will have full say in our contract agreement, and I will make sure it's known that both you and Mr. Brown want a full agreement over any contract that is made with the team of your choice.

Does that cover it for you, Mr. Prince?"

TaSean looked at his mother and saw the smile she had for him as she gave her nod of approval. TaSean then looked back at the agent and held out his hand to Brian.

"I guess we got a deal!"

* * *

TaSean returned to the hotel after leaving the park once the conversation with Brian was finished. He then jumped into the shower to get ready to meet up with his family for dinner. He spent longer than he intended until he heard his cell phone begin ringing, which snatched him from his thoughts.

TaSean hopped out of the shower, dried off, and then walked naked toward his bed. He grabbed his cell phone from the dresser and saw Alexus's name.

"Alexus! What's good, ma?"

"Handsome, what you doing?"

"Just jumped out of the shower. I'm about to meet up with my mom and sister for dinner. What up with you?"

"Thinking about you, but I wanted to ask you

something though."

"What up?"

"Who was that Spanish-looking girl you was with after the game?" Alexus asked him. "I saw her when I was leaving with my girls."

"You sounding real jealous right now, ma!"

"I'm just making sure what's mine stays mine!"

"And what exactly is yours, shorty?"

"You are!"

"Is that right?"

"Yes!" Alexus answered with a sureness. "But listen, handsome. I need to handle something real fast, but I'ma call you later tonight. I wanna see you before the game tomorrow, all right?"

TaSean hung up with Alexus after agreeing to meet up with her later in the night. He finished getting dressed and put on a pair of black metallic Polo jeans, a light gray-over-white Polo sweater pullover, and a long-sleeved shirt. He then stepped into a pair of gray Tims, just as there was a knock at his room door. He walked over and opened it.

"Hey, you!" Nina said as soon as TaSean

answered the door. She smiled as she saw how he was staring at her. "You gonna say something?"

"Damn!" TaSean got out as he looked Nina over.

She was wearing a white, body-hugging, mid-thigh skirt that hugged her perfectly rounded and perky C cups, along with the black jean jacket and black stiletto heels.

"You're gorgeous, ma!"

"Thank you!" Nina replied, blushing as she brushed back her straight and silky hair.

TaSean saw her blushing and kissed her forehead.

"Let me get my keys, and then we can see what's up with my cousin."

"Anthony and Vanessa already left to go meet his mom and sister," Nina told him, laughing after seeing the look TaSean gave her as he picked up his white-on-white White Sox fitted cap.

"So, those two kicking it, huh?" TaSean asked as he headed back to the door where Nina was waiting for him.

"Something like that!" Nina answered as TaSean

locked the room door behind them. "She finally admitted she likes Anthony more than she was willing to admit at first."

Once they were down in the parking lot walking out to TaSean's Escalade, Nina waited until he unlocked and then held open the passenger door for her.

"Thank you!" she replied with a smile as she got up into the truck.

"Not a problem!" TaSean answered back before he closed the door for her.

TaSean then walked around and climbed up into the truck behind the wheel. He got the Escalade started and was backing out of his parking space when Nina said his name.

"Yeah!" he answered, looking over to Nina.

"Are you thinking about talking to that white girl I saw you with earlier?"

"Why you asking?"

"I was just wondering, that's all!"

"You was just wondering, huh?" TaSean asked as he cut his eyes over to her with a small smile on his face. "Truthfully, she asked. But we really ain't talk too much about it."

"Do you want to talk to her?" Nina wanted to know.

"Let me ask you something!" he switched up without answering her question. "You serious with this dude Derrick?"

Nina stared at TaSean and then asked, "You don't like him, do you?"

"Not at all!" TaSean replied truthfully. "I also caught that you didn't answer the question I just asked you either."

"Neither did you answer mine!" she told him, only for the both of them to burst out laughing at the same time.

"Okay, TaSean!" Nina stated after getting control of herself. "I'll be honest if you'll do the same thing with me."

"Deal!"

"All right! Yes, I'm serious with Derrick. I do love him, but I'll admit that I am attracted to you as well."

"I guess it's my turn now, huh?" TaSean asked, smirking at Nina.

"It sure is!" she told him with a smile.

"A'ight! Yeah, I'm feeling the white girl. I like her voice, but I'm feeling you also. It's just that since you kicking it with dude, I've been doing the respect-ya-space-and-relationship thing."

"So, now that that's out, what are we gonna do?" she asked, turning as much as her short skirt would allow her to face TaSean.

TaSean glanced back over to Nina and met her hazel-green eyes a moment before focusing back onto the road.

"I guess I've got a new best friend!"

"I was hoping you'd say that, because I don't want to lose you after this tournament is over, TaSean!" she told him truthfully. "I understand you're in New York and I'm in Chicago, but you need to get an iPhone 8 so we can not only talk, but we can have some FaceTime so I can see you while we talk. Can you do that for me, TaSean?"

TaSean smiled as he looked back over to Nina

and met her eyes again. He reached over and used his pointer finger, and he gently pushed back some of her hair out of her face.

"I'ma make sure I take care of that real soon, shorty!" TaSean promised her.

Chapter 7

TaSean acted a fucking fool inside the tournament on Saturday morning. He intentionally went out of his way to embarrass Derrick, refusing to let the clown-ass nigga score. He kept him running all over the court stumbling and tripping all over his own feet while trying to play defense against him, until he ended up twisting his ankle after a crossover that he tried to stop. TaSean laughed with Anthony and the rest of the team as a cussing and yelling Derrick was carried off the court, causing his team to be one man short and eliminated from the tournament final. The commissioner and judges then named team #4 the champions of the new Orlando Five-on-Five Bigfoot Hoops Tournament.

TaSean caught Alexus as she flew down from the stands once team #4 was named the winner. He found himself being tongue-kissed in the middle of the court that was now crowding with fans and reporters.

"Yo, Cuz!"

TaSean had heard Anthony but then felt him

pulling his arm. TaSean broke the kiss with a smiling Alexus, only to find cameras and reporters in his face, with questions being yelled at him from every direction.

TaSean answered a few questions that he heard and then peeped Brian Adams a few feet away talking on his phone. Brian could only smile while staring at TaSean.

TaSean ended the interviews and allowed Alexus to lead him away from the cameras and reporters. He then noticed his cousin surrounded by reporters and more cameras.

"TaSean!" Brian yelled over the noise as he jogged over to catch up with him.

"What's up?" TaSean answered as he turned to face the agent as Alexus wrapped her arm around his waist.

"I just got off the phone with my guy with the Knicks, and he watched you play in the tournament. In fact, he was the one that called me after he got my message about me talking to you about trying out for the team. He wants you in New York in two days, so

I already got on the phone with the airlines and got two tickets to New York. We're leaving in two hours!"

"Whoa!" TaSean said. "What about my truck?"

"Babe, don't worry about your truck!" Alexus spoke up, drawing both TaSean and the agent's attention to her. "I'll drive your truck back for you. I've also got a place in New York you can stay at, and I'll meet you there when I get there."

"Who's this woman, TaSean?" Brian asked with a smile. "I like her!"

"I'm his girlfriend!" Alexus answered as she smiled up at TaSean.

"All right, let's get on the move!" Brian stated as he was getting back on his phone.

TaSean found his mother and the rest of the family waiting by the stands receiving hugs and a few kisses to the cheek. After he introduced Alexus to the family, he caught the smile she gave him after mentioning she was his girlfriend.

TaSean then explained about having to leave and fly to New York, letting his mother know what was going on and where he was going. He was hugging his mother when Anthony and the rest of the team walked over.

"Cuz, what's up? We going out to celebrate or—?"

"He can't!" Tiffany spoke up, cutting Anthony off. "He's leaving for New York."

"What?" Anthony, Kyle, Tim, and Howard all said at the same time in surprise.

"TaSean, we need to get going!" Brian stated as he walked over next to him.

"Babe, I'll explain to your cousin what's up!" Alexus told him as she kissed TaSean on the lips and then said, "Get going, and call me when you get to New York."

After kissing his mother and Auntie Patricia one last time, TaSean winked at Alexus before walking off with Brian, who went straight into explaining what he would have to expect, just as Alexus caught up to them.

"Babe, here!" she said as she handed him three keys. "That's the key to my place, and this one is for the car that's still there. Call my phone when you land, and I'll give you the address to where I live in the city."

TaSean accepted one last kiss from Alexus before she turned and walked off. He smiled as he shook his head and began following beside Brian.

* * *

TaSean stopped back at the hotel and picked up his clothes as he and Brian then drove out to the airport. TaSean finally relaxed once he was on the plane, still dressed in his gear from the big tournament.

"Wake me when we get to New York!" TaSean told the agent as he laid his head back.

Brian texted a bit on his cell phone before he also laid his head back and closed his eyes.

TaSean was unsure when he fell asleep, but he felt the agent waking him up, nudging him in his side. TaSean sat up and looked over at Brian.

"We're about to land now!" Brian told TaSean as he was getting himself ready.

Once the plane landed and the passengers were

allowed to disembark, TaSean and Brian headed to the baggage claim.

"Go ahead and get your luggage, TaSean. I'll get the car," Brian informed him, leaving TaSean in the baggage area.

TaSean walked out of the airport five minutes later with his bags, just as a 2018-model Jeep Grand Cherokee SRT pulled to a stop in front of him. As the passenger window slid down, TaSean stared at the driver.

"Come on!" Brian called out to TaSean.

Once inside the Jeep with his bags tossed onto the back seat, TaSean slammed the passenger door shut, just as Brian began to pull off.

"Sorry about the Jeep!" Brian apologized, glancing over at TaSean. "It's all I could find at the last minute."

"It's cool!" TaSean stated, laying his head back and shutting his eyes. "So, how all this supposed to go? What's about to happen?"

"Well, right now you're just going to meet with the coach and a few of the staff members, so they'll get a feel of who you really are and ask you a few questions."

"When do tryouts start?"

"In a few weeks," Brian answered, but then reminded TaSean to call his girlfriend.

"Shit!" TaSean said, forgetting about the whole phone call to Alexus. But he also remembered the promise that he made to Nina. "Yo Brian! I'ma need a new iPhone 8!"

"I'll take care of it!"

* * *

Nina arrived back at the hotel after leaving the hospital with a still pissed-off Derrick. She helped him from the truck and handed him a pair of crutches that the doctor had given to him.

"You okay?" Nina asked as she walked alongside Derrick, only to receive a nasty look as a reply.

She could only shake her head when she spotted TaSean's Escalade.

Nina helped Derrick as much as he allowed her to, up the stairs. She then walked ahead and opened her hotel room door. She went inside and made room for Derrick on the bed as he finally made it into the room a few moments behind her.

"You want me to help you into the shower?" she asked him as he sat down onto the couch next to the room window.

"I want you to leave me the hell alone right now!" Derrick barked at Nina.

Nina rolled her eyes at his attitude and then turned around and headed for the door.

"Where the hell are you going?" Derrick asked her, watching her leave.

Nina heard Derrick, but she ignored his question as she walked out the hotel room and slammed the door behind her. She went next door and was just about to knock on TaSean's room door, when it opened.

"Nina, right?" Alexus asked after seeing the Spanish girl standing in front of her, who TaSean claimed was his friend.

"Alexus?" Nina asked.

"That's me!" Alexus answered as she set down TaSean's bags. "You looking for TaSean, right?"

"Where is he?" Nina asked, looking down at the bags at Alexus's feet. "Aren't these TaSean's bags?"

"TaSean is in New York!" Alexus told the Spanish girl, smiling when she saw the surprised look that appeared on Nina's face. "You may already know since TaSean seems to care about you more than I approve of, but he left to meet with the people with the New York Knicks, and he left with his agent a little while ago."

Nina opened her mouth to ask another question, but instead just thanked the white girl and walked down the hall and knocked on Vanessa's room.

"Hey, girl!" Vanessa called, smiling as she slipped out of the room and shut the door behind her. "You just get back?"

"Yeah, girl!" Nina replied. "Derrick's ass is back in my room, but what's this about TaSean flying back to New York? He's not playing in the tournament's all-star game this afternoon?"

"Girl, TaSean went to see those people with the New York Knicks," Vanessa told her. "Anthony has to see the people at Miami Heat Arena in two days."

"Baby, what's up?" Anthony asked after opening Vanessa's room door to see Nina. "Oh shit! What's up, Nina?"

"Hey, Anthony!" Nina replied, shooting a look at Vanessa, who stood with a big smile on her face.

"You looking for TaSean?" Anthony asked. "He flew back to New York with his agent. He's about to try out for the New York Knicks, so he had to leave now. But Cuz told me to tell you he's gonna hit you up when he gets the chance to."

"Thank you!" Nina told him as she smiled and then looked back and forth at Anthony and Vanessa. "So what, you two an item now?"

"She's not going nowhere!" Anthony stated as he grabbed Vanessa around her small waist from the back and pulled her up against his front.

Nina watched her best friend smiling and leaning back against Anthony as he was kissing all over her neck.

Nina shook her head and said, "I'ma leave you two alone before y'all start something out here in this hallway!"

"I'ma call you later!" Vanessa told Nina as she followed Anthony back into her hotel room.

* * *

Nina lay in the bed beside a sleeping Derrick, who was snoring softly. She was watching the highlights from the tournament's all-star game, but she couldn't help smiling when she heard the news reporters express how disappointed they were that TaSean Prince was unable to play in the game. But they enjoyed Anthony Brown as he showed up in the game, scoring twenty-five points, with eight blocks, six rebounds, and four assists.

Nina heard her cell phone begin to ring, so she snatched it up immediately, answering before it woke up Derrick.

"Hello!" she whispered into the phone.

"You asleep, ma?"

Nina smiled at the sound of TaSean's voice. She climbed out of bed and made her way outside her room into the hallway.

"Hey, you! I was wondering when you were gonna call," she said in a normal voice.

"Didn't Anthony tell you what I said?"

"He told me!" she admitted. "That's why I'm still up. So how'd the meeting go with the people with the Knicks?"

Nina listened to TaSean as he explained how his meeting went. She found herself smiling as she could feel the excitement in his voice. But she was caught off guard when he suddenly changed the subject and asked her when they were going to see each other again.

"I have a photo shoot next month in New York for *Straight Stuntin' Magazine*, and then there's a party afterward at Club Angels. You want to go with me?"

"You shouldn't even have to ask me that!" he told her, but then said, "I'll have that iPhone 8 tomorrow just as I promised you I would."

Nina smiled at his words and then leaned against the rail with her eyes closed. She then pulled up a mental picture of TaSean already missing her.

Chapter 8

"TaSean!"

TaSean heard Alexus when she walked through the front door of the penthouse in which the two of them were living in New York City for the last three weeks. He then looked up from where he was laid out across the sofa watching the 42-inch screen television to see Alexus and her girls walk into the den. Gina was cute with dark skin and a phat ass that she loved to show off, while Erica was a green-eyed, dark-haired white girl who reminded him of a thicker and curvier Katie Holmes.

"Hey, handsome!" Alexus said, kissing TaSean as she stopped in front of the sofa.

He tossed the bacpack she was carrying onto the glass coffee table as she sat down on the sofa in front of him.

"You hear from the Knicks yet?"

"Naw!" TaSean answered as Alexus lay back against him. "I got at Brian, and he was supposed to get at the management and find out what the deal was. It's been almost two weeks since I tried out for the team!"

"Couldn't they have told you the same day you tried out, pretty boy?" Gina asked him.

"Naw!" he answered, just as his iPhone began ringing on the coffee table. He continued as Alexus picked up the phone. "They gotta make a decision between picking a walk-on—me, in this case—or deciding if they wanna pick somebody out of the draft."

"Baby, it's Anthony!" Alexus told TaSean as she handed him the phone.

He took the phone from her and then watched her stand up and pick up her backpack as she, Gina, and Erica walked out of the den.

TaSean got on the phone and asked, "What up, Cuzo?"

"Cuz, I'm on!"

TaSean heard Anthony yell something about being on, but he was unable to really hear what the hell he was yelling about. TaSean had to yell to his cousin to get him to slow down.

"What the fuck is you saying? Slow the fuck down, dude!"

"Cuz, I'm on!" Anthony repeated, sounding excited as hell. "Sean, I made the team, Cuz! The Heat just called me and told me I made the team! I gotta go in and sign the contract today!"

TaSean was surprised and so happy for his cousin, but he felt some type of way since he had still not heard from his agent or the Knicks. TaSean finished talking with his cousin, and as soon as Anthony had finished and hung up the phone, TaSean tossed it onto the coffee table and then sat a moment and stared into space.

"I can't believe this shit!" TaSean said, running his hands over his wavy hair. He then suddenly snatched up his keys from the table and headed for the door, leaving the penthouse.

* * *

Alexus heard the loud ringing coming from the front of the penthouse while she and her girls were counting the money they took in from that week's intake. Alexus ignored the ringing for a few moments, only to hear it begin again.

"What the fuck! TaSean!" Alexus yelled out to her boyfriend, only to receive silence in return. "Gina!" Alexus called her friend before she just as quickly waved her hand dismissively.

She then stood up herself from her seat around the cherry wood table. She left the room that she used as her private study and walked back out to the front of the penthouse.

"TaSean!" Alexus yelled out again after walking into the den and finding him gone.

She spotted his cell phone on the coffee table.

Alexus picked up the ringing phone once it started back up and answered.

"Hello!"

"TaSean, we did it!"

"What?"

"Wait! Who's this?"

"Who the fuck is this?"

"This is Brian Adams. Is TaSean Prince around?"

"Brian, this is Alexus!" she told him while looking through the penthouse for TaSean. "I don't think TaSean's here right now. You want me to tell him something!"

"Alexus, you need to find him! I just got off the phone with the general manager with the New York Knicks. He's been drafted, Alexus! The Knicks want TaSean to play for them, and I need to speak with him about his contract signing!"

"He's not in the—! Wait!" Alexus said as an idea came to her. She smiled since she was sure she knew where TeSean was.

"Brian, TaSean's gonna call you right back!"

* * *

TaSean pulled up in front of Brooklyn Park a few blocks from his mother's house and saw the park was filled with its normal crowd of ballers. TaSean shut off the engine to the new 2018-model Mercedes-Benz GLS 450 that was a gift from Alexus after she sold his Escalade, giving him the money after already buying him the new Benz truck.

TaSean climbed from the Benz and walked out to the court. He heard his name called, and he looked over to his right to see a group of boys rushing at him.

TaSean smiled after realizing he was recognized because of the tournament. He stood answering questions and listening to the young boys excitedly tell him about watching him play in the televised tournament.

"Yo, TaSean!"

TaSean heard his name yelled out. He looked out onto the court and saw four guys staring at him.

"What's up, Superstar? You wanna run a two-on-two with us, or you too big to play with niggas like us now, B?" one of the four guys called out to TaSean in a challenge.

TaSean smirked as he began pulling off his T-shirt, which caused the crowd of boys to get hyped up and yell excitedly. TaSean started out onto the court.

"Let's get one in!" TaSean told the guys, catching the basketball that was tossed to him.

* * *

Alexus spotted TaSean's Benz truck as soon as she pulled up in front of the park. She smiled since she knew his ass would be there. She parked her

E350 Mercedes-Benz drop-top, climbed from the car, and stared at her man doing his thing on the basketball court.

"What's good, ma? Who you out here to see?" a guy asked, looking over Alexus's fine-as-hell body for a white girl.

"You really wanna know, playboy?" Alexus asked, smiling as she showed off her golds. She nodded out to the court and said, "My daddy's out there playing ball."

"Oh yeah!" the guy stated as he reached out and started playing with a few strands of her hair. "Well, since your dude's over there playing on the court, why don't you let the kid get in a few minutes with you?"

Alexus shifted her eyes and looked at the hand that was touching her hair. She brushed the guy's hand away.

"You really don't wanna touch me!" she told him as she pushed her hair back behind her ear with her right hand.

"I'm just saying, baby. I'm just trying to get to

know you!" homeboy told Alexus as he attempted to touch her again, only to freeze with his hand in mid-air after feeling the razor blade that was pressed against his throat.

"I just told you not to touch me!" Alexus told the guy again in a voice a little above a whisper. "This is what you will do though. You're gonna get the hell away from me and continue to breathe, unless you ready to die out here! Which is it gonna be?"

"You got that, shorty?" homeboy stated, holding up both hands as he backed away. He walked off from the crazy-as-hell white girl, shook his head, and said, "I won't do that again!"

* * *

"Game time!"

TaSean heard the crowd from the sideline right after he made the game-winning shot against the guys who had initially called him out to play. TaSean then looked at his teammate and winked at the boy.

"Collect the money, youngin'!" he told the young boy with a smile.

After leaving the court, TaSean headed over to

the young boy with whom he left his shirt, only to see the boy no longer had his shirt and was instead kicking it with a young girl.

"Hey, handsome! Looking for this?"

TaSean recognized the voice and smiled after turning around and seeing Alexus. She stood there with a big smile on her face.

"What's good, shorty?"

"You!" Alexus answered as she reached up and locked her hands behind TaSean's neck.

"Why didn't you tell me you were leaving?"

"I just needed to get out of the house and think!" he told her, just as his young teammate walked up beside him.

"Big homie, here's the money!" the young boy told TaSean, holding out the $300 for which they played.

"That's for you, lil' homie!" TaSean told the young boy, which earned him a smile. He dapped up with the kid before the boy took off running away.

Alexus smiled after watching her man and what he had just done. She kissed his lips and then released her hold on his neck, only to take his hand and lead him back out to his and her Benzes.

"How'd you know I was out here?" TaSean asked once he and Alexus were standing in front of her car.

"I remember your mom saying once that this was where you loved to be!" Alexus told him. "But I came out here because Brian called and said he needs to talk to you!"

"About what?" TaSean asked as he took the cell phone Alexus pulled out and was holding up to him so he could talk.

"Call 'im!" Alexus told him, leaning back against the front of the car.

TaSean did as he was told and called his agent and stood listening to the line ringing twice before it was finally answered.

"Adams!"

"Brian, it's TaSean! You called?"

"Where the hell you been at?" Brian asked. "Never mind all that! We did it! You're on the team!"

TaSean looked back at Alexus and saw a huge smile on her face after hearing the news that Brian had just given him. He then heard his agent says something about signing the contract right before he grabbed and picked up Alexus causing her to scream as she threw her arms around his neck as he kissed her directly on the lips.

Chapter 9

Nina was more nervous than she ever was in her life after hanging up the phone from talking with TaSean after he called to let her know he was a few minutes away from her hotel. She arrived in New York late the night before and was up early that day for her photo shoot with *Straight Stuntin' Magazine*. She was now waiting for her sweetheart to arrive so they could go the magazine's party together.

Nina looked herself over one last time in the mirror, making sure she looked perfect in her blue jean jumpsuit that was actually a short set with some mid-thigh length caramel-brown leather boots. She made sure her curly hair was still looking tight, just as her cell phone began ringing again.

Nina saw that TaSean was calling. She looked one last time in the mirror at her Dolce & Gabbana outfit, and then headed toward the hotel room door.

"I'm on my way down now, TaSean!" she told him after answering her phone while out in the hallway and heading toward the elevator.

Nina took a deep breath once she got on the elevator. She tried to calm herself since she was both nervous and excited about seeing TaSean after almost four weeks. She stepped off once she reached the lobby level. She made it three feet, when she saw the all-too-familiar figure walk into the hotel.

"Oh my God!" Nina heard herself say as she stared at TaSean wearing a Gucci outfit and Gucci loafers. She locked eyes with him as he turned his head and met hers. He immediately broke out in a smile at the sight of her.

Nina moved before she realized it and found herself in his arms and tightly hugging his neck.

"I guess you missed me, huh?" TaSean asked once Nina released him.

She smiled as she stood looking him over.

"Boy, look at you!" Nina said, seeing the ice in his ears and around his wrist. "You really look good, TaSean!"

"I was thinking the same exact thing about you!" TaSean stated honestly, unable to stop himself from looking at the way the jumpsuit she was wearing hugged her thighs and ass, showing off her perfectly curved hips.

"You ready to go?" Nina asked, noticing the way TaSean was looking her over.

"Umm, yeah!" he replied as he followed her to the door.

Once she was outside, Nina following alongside TaSean over to a new model Benz truck.

"I see NBA money has been good to you!" Nina commented.

"Naw!" TaSean stated as he opened the passenger side door to the Benz to let Nina into his truck. "This actually was a gift from Alexus."

Nina was surprised at what she had just heard, but she watched and waited until TaSean walked around his truck and got inside.

"TaSean! Alexus bought you a 2018-model Benz truck?"

"Yeah!" he answered as he was starting it up. "She sold the Escalade and bought me this!"

"Wow!" she said in surprise. "I guess you two are doing better than I thought you'd be, huh?"

"We good!" TaSean said as he caught the way Nina had asked the question. He then looked over at her and asked, "What's up with you and your boy Derrick?"

Nina waved her hand dismissively at the mention of her sorry-ass boyfriend. "Derrick is being who his ass been and can only be!"

"I take it you two are not doing so good?"

"TaSean, he's still having a temper after what happened at the tournament. But then it got even worse once he saw you on the news and found out that you got signed with the Knicks. He feels like it should be him playing for the team and not you!" Nina said with a sigh.

"So he's still tripping then, huh?"

"Is he?" Nina stated, shaking her head before she changed the subject. "So, when do you start playing in the summer league you were telling me about?"

"Actually, the first game starts this Wednesday again the Brooklyn Nets."

"And how many games is it again?"

"Eight!"

"So this league is really just supposed to show your coaches what they can expect out of you, right?"

"Pretty much!" TaSean answered, but then added, "It's really just another tryout, but just for the possibility of getting a back-up position to get onto the court and into an actual game."

"You'll be starting as soon as they see how good you really are!" Nina told him.

She smiled as she leaned over and kissed TaSean on his cheek, only to receive that gorgeous deep-dimpled smile he seemed to have only for her in return.

They continued their conversation until they pulled up in front of Club Angels and saw that the place was packed. TaSean parked the Benz a short ways up the block, and then both he and Nina walked back up the street to the club.

"Nina!"

Nina heard her name and recognized a few model friends in line. She exchanged a few words with the girls until they began asking about TaSean. When the women turned around, they could see that he had drawn his own crowd of models and partygoers.

"Excuse me, ladies!" Nina stated as she turned away from her friends and walked over to get TaSean.

"Sorry, ladies!" Nina apologized as she took TaSean's hand and led him into the club after seeing that the doorman also recognized him.

Once they were inside the crowded club with people everywhere, Nina leaned into TaSean and asked if he wanted something to drink. She then led him over to the bar to order drinks, only for the female bartender, who was also a famous model, to recognize TaSean.

"Nina, girl! I ain't know your man was TaSean Prince!" the bartender/model cried, smiling as she gave the two of them their drinks. She then added, "It's on the house, Prince!"

"Good look, ma!" TaSean told the girl, winking his eye at her.

Nina watched the entire exchange between TaSean and the bartender/model. She stood there and smiled and waited until the two of them walked away from the bar.

"I see you easily took to being famous."

"Look who my girl—! I mean my best friend is!" TaSean told Nina.

Nina caught the slip-up, but she didn't react to it since she could see that he didn't really mean it.

"You gonna dance with me, right?" she asked, immediately changing the subject.

"I'll see what I can do for you, shorty!" TaSean told her, smiling at Nina with a playful smirk.

* * *

Jennifer spotted TaSean as soon as his ass walked into the club with the Spanish-looking bitch who looked familiar. They were now all up on each other on the dance floor, which was a little too close for her liking. Jennifer left the bar and the friends she was with and started toward TaSean and the bitch he was all up on in the club.

"TaSean!" Jennifer yelled, grabbing and snatching TaSean away from the bitch he was with, only to get all up in his face. "What the fuck is you doing? Who's this bitch you got up in here all over you?"

TaSean recognized Jennifer and saw the bullshit about to jump off. He grabbed Nina's hand and attempted to walk off, only for Jennifer to grab his arm again.

"Jennifer, look!"

"Look, bitch!" Nina yelled as she got up into the face of the girl who kept grabbing TaSean's arm. "I don't know who the fuck you is, but grab TaSean one more time and I'ma whoop your ass!"

"Bitch, who—?"

Nina went straight into the girl's mouth in the middle of what she was saying. Nina then went in on the girl, keeping her word and beating the girl's ass until somebody pulled her off of her, just as security showed up.

"Put me the fuck down!" Nina yelled, fighting to get free and back to the shit-talking hoe she was just beating on.

"Nina, relax, ma!"

"Fuck that! Let me go!" Nina yelled.

Nina snatched away from the guy that carried her

out of the club, only to be pulled back around and kissed on the lips.

Nina fought her way to push the guy off of her at first, but she felt familiar hands on her waist, gripping her there. Nina somehow knew who was kissing her and was soon returning the kiss.

"You feel better now?" Nina heard after the kiss ended and she slowly opened her eyes to find herself staring into the familiar light grayish eyes that belonged to TaSean.

"What! What was that?" she asked, still surprised after what had just happened.

"It was the first thing I could think of that I figured would get you to calm down and talk to me!" TaSean explained to her.

Nina looked around and saw people watching them. She then grabbed TaSean's hand and said, "Let's get out of here!"

* * *

TaSean drove around for a while after leaving the club. The both of them were quiet the entire time, until Nina broke the silence and told TaSean to take her back to her hotel. She sat staring out the window in deep thought, never realizing when they pulled into the parking lot of the hotel.

"Nina!" TaSean spoke up, saying his first word since leaving the club.

Nina lost her train of thought and looked over to TaSean. She then realized they weren't moving and were back at her hotel.

"Come up!" she told TaSean, looking away from his stare as she opened the truck door and got out.

She waited for him at the back end of his truck until he finally joined her. She took his hand in hers and then led him into the hotel.

Once they were on the elevator, Nina waited until the door shut and then she turned to face TaSean. Before he could say anything, she was kissing him and pressing her body against him.

"Nina!"

"No talking!" she told him, pressing her lips back against TaSean's lips, which she instantly fell in love with at how soft they were.

Once they arrived on her floor and the door slid

open, Nina took TaSean's hand and led him off the elevator and to her hotel room door.

"Nina, are you—?"

"I told you no talking!" she told him, pulling TaSean into the hotel room and shutting the door behind them and locking it.

Nina went directly into pulling open TaSean's button-up. She then looked up into his eyes once he grabbed both her wrists.

"Nina, what's all this?" TaSean asked her, staring straight into her hazel-green eyes. "Ma, you know what you doing?"

"I know exactly what I want!" she told him, pulling herself free from TaSean's grip. "TaSean, this doesn't have to change anything between us, but tonight I need this! I need you!"

Nina kissed TaSean's lips once more, feeling him responding after a brief moment. She wrapped her legs around his waist once TaSean picked her up and then began carrying her over to the bed.

"Take off your clothes!" she told him as he stood in front of her after gently laying her down onto the bed.

She also began undressing herself, rushing while never taking her eyes off of TaSean.

"Condoms!" Nina stated in a hopeful tone.

Nina watched as TaSean picked up his pants and pulled out his wallet. She smiled when he pulled out a gold-wrapped Magnum condom.

"Hurry!"

Chapter 10

Nina was seated in front of her 38-inch wall unit, flat-screen television, waiting for the start of TaSean's first game with the summer league. She was missing him since the last time she saw him six days ago. She let her head fall back against the sofa and groaned loudly in frustration, wanting to call and talk to him, but she was unsure why she still had not since returning to Chicago.

Nina heard a knock at her condominium front door, which interrupted her train of thought. She sighed loudly and deeply as she pushed herself up from the sofa and left the den to answer the front door.

"Damn, bitch!" Vanessa cried out in surprise as soon as Nina opened the front door looking like a hot mess! "What the hell is wrong with you, and why haven't you been answering your phone?"

Nina stepped aside as Vanessa entered the apartment. Nina closed and locked the door behind her and then returned to her spot on the sofa.

"Nina!" Vanessa called out, following her friend back into the den and seeing how she was living.

There was garbage all over the coffee table from different fast-food restaurants. There was also a blanket and pillow lying across the sofa beside her.

"What the hell is wrong with you? What's all this mess around here?"

Vanessa received no response at all from her best friend, so she made room on the sofa and sat down beside Nina.

"Nina, what's going on, girl? What's gotten into you?"

"Be quiet!" Nina finally spoke up as she sat forward seeing that the game was about to start. "The game is starting!"

"Game?" Vanessa repeated, looking at the flat-screen. "What game?"

"TaSean's first game in the summer league is starting!" Nina answered, smiling when the camera zoomed in on TaSean as he and his team jogged out onto the floor, listening as the commentator spoke about TaSean winning the Bigfoot Hoops

Championship tournament, and even mentioning his cousin Anthony, who was now playing for the Miami Heat.

Vanessa watched her best friend as Nina sat smiling and staring at the screen. Vanessa then realized what was wrong with her friend.

"Nina, you slept with TaSean, didn't you?"

"What?" Nina asked, barely glancing over at Vanessa. "What are you talking about?"

"You did!" Vanessa stated, smiling as she sat staring at Nina. "That's what all this is about. You went to New York and ended up sleeping with TaSean, and now you can't take it!"

"Vanessa, it's bigger than that!" Nina told her friend, turning to face her.

"So you really did sleep with TaSean?" Vanessa asked, smiling as she sat watching Nina nod her head yes. "So what's with all this?"

Nina looked around after Vanessa waved her hands around her den. Nina sighed as she fell forward and lay her head against Vanessa's shoulder. Vanessa wrapped her arms around her, which caused the tears to begin falling.

"Nina, what's wrong?" Vanessa asked in real concern after hearing her friend begin to cry. "What did TaSean do to you?"

"That's just it!" Nina got out past her tears as she sat up from Vanessa's shoulder and met her eyes. "TaSean was perfect the whole time!"

"So, what's wrong?" Vanessa asked with a confused look on her face.

"I'm afraid I may end up pregnant!" she told Vanessa, seeing the look that now appeared on her friend's face.

Nina went into the story of how everything happened. She told her how it started with a fight between her and who she found out was TaSean's ex-girlfriend. She continued with how that led to the two of them going back to her hotel and having sex.

"So, you and TaSean didn't use protection then, right?" Vanessa asked once Nina was finished with her story.

"We used one, but it just popped, Vanessa!" Nina admitted. "We didn't even know until it was over and

TaSean was pulling out of me!"

"What did TaSean say?" Vanessa wanted to know. "How did he react?"

"He said that he wants us to be together if I'm pregnant."

"So, what's the problem other than Derrick?"

"That's just it, Vanessa. I'll leave Derrick for TaSean. I've fallen in love with TaSean, but he only wants to be with me if I'm pregnant! I want him whether I'm pregnant or not, and he's not feeling the same way."

"Have you talked with him about all of this?"

Nina shook her head and said, "I haven't spoken to TaSean since I left New York and came back home."

"Hasn't he called you?"

"He calls every day, but I don't answer his call; and before you ask, no, I haven't called him either!"

"Why not?" Vanessa inquired, staring at Nina like she had lost her mind. "You just sat there and said that you're in love with TaSean! Why won't you call him?"

"Vanessa, I don't even know!" Nina admitted, just as she heard the yelling coming from the flat-screen.

Nina and Vanessa looked at the screen just in time to see the replay of TaSean throwing the alley-oop to the rookie power forward, causing the Knicks fans to get up out of their seats and start to yell and cheer.

"I know one thing!" Vanessa stated, smiling as she looked from the flat-screen back at Nina. "You better hurry up and make up your mind before that white girl seeing TaSean gets smart or some other bitch gets her hands on your man, Nina! TaSean is an extremely good-looking guy, and both you and I know a lot of women who want him. Are you gonna let them have what belongs to you?"

Nina looked back at Vanessa and met her best friend's eyes after hearing what was just said. Nina changed the subject as she looked back toward the game to see TaSean being taken out of the game.

"What's going on with you and Anthony?"

Vanessa smiled at the mention of his name.

"Actually, I'm going to Miami this weekend to see my baby play against Oklahoma City. You wanna come with me?"

* * *

TaSean played seven minutes in the first game against the Brooklyn Nets and never returned to the floor for the rest of the game. In fact, he played even less time the next game they played against New Orleans. And just like the first game, when he was taken out, he wasn't allowed back on the court. TaSean found himself playing five minutes in the game against the Lakers, and again after five minutes of play, he was taken out of the game and not allowed back.

TaSean didn't know how he was feeling during the next five games of the summer league, when his play was still limited. But he was certainly looking forward to playing the Chicago Bulls after seeing Nina, Vanessa, and Gina in the stands. But he became very upset when he found out that Nina had left and then she wouldn't answer his call when he phoned her before the team was getting ready to leave town.

Once they were back in New York, all the rookies were attending orientation concerning different issues, such as opening a new bank account, hiring an accountant, etc. TaSean was pulled away from the class when he was told that Coach Hans wanted to speak with him.

"What's up, coach?" TaSean asked after stopping in front of the coach's office door that was wide open.

"Come in and shut the door behind you, Prince!" Coach Hans told TaSean as he set down the papers he had been looking over. The coach then sat back in his desk chair as the young ballplayer stepped around in front of the desk. "I'll make this quick and straight to the point, Prince. I've made the decision to put you in as De'Nard Green's back-up at point guard. Can you handle that?"

"Hell, I mean, of course!" TaSean answered after correcting himself.

Coach Hans nodded his head after receiving his answer, and then went back to the papers he was reading over.

"Get back to orientation, Prince!" the coach said.

After leaving the coach's office and feeling much better about the whole summer league situation with not playing much, TaSean pulled out his cell phone and paused at the thought of calling Nina. But he remembered she was basically letting him know she wanted nothing else to do with him; so instead, he called his current girlfriend.

"Hello!" Alexus answered at the start of the second ring.

"What's good, shorty?" TaSean asked, standing outside of the orientation room.

He then went straight into telling Alexus the good news of him getting the backup position for the starting point guard.

* * *

TaSean was leaving the New York Knicks' arena and heading home, but at the last minute he changed his mind and direction. He found himself pulling up in front of his mother's place, just as she was parking her Lexus GS 350 and getting out.

"Hey, baby!" Yolanda said happily as her son got out of his truck and then jogged over to take in the bags she was holding. She then accepted the kiss he gave her. "What are you doing here?"

"I just got out of orientation and wanted to see how you was doing!" he told his mother, following her from the Lexus up to the front door of the apartment.

"Where's that girlfriend of yours at?" Yolanda asked as the two of them entered the front door.

"She was back at the penthouse when I talked to her last," he answered his mother as he followed her into the kitchen. "Ain't no telling where she is now though!"

"What you mean?" Yolanda asked, looking at her son as she began putting away the groceries.

She then noticed her son's dismissive wave of his hand and also saw the look on his face

"How was your day, Momma?" TaSean asked his mother as he helped her put the groceries away.

Yolanda set down two loaves of bread and then turned to face her son. She followed him with her eyes as he continued helping her.

"What's wrong, TaSean?"

"Huh?" he said, looking at his mother before going back to doing what he was doing.

"TaSean, don't play with me, boy!" Yolanda told him, getting his attention. "You may have wanted to see me, TaSean, but I know you! What's bothering you, baby?"

TaSean sighed as he grabbed a bottle of water from the refrigerator. He then turned and leaned back against the fridge and said, "I think Nina's pregnant, Momma!"

"Does Alexus know?" Yolanda asked as she shook her head and deeply sighed.

"No!"

"When did you sleep with Nina, TaSean?"

"Almost two weeks ago now," he answered. "Well, fifteen days exactly."

"Has she attempted to call you?"

"No!"

"Have you attempted to call her?"

"I've been calling her since we was together last,

Momma!" TaSean told her, but then added, "It's like every time I call, she doesn't answer or I'm getting her voice message."

Yolanda sighed again and thought for a few moments before looking back at her son.

"TaSean, you need to go to Chicago and see her. Do you know where she lives?"

"She never told me!" he admitted, but then smiled and said, "But I think I know how to find out though. Thanks, Momma. Love you!"

After kissing his mother's cheek, TaSean headed for the front door. He met his step-father at the door as he was coming in. He spoke as he shot out the door.

"What was that?" Aaron asked, looking from his fleeing step-son to his wife and seeing the smile on her face as she walked up beside him at the front door. "You gonna tell me what just happened?"

Yolanda was still watching her son as he was driving off.

She then looked at her husband and said, "I think we're going to be grandparents really soon, sweetheart!"

Chapter 11

Nina was tired from flying from one photo shoot to the next, and she was already booked up for the next coming week for more shoots as well as a few parties she was being paid to attend. Nina didn't bother unpacking her bags from last night after getting back from the Bahamas on a photo shoot for *Smooth Girl Magazine*.

Nina groaned in aggravation when she heard her house phone begin to ring. She reached over to the bedside table, first knocking over something before she picked up the headset.

"Who is it?" she answered in what came out like a growl.

"What's up, ma?"

Nina's eyes popped open at the sound of the familiar voice, and she shot up into a sitting position.

"Who is this?"

"Come on, shorty! We both know you know whose voice this belongs to!"

Nina remained quiet for a moment, unable to

believe who was on the other end of the phone.

"How the hell did you get my home number, TaSean?" she asked angrily.

"Why have you been ignoring me, ma?" he asked, ignoring her question.

"Did you hear me?"

"Yeah! But I'm only concerned about you telling me why you ignored my calls."

"Because we have nothing to talk about, that's why!"

"I heard we do!"

"What?" she yelled. "What the hell are you talking about?"

"Why didn't you tell me, Nina?"

"Tell you what, TaSean?"

"Tell me you was pregnant!"

Nina remained quiet for a moment after hearing what TaSean had said, but she soon got control of herself.

"For your information, I'm not pregnant from you, and I need to go. Please do not call me back!"

Nina hung up the phone in TaSean's face. She

was unable to believe he knew about her pregnancy. She instantly thought about Vanessa, just as the knocking started at the front door.

"This better not be this hooker!" Nina said as she got out of bed and marched to the front.

She looked out of the peephole and froze in place at what she saw.

"Oh shit!" she cussed as she stepped back from the door, staring at it as if it had just grown a face.

"Nina, open the door, ma!" TaSean called out from in the hallway. "I know you're in there since I just heard you cussing."

"What are you doing here, TaSean?" she yelled back. "Did Vanessa tell you where I lived?"

"Open the door, ma! We need to talk!"

"We have nothing to talk about, TaSean!"

"Nina, open the door. Please, ma!"

Nina was softened by his plea and her need to really see him. She was back at the front door and unlocking it before realizing what she was doing.

She broke down as soon as her eyes lay on him, falling into his arms as she began to cry.

Nina then felt TaSean lift her off her feet and hold her in his arms. She wrapped her arms around his neck, and she laid her head against his chest, only to soon be laid down onto her bed. She felt TaSean lay down beside her as his arms went around her.

"TaSean, I'm sorry!" Nina cried as she rolled over toward him, burying her face into his chest as he held her tighter.

He then began kissing her on the top of her head, telling her that it was okay and that he would make everything better.

* * *

Nina was unsure when she fell asleep, but she slowly opened her eyes to find herself staring into TaSean's extremely handsome face. She realized at that moment that she hadn't dreamed what she was remembering, but that he actually showed up at her place to see her.

Nina lay where she was and stared at TaSean, as he was asleep. She quickly rolled over and snatched up her cell phone as it began loudly ringing.

"Hello!" Nina answered the phone.

"I'm guessing TaSean's there since your ass is whispering!" Vanessa asked with a little laugh.

"I can't talk now, Vanessa. TaSean's sleeping, and I don't—"

"It's cool, ma!"

Nina looked back at TaSean to find him watching her. She held his eyes as she told Vanessa that she had to go, and then she hung up the phone on her best friend.

"Come here, ma!" TaSean told Nina as she sat staring at him.

Nina placed her cell phone back onto the table next to her and crawled back across the bed to TaSean, only for him to sit up and gently push her down and onto her back. He then positioned himself between her legs while still continuing to hold her eyes. She met his lips as he leaned down to kiss her.

Nina moaned at the touch of TaSean's hands on her breasts as their kiss turned passionate. Nina then helped as TaSean began undressing her, working off her panties once he had her jeans off.

"TaSean!" she cried out once she felt his mouth

on her womanhood.

Nina arched her back and gripped the side of TaSean's head as he ate her pussy in a way she never had done to her before. Within minutes, she was screaming out his name, and she climaxed so hard that she thought she blacked out. Before she realized it, TaSean was completely naked and slowly sliding inside of her.

"Oh God!" Nina cried as she pulled TaSean down against her body, wrapping her arms around his neck as he began moving in and out of her. "TaSean, I love you! I love you so much!"

"I love you too, ma!" he told her, softly speaking into her ear. "I want us to be together. Be a family, Nina! Tell me you'll be mine!"

"Yes, TaSean!" Nina cried as he pushed deeper inside of her, hitting her spot just right. "Baby, you can have whatever you want, TaSean. I love you! Oh God! I'm about to cum again!"

"Cum for ya man, ma!" TaSean told her as he began grinding up into her the way he remembered she liked the last time they were together, only to cause her to scream out his name as she exploded once more.

* * *

They showered together and talked while under the hot water washing one another. Nina expressed her fear of him only wanting to be with her because of the baby that she recently just found out she was carrying. She admitted that she had not told Derrick she was pregnant or that she wanted to end their relationship. She also discussed how she felt about the two of them living apart if they were going to be together.

After getting out of the shower and drying off, TaSean put his boxer briefs back on while Nina wrapped a long towel around her body. She was drying her hair as the two of them left the bathroom and went back into the bedroom.

When they were back in bed together and under the blanket, Nina laid her head onto TaSean's chest and was running her fingers up and down his trail of hair that ran down the center of his lower abdomen.

"TaSean, how are we going to do this?" Nina

asked as she continued to play with his trail of hair.

"I was just thinking about the same thing!" TaSean admitted. "I know you're settled out here in Chicago, and I don't wanna ask you to up and leave since I know this is where your family, friends, and agent are."

"So, what are you planning then?"

"I just found out that I made the backup position for the starting point guard for the Knicks. But I was thinking about talking to Brian to see if he can get me traded from New York to the Bulls."

Nina lifted her head and looked over at TaSean.

"TaSean, are you serious?"

"You do want me out here, right?" he asked her with a smile.

"Of course!" Nina replied with a smile as she hugged his neck tight and then kissed him on the lips. "How long is it gonna be before you can get a trade?"

"I gotta holla at Brian and talk to him about it first!" TaSean admitted, but then said, "But until I can make the move, you need to answer that phone when I call or we gonna have a problem."

"Yes, papi!" Nina replied with a grin as she kissed TaSean's lips again and felt him pull her on top of him, with his hands gripping both of her butt cheeks.

* * *

TaSean discussed the issue about Alexus and a few other things, when they were interrupted by knocking at the front door at the same time Nina's cell phone started ringing. TaSean put on his jeans and wifebeater while Nina answered her cell phone. He left the bedroom and went out to answer the front door.

"Where my girl at?" Vanessa asked as soon as TaSean opened the front door, where both she and Shawna pushed inside past him.

TaSean shook his head and smiled before he looked back to see his smiling cousin in the doorway.

"What up, Cuz?" Anthony said as he and TaSean embraced each other.

"I see Vanessa got ya ass out here too, huh?" TaSean asked as he closed and locked the door.

"Yeah!" Anthony admitted, following his cousin

through the condo and into the den.

They both sat down on the couch as TaSean snatched up the remote from the coffee table and turned on the television

"Is it true or not, Cuz?"

TaSean found ESPN on the flat-screen, and then looked back over at Anthony with a smile on his face.

"Oh shit!" Anthony said, seeing the look on his cousin's face. "Nigga, you actually got Nina's fine ass pregnant, Cuz?"

"Excuse me?" both Anthony and TaSean heard, just as Vanessa, Nina, and Shawna walked into the den.

"Don't play with me, Anthony!" Vanessa told him as she sat down beside him, pushing him over only to get right back under him.

Anthony shook his head as he dropped his arm around Vanessa. He then looked over at his cousin to see TaSean and Nina locked in a deep kiss.

"Excuse us!" Vanessa cried out. "We do not want to see that mess!"

Nina smiled after pulling out of her kiss with

TaSean. She then curled her feet up underneath her and then leaned in against TaSean.

"Where y'all just coming from?" she asked her friends.

"We just picked Anthony up from the airport," Vanessa answered. "We were talking on the way here. Y'all wanna go out tonight?"

"Where to?" Nina asked.

"Club Chocolate!" Vanessa answered before she continued. "Miss Shawna's new boyfriend owns the club, girl!"

Nina looked over at a smiling Shawna in surprise and shook her head, and then turned back and looked at TaSean.

"Baby, you wanna go?"

"I don't know!" TaSean answered. "Last time we went out, you ended up beating on some female."

"But you ended up getting some too!" Nina threw back at him.

"In that case! We are leaving!" TaSean said, causing everybody to burst out laughing.

Chapter 12

TaSean met with his agent, Brian Adams, and talked about a possible trade to the Chicago Bulls. However, he found out that they would have to wait at least a month into the regular season before a trade was even considered. They further needed to find out if Chicago was willing to make a trade for him or not. TaSean relayed the message to Nina over the phone one night when she called from California at a photo shoot.

Once the preseason started up and the Knicks were supposed to play the Milwaukee Bucks in an away game, TaSean played behind De-Nard Green a total of thirty-seven minutes. He scored eighteen points and made three steals, one block, and nine assists.

TaSean talked with Nina on FaceTime as the team was headed back home. He found out that she, Vanessa, and Shawna went back and forth between games watching the Knicks and the Miami Heat play against the Utah Jazz in a home game.

"Baby, you was amazing, TaSean!" Nina told him while FaceTiming with her boyfriend. "We liked you better than that guy you played behind. What's his name?"

"De'Nard Green!" TaSean answered with a grin. "But then I'm pretty sure you and ya girls were being biased."

"So!" Nina replied as both she and TaSean began laughing together.

"I love your ass, TaSean!" Nina told him. "Also, I talked to Derrick."

"What did homeboy say?"

"He got mad, but then claimed that he was seeing someone else anyway. I just hung up on his ass. He called back a few times, but he hasn't called back since."

"So I ain't gotta fly back there, right?"

"Boy, no!" Nina answered, laughing at her baby daddy's crazy ass.

* * *

Once he was back to New York, TaSean wasted no time leaving the arena, since he wanted to get home and lay down. He hopped into his truck and headed for home as he began thinking about Alexus and how he was going to break the news to her, first about Nina's pregnancy and then about his decision to end their relationship.

Once he got to his high-rise apartment building and parked in the garage, TaSean took the elevator up to his floor and stepped off, just as his cell phone began to ring.

TaSean dug out his phone to see a name and number he didn't recognize. He answered the phone just as he was letting himself inside the penthouse.

"Hello!"

"Good evening, is this Mr.—?"

"What the fuck!" TaSean got out as soon as he stepped into the penthouse and saw the place ripped apart. Shit was all over the place and tore the hell up. "What the hell happened in his shit?"

"Yeah!" TaSean answered while still looking around.

"Mr. Prince?" TaSean heard.

"Yeah! What's up?"

"Mr. Prince, my name is Keith Davis, and I'm an attorney representing Miss Alexus Kristen. She asked that I call you and let you know that she would like you to come and visit her at—!"

"Whoa!" TaSean spoke up, interrupting the attorney. "Where the fuck is Alexus?"

"I was just telling you, sir, that Miss Kristen was arrested and is being held on the island at this moment. She wants to see you as soon as you can get out there, sir."

"Yeah, I hear all that!" TaSean stated, but then asked, "You know what the hell happened here?"

"I'm assuming you're at Miss Kristen's penthouse residence, correct?"

"Yeah! What the fuck happened?"

"I'm not at liberty to discuss the case over the phone with you, Mr. Prince. I was only told to relay the message that Miss Kristen asked me to, which is what I just did. If you wish to know anything further, my advice is that you visit Miss Kristen. Oh, and one last thing, you should find a new residence soon before the penthouse is impounded by the DEA! I need to go, Mr. Prince! Have a good night."

TaSean couldn't believe what the fuck he had just heard, and he still didn't have any idea what the hell was really going on. TaSean went ahead and took the attorney's advice and started packing up before the DEA actually did show up.

* * *

TaSean left Alexus's penthouse after getting his things out and packing them into his Benz truck. He headed straight to his mother and step-father's place. He parked in front, hopped out of his truck, and walked up and knocked on the front door.

He saw the light go on in the front room and heard the door being unlocked. TaSean came face-to-face with his step-father and saw his mother standing behind him.

"TaSean!" Yolanda cried in concern at the sight of her son stopping by so late at night.

"TaSean, what's wrong, son?" Aaron asked his step-son, when he saw the expression on his face.

"Aaron, let him in!" Yolanda told her husband as she reached for her son.

TaSean stepped forward to enter the apartment, and he allowed his mother to lead him over to the couch and sit with him. He then laid his head back and sighed deep and loud.

"TaSean, what's happened, sweetheart?" Yolanda asked her son. "Did you and Alexus get into a fight?"

TaSean shook his head and then lifted it as he saw both his mother and step-father watching him and waiting for him to say something.

"I'm not sure what's happened, Momma!" he admitted before he then told them everything he knew.

"So you don't know why Alexus is in jail, and all an attorney told you was that she was at Rikers Island and wants you to come and visit her, right?" Aaron asked TaSean. "And if you need a place to stay until you can figure all of this out, you're obviously welcome to stay here, son."

TaSean heard his step-father but simply stared into nothingness. He laid his head over onto his mother's chest as she wrapped her arms around him and began rubbing the back of his head.

* * *

"Kristen!" Officer Jones yelled, kicking the side of the inmate's bunk. "Inmate Alexus Kristen, wake up!"

Once she opened her eyes, she immediately gripped the homemade knife that was under her pillow as she looked around to finally lay eyes on the butch female standing too close to her. Alexus then released her grip on the knife and sat up.

"What's up, officer?" Alexus asked the dike-ass female officer.

"You've got a visit!" Officer Jones announced, looking at Alexus's perky breasts that were covered up in the sports bra. "You've got five minutes to be ready."

Alexus caught the way the pussy-eating bitch was eye-fucking her titties. She then shook her head as she got up out of her bunk to get ready for her visitor. She just hoped it was who she had been waiting for since the last time she spoke with her attorney.

Alexus was escorted to the visitation room fifteen minutes after she was dressed. She entered the visitors' room and saw a few other females already inside different booths as she passed, until she stopped in front of a booth with a gorgeous and really familiar face looking back at her.

Alexus smiled at the sight of her man and then picked up the phone receiver as TaSean did the same on the other side of the glass.

"Hey, handsome!"

"What up, shorty? You good in there, ma?"

Alexus smiled a little harder after hearing her man's concern for her.

"I'm good, baby! I know you're wondering what's going on, right?" she said.

"The thought did cross my mind!"

Alexus heard TaSean's sarcasm, which let her know he was upset, since he was extra sarcastic when he was mad. Alexus then took a deep breath and after releasing it, opened up and admitted the truth to her man. She told him about the weed, mollies, and even cocaine she was selling.

"So, let me see if I got this right!" TaSean spoke up once Alexus had finished explaining. "You basically a dope girl and never thought to tell me?"

"That's just what they're charging me with, TaSean!" Alexus told him before she then pointed to the phone receiver while mouthing that he needed to be careful about what he said.

TaSean nodded his head in understanding and then questioned, "So, how do things look for you getting out of all of this? Can I bond you out?"

"I've got a federal hold!" she told him. "I can't bond out, but I've got a strong team of lawyers, and the DEA really doesn't have nothing on me, but he says, she says."

"You need anything in here?" he asked her. "Everything good in there?"

"For now, I'm good, handsome," Alexus told him, smiling at him as she then said, "I saw your game last night. You did your thing with eighteen points, three steals, one block, and nine assists. I just don't like that they kept pulling you out of the game so much! I love you over that clown De'Nard

Green!"

"Thanks for the vote, ma!" he told her, showing a small smile.

"Kristen! Visitation is over!" both Alexus and TaSean heard the officer announce.

Alexus stood up from her seat as did TaSean.

"I've got some news for you. I had planned on telling you last night before all this jumped off, but when you come back to visit, I'll tell you then. But I love you, TaSean!"

"Kristen, that's it!" the officer yelled again.

Alexus winked at TaSean and then smiled as she set down the phone receiver, turned, and left the visitation booth.

Chapter 13

TaSean played against the Miami Heat on the same day he moved into the penthouse that his agent, Brian, made arrangements for him to rent. TaSean sat out the whole first quarter but sat watching his cousin doing his thing out on the court for the Heat.

TaSean smiled after seeing the ten-footer jump shot Anthony made for the Heat, which pushed Miami up by six points, with the score 34-28.

"Prince!"

TaSean heard his name and looked over at Coach Hans, who told him to check in for Green. TaSean did as he was told and checked in at the sub-desk.

Once the substitution was made and Green angrily left the court, TaSean got onto the floor with the Knicks on defense. He got the inbound ball that was tossed in by the power forward.

He walked the ball up the floor after the inbound. TaSean eyed the floor, but he fucked up the defender when he pulled up for the three from the top of the key.

TaSean got back on defense after making the three and getting the home crowd up out of their seats yelling and cheering. TaSean was already on the move when he saw the pass that was meant for Anthony. He intercepted it and heard Anthony yell as he was already pushing the ball up the floor.

TaSean put on a show, stepping off his right foot from the free throw line and setting up for the one-handed tomahawk. But he changed up at the last moment and switched from his right to his left hand, tossing up the left-hand layup and scoring off the glass.

TaSean smiled at his cousin once he and Anthony locked eyes. He could see the smile on his cousin's lips. TaSean got right back onto defense as Anthony and his team got back on offense.

* * *

By the end of the fourth quarter, TaSean's team had lost to Miami 97-82. TaSean finished with fifteen points and seven assists. He embraced his cousin after the game in the middle of the court, only to be quickly approached by the reporters and cameras.

TaSean did a quick interview and answered a few questions concerning the two of them playing against each other and their feelings. Both TaSean and Anthony weren't surprised when the reporter asked if the two of them could see themselves playing together again on the same team.

"We'll see!" TaSean stated with a smirk on his face before he and Anthony walked off together.

* * *

After showering and changing back into his own clothes, TaSean listened to the players joke with the starting point guard, De'Nard Green, about his position being taken and given to the rookie. TaSean peeped Green's face, and he saw that even though dude was smiling, he wasn't really feeling what his teammates were saying.

After leaving the locker room and meeting up with Brian in the hallway, TaSean fell into step with his agent.

"So, what's good, Brian?"

"I've got some good news about this Chicago

request you wanted with this trade."

"What up?"

"I spoke with Chicago and they're really interested in you, and they're planning to make an offer to the Knicks for you as a trade."

"Yo, you bullshitting?" TaSean asked as he stopped at the exit that led to the players and administration's parking lot. He turned and faced his agent. "You serious, B!"

Brian smiled as he answered TaSean's question.

"I'm not sure if you're aware of the Bull's starting point guard, Jason James, who recently injured his Achilles tendon. Supposedly, he's out for the rest of the season, so they're really interested in you!"

TaSean was hyped the hell up after the news he had just received. He listened to the rest of what his agent had to say, but he then said he would call him later as he was walking out the exit. TaSean barely heard the door slam shut behind him when he heard a familiar voice.

"Hey, baby daddy!"

TaSean turned around to see Nina standing with Tina, who was the small forward A. J. Hill's wife, along with the female security guard that patrolled the parking lot. TaSean broke out in a smile as Nina rushed toward him.

"Hey, baby!" Nina cried happily, throwing her arms up and around his neck and hugging him.

TaSean passionately kissed Nina's lips, breaking the kiss moments later to see his baby mother's eyes closed as her lips still held the form as if she was still being kissed.

"What was that?" Nina asked as she finally opened her eyes and smiled up at her man.

"I miss you!" he admitted. "You ready to go?"

"Sure is!" Nina answered as she waved to the two women and then walked off with TaSean.

"Where's your car?" TaSean asked as the two of them approached the Benz truck.

"At your mother's house!" Nina replied as TaSean opened up the passenger door for her. She caught the way he looked at her after mentioning her car was parked at his mother's house. "I'll explain everything once you get in the truck, TaSean."

After shutting the door, TaSean walked over to the driver's side and got behind the wheel. He then tossed his team gym bag into the bag seat.

"You played good tonight, baby!" Nina told him as TaSean was backing out the Benz from the parking spot and began driving toward the exit. "I didn't know you could jump so high either, TaSean."

"I'm more of a ground player and a shooter!" he told her, but then asked, "How'd you know where my mom lived at?"

"The same way you found out where I lived!" she answered him.

"Vanessa!" TaSean asked with a grin as he looked over at Nina and saw her smiling and nodding her head. He shook his head but then remembered his conversation with his agent. "Yeah! I've got some good news."

"What is it?"

"Remember what we talked about, about me getting traded from the Knicks to the Bulls?" he asked Nina. "Well, Chicago is interested in me playing for them since their starting point guard got injured and can't play. They're going to make New York an offer!"

"Baby, are you serious?" Nina asked with a huge smile on her face.

TaSean nodded his head, only to have Nina throw her arms around his neck and hug and kiss him on the cheek. He turned his head and kissed his girl and baby mother.

"I love you so much, TaSean!" Nina told him, still smiling as she moved back into her seat and stared at her man.

TaSean smiled when he winked at her, and then he accepted her hand as they intertwined their fingers.

* * *

TaSean hung out at his mother's for a little while, but he got tired and needed to get some sleep, since the first game of the regular season was the next day against the Chicago Bulls. TaSean left his mother's place with Nina trailing behind him, and was halfway there when he was suddenly pulled over by the

NYPD for no reason.

TaSean spoke with the officers and found out that the truck was a match to one the DEA was looking for. After telling the officers his name, TaSean was asked to step out of the truck. The officers then explained to him that it was being seized due to orders to pick it up once found.

"This is some bullshit!" TaSean stated angrily as he climbed his six-foot-five frame into Nina's rented Audi RS7.

"TaSean, what's going on?" Nina asked, looking from the two police officers over to a pissed-off TaSean. "Are they taking your truck?"

"Let's just go, Nina!" TaSean told her, laying his head back against the headrest.

They arrived at the rental penthouse a short while later, and Nina parked inside the garage. They took the elevator up to the top floor. TaSean led Nina from the elevator to the front door of the new place. He then headed straight toward the west side of the four-bedroom, five-bath penthouse with Nina right behind him.

"Baby, are you gonna tell me what the hell just happened?" Nina asked him as she tossed her keys, purse, and cell phone onto the bedside table closest to the door.

"It's just bullshit, Nina!" TaSean stated as he undressed down to his wifebeater and boxer briefs and then climbed into bed.

"TaSean, don't play with me!" Nina told him as she stood beside the bed in nothing but her panties and bra. "I asked you why your truck was taken, and I would like a real answer, please!"

TaSean sighed as he lay in bed watching Nina go through his dresser until she found one of his T-shirts. He remained quiet and just thinking until she got into bed beside him and crawled over to lay her head on his chest.

He then told her about Alexus getting locked up for selling drugs and the DEA seizing the penthouse that the two of them lived in together. He then told her about his visit to see Alexus and the warning that he received about the truck possibly being taken.

"So, what's happening with Alexus?" Nina asked

once TaSean was finished talking.

"Right now, nothing!" he told her. "She believes though that she'll beat this case that the DEA is building against her."

"So I'm guessing you didn't tell her about us, huh?"

TaSean looked down at Nina as she lifted her head up to look up at him.

He sighed again and then said, "No, Nina! I didn't tell her, because I didn't feel like it was the best time to tell her that I was breaking up with her to be with my best friend-turned-girlfriend/baby mother."

"TaSean, relax!" she told him as she began to rub his chest. "I'm not upset or didn't mean to make you mad. I was just asking you."

TaSean kissed Nina's lips as she lifted up and leaned forward to kiss him. TaSean laid his head back against his pillow and reached over and hit the lights as the room went dark.

"I love you, TaSean!" Nina told him as she closed her eyes, wrapped her arm across his chest, and kissed him softly.

Chapter 14

Two weeks after playing the Bulls and winning by four points, TaSean got the call from his agent that he had been waiting for. He received the call at 10:45 p.m. on Friday night and found out the Chicago Bulls traded two of their draft picks for him. One was the number one pick center that really got the New York Knicks' attention.

TaSean flew out to Chicago the next morning to sign his new $7.5 million, three-year contract. He met with the head coach and the general manager at the signing, and even got to meet a few players on the team who seemed to be happy that he was on their team. He dapped up with shooting guard Tyrone Baily, who remembered him after the shootout the two of them had when the Knicks played against the Bulls.

TaSean got through the transition of his trade from New York to Chicago and explained to Brian what he wanted done and needed. TaSean got in his first practice with the Bulls and found out that he was going to get to try out as starting point guard, which was 100 percent cool with him.

TaSean was dealing with an overly excited and happy Nina once everything was finally finished, and he was assigned a Chicago Bulls #3 jersey. He finally got the chance to meet Nina's parents and even her younger sister and brother, who took an instant liking to him.

He also received a surprise visit from his mother, step-father, Auntie Patricia, Eddie, and Steffaine. He found out that Nina set up the visit together with his family. TaSean convinced his family to stay until after Saturday, since that was his first game with the Bulls against the San Antonio Spurs. He offered to put his family up in a hotel to make sure that both his mother and step-father had their own suite, while his auntie, Eddie, and cousin had their own suite as well.

* * *

TaSean spent Saturday morning taking his family out and even bought a new 2018-model G63 Mercedes-Benz G-Wagen for himself, since he needed some wheels now that he was in Chicago.

TaSean left Nina and her girls with his family as it got closer to game time. He headed back to the condo that he and Nina shared while waiting for the new house that Brian was working on getting for him.

TaSean got himself together and packed his team gym bag. He then left the condo and started toward the United Center, when his cell phone started ringing while he was driving out of the parking garage.

He looked down and saw Nina was calling.

"Yeah, ma! What up?"

"Hey, papi! I just wanted to tell you good luck tonight, and I love you!"

"Love you too, shorty!" TaSean replied with a smile.

* * *

Nina made it to the Chicago Bulls arena five minutes before game time and got inside with no problem after she mentioned who she was. She then led TaSean's family and her younger brother, Jonathan, to their second-row seats on the court.

"How many of TaSean's games have you been

to, Nina?" Yolanda asked her son's girlfriend while looking around at how packed the arena kept getting as more people showed up.

"I've been to a few while he was still in New York!" Nina admitted. "I'm just happy he's here now though, so I'll be able to see more of his games."

"And what about the baby?" Yolanda asked her. "How's my grandbaby?"

"The baby's doing fine!" Nina answered just as Steffaine cried out and pointed at the Bulls and Spurs jogging out onto the floor from their opposite tunnels.

"There goes TaSean!" Patricia said while pointing at her nephew.

Nina saw her baby and smiled at just the sight of him. She stood up from her seat. As if TaSean sensed her, he looked over at her, smiled, and then winked when they made eye contact.

* * *

TaSean set up for the tip-off after the Bulls' and Spurs' starting five were introduced. TaSean touched fists with each of his teammates as center Samuel

Forster stepped up to center court for the tip-off against the Spurs' center.

Once the referee tossed the ball up and Forster got the tip-off to power forward Chris Young, TaSean caught the pass from Young as the rest of the team went down court to set up for offense.

TaSean pushed the ball up the floor as the Spurs point guard got up on him to play defense. TaSean shot the pass off to his right to small forward D. J. Jackson, but then took off to his left. He cut back to his right, running through traffic and coming back out at the top right side of the court, to catch a pass from Tyrone Baily at the top of the key.

TaSean pulled up a three just as his defender was pulling up on him. TaSean switched up and shot the pass to the middle to Chris Young, and watched the power forward take flight with a two-handed dunk straight to the middle.

* * *

TaSean crossed over right and swung the ball back left around his back, leaving the defender leaning in the opposite direction. He then took off past the defender, driving toward the basket. He spun off another defender into the inside but shot a no-look pass back outside to his left, catching D. J. Jackson rushing as the small forward caught the ball on the move.

The fans erupted into yells and cheers for the team when they watched Jackson score with the tomahawk one-handed dunk. TaSean was already on the move, seeing the ball being thrown inbounds. He caught the player that was reaching the ball off guard, just as the player that threw the ball in yelled out in a late warning.

TaSean snatched the ball free from the Spurs' point guard, and then he spun off and went toward the basket, just as the power forward tossed the ball inbounds. TaSean took flight as the power forward attempted to jump up for the block.

TaSean made a two-handed dunk, knocking the Spurs' power forward out of the air. He then hung from the rim, yelling at the top of his lungs as the Bulls fans screamed along with him.

* * *

"What a game you've had tonight, Prince!" the reporter stated after the Chicago Bulls victory against the San Antonio Spurs, with the Bulls winning 110-96.

TaSean finished with thirty-two points and ten assists, four steals, and six rebounds, and TaSean shot nine for nineteen at the three. He stood answering questions that were asked by the reporters while a few of his teammates made it over to him playfully roughing him up and letting him know he played well.

Once he finished with the interview, TaSean turned to see security waiting to escort him back to the locker room. But first he jogged over to his family and kissed and hugged Nina, who was extremely happy and excited. He then hugged his mother and then his auntie. They were both smiling and crying at the same time, telling him how proud they were of him.

TaSean finally made it to the locker room, only for the team to rush him all hyped up to let him know how well he played. Coach Phillip Green yelled to get his attention and waved him into his office. TaSean broke off from the rest of the team and walked over to the coach's office. He walked inside, where he also saw the assistant coach waiting.

"Prince!" Assistant Coach Reed said, nodding his head toward the young ball player.

TaSean nodded back at the assistant coach and then looked over at Coach Green, just as the older white man was sitting down behind his desk.

"What's up, Coach?" TaSean asked. "Everything okay?"

"Everything's fine, Prince!" Coach Green told him. "Good game tonight."

"Thanks, Coach!"

Coach Green nodded his head in response to the young ball player's thanks.

"We've got a game against the Denver Nuggets this coming Tuesday. You think you can maintain this position, son?"

TaSean felt the smile pulling at his lips as he answered, "Relax, Coach. I'll take care of it!"

The coach lightly laughed, unable to catch it before it slipped.

"You've got the position, Prince! Go ahead and get outta here!" he said, shaking his head.

* * *

"What do you think?" Assistant Coach Reed asked, once point guard TaSean Prince left the office.

Coach Green looked over at Assistant Coach Reed as a small smile appeared on his face after the young ballplayer left his office. Green then sat back for a moment just thinking.

"I do believe that young man may just be the piece to what this team needs to get us to the championships, Reed. Now the question is if he can help up get a win during his rookie year!"

"I think the young man can possibly do it!" Reed stated. "I'm going to personally see to his training whenever he's not training with the team. I really see something in this young man!"

Coach Green nodded his head in agreement and then said, "Go ahead with that plan, Coach. I agree with it."

Assistant Coach Reed nodded his head in response to what the head coach had told him as he pushed away from the wall and headed for the office door.

Chapter 15

Alexus heard her name being called and found out that she had a visit, which surprised her since her girl, Regina, and another person she hadn't expected to see came earlier in the week. Alexus got herself ready and ended up waiting a little over five minutes until she was finally escorted down to the visitation room.

"Ain't this a bitch!" Alexus stated as she stood up in front of TaSean, with only a thick piece of glass between them.

Alexus picked up the receiver while never taking her eyes off of TaSean, even as he picked up the receiver on his side.

"You finally found time to visit me, huh?"

"I've been a little busy, Alexus."

"I'm fully aware of that since you're now playing against our home team, since you switched out and got traded to Chicago," she told TaSean. "Good games against the Spurs and the Nuggets. In both games you scored over thirty points and helped

Chicago win two more. You're showing that ass out there in Chicago, I see."

"How you been doing, Alexus?" TaSean asked, taking the conversation off of his ball playing.

"Let me see!" Alexus stated, putting on a show as if she was in deep thought before she balled up her face. "Well, considering I'm in jail fighting for my life and my supposedly boyfriend and father of the baby I'm carrying moved off to a whole other state to play not just for some other team, but also with some other bitch that he claimed was his best friend but is now the new bitch he's fucking and also got pregnant and is all over TV kissing and hugging all up with, not too good. But other than that, I'm doing great, TaSean! How you doing?"

TaSean wasn't surprised to hear that Alexus knew about him being with Nina or the fact that she also knew Nina was pregnant, since it seemed to be all over the news. It was also not surprising for her to find out since Nina was a very well-known and popular urban model and was suddenly being invited onto different talk shows as well. TaSean sighed and opened his mouth while attempting to say something, only for Alexus to beat him to it.

"I tell you what, TaSean! Go ahead and enjoy yourself with that bitch you're fucking while I'm in this shit because I can't do nothing for you now. But understand this. Once I'm out of this place and back on the streets, you will be seeing me again, because I will be coming to get what belongs to me. You! Enjoy for now!"

Alexus slammed down the receiver and walked off from the visitation booth. She released the tears she had been holding and allowed them to run down her face as she began banging on the door and yelling for the guard to come and get her.

* * *

Once Alexus returned to her dormitory-style jail cell, she walked directly over to the bank of wall phones. She used the phone card she had and made a quick call out.

"Hello!"

"Regina, call my lawyer!"

"Alexus, what's wrong, girl?"

"Bitch, this nigga's ass finally decided to bring his ass back out here to see me, and then he ain't got shit to say now since I told his ass about knowing about that bitch he fucking with being pregnant. These lawyers need to do something to get me the fuck outta this shit! I am not letting that hoe have my man!"

Chapter 16

TaSean focused his attention on the upcoming game against the Golden State Warriors, who were last season's champions. He blocked out the visit with Alexus and all her bullshit, especially since it was she who had put him in the middle and left him blind to all the drug selling she was into.

TaSean told Nina about his visit to see Alexus and how it went. He wanted her to know about him flying back to New York, and he even mentioned the fact that she knew about their relationship. TaSean made sure he stressed that he wanted Nina to be careful whenever she went out, and even went as far as hiring a personal bodyguard that would now be escorting Nina around, whether it be on a photo shoot or during her day-to-day activities.

TaSean found himself in game mode and found himself training hard with the team and even harder with Assistant Coach Reed, who seemed to be pushing him harder than the others. TaSean said nothing and accepted the extra training. He figured that it was because he was still a rookie and now starting point guard.

TaSean was not only doing a cover photo shoot for *Slam Magazine*, but he was also having a four-page Q & A spread inside. Afterward, he got a call and found out that Nike, Adidas, and Under Armour were all offering him a shoe deal.

After talking with his agent, Brian, TaSean let him know that he liked all the shoe deals from the big companies, but he expressed an interest in seeing what And1 was willing to offer, surprising his agent at the request.

* * *

TaSean made the trip out to Oakland to play Golden State. He started the first quarter off with an assist to shooting guard Tyrone Baily at the left side corner. He smiled and nodded his head to Baily after making the wide-open three-pointer.

They beat the Warriors 110-107. TaSean finished with twenty-eight points, ten rebounds, four steals, and eleven assists, and earned his first triple-double. He did two interviews with two reporters after the game and heard the same questions concerning the winning streak. Both reporters wanted to know how he felt about the Bulls getting to the playoffs and NBA finals.

"We'll see you come game day, Angela!" TaSean told the reporter before he turned and walked away.

* * *

TaSean was happy to be back in Chicago and able to lay back and relax, since the next game was against the New Orleans Pelicans. In that game, he had to play against Anthony Fields and Keon Jackson. He also received the phone call from his agent finding out that And1 actually wanted to make him a shoe deal.

TaSean met with And1 and talked about the different deals they wanted to offer him. After negotiating, both parties agreed on a six-year contract for $53 million. TaSean stressed that he wanted to have a part in designing the shoes as well.

The next day, TaSean went with Nina to her doctor's appointment, where they found out they were having a baby boy. TaSean was hyped after finding out about his son. He immediately got on the phone and called his mother. Then he called his Auntie Patricia and cousin Steffaine about the news.

* * *

The Bulls lost to the Pelicans 101-99, ending their winning streak. TaSean left the game pissed off, hating how things went in the game and refusing any interviews. He headed straight home afterward. He hated that Nina was staying with Vanessa and Shawna, since the three were planning a trip out of town for Nina to just relax.

TaSean lay across the bed, when his cell phone suddenly began to ring. He dug out his iPhone from his pocket and saw his cousin Anthony was calling.

"What up, Cuzo?"

"What's up? You good?"

"Why you asking me that?"

"I saw ya game, Cuz! You looked heated as hell after losing. What happened to D. J. Jackson?"

"Last I heard, the team's making another trade and Jackson wanted off the team!" TaSean told Anthony. "Why? I have no fucking idea, but now we playing with this kid, Tim Holmes. Dude's got a sweet game, but it's like he froze up when he went up against Anthony Fields."

"Relax, Cuz! That's just one game! You can't win every game you play in!"

"I plan on trying though!"

"That sounds like some shit you would say!" Anthony told him as he and TaSean began laughing. "So, is it true? You having a little man, Cuz?"

TaSean smiled at the mention of his son and said, "Yeah, Cuzo! I'ma have me a lil' mini-me running around here in a little while!"

"Congratulations, Cuz!" Anthony told TaSean.

The two cousins continued their phone conversation a while longer until Anthony said he needed to go. But he told TaSean he'd call him back the next day. TaSean hung up with his cousin and tossed the phone down onto the bed. He was just about to climb off the bed and head to the kitchen to get something to eat, when the phone rang again.

TaSean picked up the phone and then started from the bed. As he walked out of the bedroom, he answered the phone.

"Yeah!"

"Hey, handsome!"

TaSean paused right where he was in the middle of the hallway after hearing and recognizing the voice on the other end of the line. He looked down at the screen and saw the name and number were blocked.

"Alexus?" he said into the phone.

"I'm impressed! You still recognize my voice. How you doing, baby?"

"What do you want, Alexus?"

"TaSean, you know what I want already. Let's not play games with each other!"

"Why are you calling me then?"

"Truthfully, I just wanted to hear your voice, and to let you know that I'll be seeing you soon, baby."

After hearing the line go dead in his ear, TaSean looked at the phone screen to see that Alexus had, in fact, hung up on him. He sighed loudly as he began walking again, ending up in the den instead of the kitchen, where he actually intended to go to get something to eat.

TaSean lay his head back against the sofa and stared up at the ceiling while just thinking. He seriously hoped Alexus didn't turn out to be a bigger problem than she already was now.

* * *

TaSean wasn't sure when he fell asleep, but he was awakened by the sound of his cell phone ringing. He realized he was still on the sofa and dressed in his clothes from last night. TaSean picked up his phone from the table beside him to see his agent calling.

"Yeah, Brian! What's good?"

"You sound like you're just waking up!"

"Naw! I was just lying down and relaxing. What's good though?"

"I just got the call from the real estate agent about the new house!" Brian told TaSean. "Everything's ready for you and Miss Ortiz to move in."

"Everything's ready?" TaSean asked, now fully awake and smiling as he sat up on the sofa.

"Everything's ready, and if you want, I can meet you there with the keys."

"Gimme twenty minutes!" TaSean told Brian, hanging up the phone right afterward.

He jumped to his feet and rushed to the back of the condo.

* * *

Brian waited at the private front gate of the 7,871-square-foot main house that had a 719-square-foot, single-story mini-mansion out back. He then saw TaSean's Mercedes-Benz G-Wagen drive up the private street and stop beside his own Mercedes sedan. Brian pulled up to the front gate and stopped in front of the security box and intercom before pressing in a security code.

Once the double gates swung open, Brian pulled inside and drove up the drive and turned off in front of the mini-mansion's front door.

Brian climbed out of his car and looked over to see TaSean getting out of his G-Wagen. They were parked in an area with a basketball court. As TaSean looked around, Brian called him over to follow him.

Brian first stopped in front of the glass front door, unlocked it, and opened it. He then motioned for

TaSean to enter his new residence. He stepped off to the side and allowed TaSean to step into the mansion first.

Brian shut the front door behind the two of them as he quietly followed behind TaSean, who walked through the mansion checking out each and every room, spending most of his time inside the separate gym. He then checked out the infinity pool and spa.

"Thanks, Brian, man!" TaSean told his agent as he stood looking out at the city view while standing on the lush manicured lawn. "Nina's gonna love this place!"

"It's my job!" Brian replied as he held out the keys to the mansion to TaSean.

"Thanks as a friend, Brian," TaSean told him, taking the keys from him and shaking his hand.

"I'll see you on Thursday before you leave for Portland to play the Trailblazers!" Brian told TaSean.

He had just turned to head for the front door, only to pause and look back at TaSean and ask, "You see the news lately?"

"News?"

"ESPN or NBA TV?" Brian asked with a smile, upon seeing TaSean shake his head. "You may want to see what's being said about your team, TaSean! I'm pretty sure you'll like what they're talking about!"

* * *

TaSean headed into the media room after Brian left. He picked up the remote control that went to the wall unit's 48-inch flat-screen and turned it on. He smiled when he instantly heard surround sound. TaSean then turned directly to ESPN, whose commentators were discussing the Bulls' loss to the New Orleans Pelicans.

TaSean was just about to turn the channel to TNT Sports when there was talk about D. J. Jackson and another two players from the Bulls being traded to Miami. He broke into a smile when he heard that the Bulls were receiving not only Anthony Brown, but also a rookie from the University of Miami.

TaSean dug out his cell phone and called his cousin's number.

"Yeah!" Anthony answered on the start of the

third ring.

"Nigga, why the fuck you ain't tell me what the fuck was going on?"

"You finally heard, huh?"

"Hell yeah!" TaSean answered excitedly, smiling as he stood up from his seat and began pacing the floor. "When the hell you getting to Chicago?"

"Cuz, you caught me as soon as I got off my plane!" Anthony admitted. "I'm already in Chicago now and heading to my hotel!"

"I'm on my way now!" TaSean told his cousin as he turned off the television and headed for the door.

* * *

TaSean found out which hotel Anthony was staying at, and he was not surprised to see the large number of reporters and cameras in front of the hotel. Once he was able to get past all them himself, after they recognized him, TaSean stepped into the hotel and onto an elevator.

Once he made it to the tenth floor, TaSean stepped off and was met with security and Anthony's agent standing outside his cousin's room. TaSean shook hands with the smiling agent and was allowed straight into Anthony's hotel room, where he found his cousin standing at the sliding glass door that led out to the balcony. He was talking on his phone.

"What up, son?" TaSean called out, getting his cousin's attention.

Anthony turned around and broke out into a smile after seeing TaSean. Anthony told his mother to hold on as he embraced TaSean.

TaSean then took the phone from Anthony once their embrace ended and got on the phone with his aunt.

"Auntie Pat!"

"Hey, baby!" Patricia cried out happily. "I see you finally found your cousin, huh?"

"I just found out he was in town and that he got traded to the team!" TaSean told her as he stood watching Anthony talking to his agent, who had just walked into the room.

"He didn't want us to tell you!" she admitted before she continued, "The trade had been in the works since you got traded from New York. You know how much your cousin loves playing with you, and then that girlfriend of his has been on his case about moving to Chicago like you did for your girlfriend."

"Well, don't worry about 'im, Auntie! I got 'em now! We good!" TaSean told his auntie as Anthony walked up and the two of them shook up happily.

"You two just better win me one of them championship titles!" Patricia told TaSean. She let him know she loved him and told him to tell Anthony to call her back later.

TaSean handed the phone back to a smiling Anthony and said, "It's about to be some muthafucking problems out here in Chi-Town!"

"That's just what the fuck I was thinking!" Anthony stated as he and TaSean gave each other another brotherly embrace.

Chapter 17

Nina and her girls finally arrived home with more bags than they could carry. They dropped everything when they saw Anthony in Chicago. Vanessa was all over the man in a moment, but she screamed when Anthony told her about the trade going through between Miami and Chicago. TaSean waited until he had Nina inside the G-Wagen, to mention the new house he had bought for them.

"TaSean, don't play!" Nina told him, staring at him with a huge smile on her face. She screamed when he handed her the keys. "TaSean, let's go see it, baby!" Nina begged as she leaned over and kissed him all over his face.

TaSean laughed as he started up the G-Wagen. He left the airport and drove out to the new mini-mansion, only to get another scream out of her once he pulled up in front of the gates. After he punched in the security code, the gates opened and he drove through.

"Oh my God!" Nina cried as actual tears began

falling from her eyes.

She climbed out of the truck once TaSean got out and came around onto her side to help her.

Nina allowed her child's father to help her up to the front door, even though she was fine walking by herself. She entered the mansion and began crying harder at the sight of how beautiful it was inside.

Nina walked away from TaSean as he answered his ringing phone. She began to look around and first entered the master bedroom. But she really fell in love with the master bath with the steam shower and sauna. Next she moved on to the home theater with wet bar. She was out back looking at the fourth fireplace that turned out to be an outdoor fire pit when TaSean caught up with her.

"So, what do you think?" TaSean asked her as he gently wrapped his arms around his woman, kissing her on the neck. "You like it?"

"Baby, I love it!" Nina told him, turning in his arms to face her man. "TaSean, I love you so much, baby!"

"I love you too, shorty!" he told her as he wiped

the tears from her eyes. TaSean kissed her on the lips and then said, "I've already set it up for someone to come out here to do whatever it is you want done to the place. I'll give you her number, and you can start whenever you're ready."

"Oh my God!" she cried as she threw her arms up around his neck. Nina laid her head onto TaSean's chest and said, "I love you so much, TaSean!"

* * *

TaSean and Anthony were both hyped up on Thursday by the time it got close to the start of the game in Portland. They were talking in the locker room and were both ready to play the Trailblazers. TaSean broke down the different styles of the shooting guard, Tyrone Baily; the power forward, Chris Young; and their big man, the center, Samuel Forster.

Once it was game time and Coach Green led the team out onto the packed arena floor, TaSean started out onto the floor to warm up, just as the coach called him over.

"What's up, Coach?" TaSean asked as he walked

over beside him.

"Prince, understand me clearly, son," Coach Green started as he looked over at TaSean and met and held his eyes. "I'm not known for putting my rookies in as my starters, but I put you in because I had a great feeling about you. And considering I know what type of damage the two of you can do together, you go let Brown know he's starting tonight. I'll then decide after tonight if he'll be my new starting small forward."

TaSean smirked as he nodded his head in response to the coach's request. He then walked out onto the court to do as he was told.

* * *

TaSean watched the tip-off and saw the Portland center get control. He then started to rush the shooting guard and saw him catch the ball. TaSean decided against it and got onto defense. He played Portland's point guard as the ball was brought down by the opposing team's shooting guard.

TaSean allowed the point guard to receive the ball, but he then played tight defense on the player.

TaSean got lucky when the point guard went to pass the ball to the small forward off to his left. TaSean then looked just in time to see Anthony get the tip of his fingers out to knock the ball away.

TaSean rushed the ball at the same time Portland's point guard took off right behind him, and he snatched it up and spun wide around the guard. He then took off up the floor on a fast break.

TaSean could see the Bulls fans standing up, expecting an air show as he came down the floor. TaSean smirked as he suddenly turned and lobbed the ball up just right in front of the basketball rim. He wasn't surprised to see Anthony shoot past him and leap into the air. His cousin caught the alley-oop and scored with a one-handed tomahawk dunk.

The Bulls fans went insane after the air shot as TaSean and Anthony bumped fists and then joined the rest of the team on defense.

* * *

"Excuse me!"

TaSean crossed the point guard, drove past him, and swung the ball behind his back to his left, getting past another defender. He shot the pass over his right shoulder behind him, catching Anthony on the follow-up. He got out of the way and saw his cousin fly through the air, scoring off the glass with a reverse layup with his left hand that he shifted around the power forward, who had leapt into the air for the attempted block.

* * *

"Do you see those two, Coach?" Reed asked as he moved up beside a staring Coach Phillip Green. "How the hell do they play like that?"

"They're related, Reed!" Coach Green informed his assistant coach.

Just then, Forster grabbed the rebound that Portland threw up for the missed shot. The coach watched as his seven-foot center passed the ball off to point guard Prince, who took off and pushed the ball.

"Here we go again!" Coach Reed said as Prince passed the ball off to shooting guard Baily, only to call for the ball back after he faked out his defender, leaving Portland's point guard leaning in the opposite direction.

Coach Green watched TaSean catch the give-and-go pass back, and he noticed small forward Anthony Brown swinging round down onto the baseline, only for TaSean to spin around the center for Portland and pass the ball off to Anthony. He went up into the air just as Portland's center was turning. Suddenly, the coach saw Anthony Brown slam down a powerful one-handed dunk.

"Jesus Christ!" Assistant Coach Reed shouted after seeing the pass and dunk from Anthony Brown and TaSean Prince. "Those two are amazing!"

Coach Green nodded his head in agreement with Reed while still watching TaSean Prince and Anthony Brown putting on a show. Coach Green then realized that he needed to have a talk with the two young ballplayers.

Chapter 18

TaSean got in some free time after the win against Portland, since the All-Star Game was coming up. During the downtime, TaSean and Nina went about getting their new place put together. Nina moved what she was keeping from her condo into the new house and sold what she no longer wanted, and then put her condo up for rent.

TaSean allowed Nina and her mother and his Auntie Patricia to take care of putting the new place together. He found out that Nina actually sent for them. TaSean soon found himself being completely ignored, so when Vanessa and Shawna came over next, he left to go chill at Anthony's place.

"Coach Green talk to you yet?" Anthony asked as he and TaSean sat in the den at Vanessa's place.

"Yeah!" TaSean said, looking from the flat-screen to his cousin. "He got at you too, huh?"

Anthony nodded his head in response and then said, "He mentioned something about us playing more with the team and not just each other."

"Yeah! That's pretty much what he stressed to me since he says that I'm the lead of the team!" TaSean said with a light laugh.

TaSean heard his cell phone ring, so he dug it out and saw that his teammate Tyrone Baily was calling.

"What's good, Ty?"

* * *

Nina watched and directed the movers to where she wanted the new furniture to be placed. She also noticed that her mother and TaSean's mother were directing the two men to put things in the dining room and gourmet kitchen.

"Nina!" Vanessa said as she walked up beside her. "We're gonna need some help once these guys leave. This stuff is too heavy for the five of us!"

"I was just thinking the same—! Wait!" she said as she came up with an idea.

Nina went to get her phone, just as it began ringing from inside her Gucci bag on top of the breakfast bar.

"Hey, baby!" Nina answered after seeing that TaSean was calling.

"What up, ma? How's everything going out there?"

"Well, everything is already here, but I've got a problem."

"What's up?"

"After the moving men leave, we're gonna need some help getting things put where they're supposed to go. I was gonna call some more friends over to help us."

"Nina, relax, ma!" TaSean told her. "I got you. Gimme a little while."

After hearing TaSean hang up the phone, Nina made a few calls to some of her girls to come over and help out.

* * *

Nina saw a few of her girls arrive and thanked them for coming. She then explained what was needed. She pointed out what was what and then noticed a few more of her girls show up a little while later, including two of her model friends, Rosia and Brittany.

"Nina!" Shawna called from the front door,

drawing Nina and Vanessa's attention. "Umm, we've got company."

Nina started walking toward the front door, when TaSean stepped inside followed by Anthony. Nina stepped to the side as more and more men walked into the house. Nina counted nine guys total and then looked over at a smirking TaSean.

"Are they who I think they are?" she asked him, recognizing a few faces.

"You needed help, so I called some of my boys from the team!" TaSean told his lady with a smile.

"Let's get this over with, Superman!" Center Samuel Forster told TaSean, drawing Nina's attention to him.

Samuel then smiled, which got a big laugh out of Nina.

* * *

Two weeks went by, and the mini-mansion was finally finished, and the Bulls were doing good throughout the regular season as well, winning more games than they were losing. TaSean finally got to see his new shoes that And1 had created with his help. He loved the style of the new shoe that came out first in white, black, and red, which matched the Chicago Bulls uniform. He got the first pair of red-over-white T.P. Attack 1s, which was the style name of his new shoes.

TaSean put his new kicks to work in the game against Detroit at their house. He put up thirty-four points and got back up from Anthony, who gave twenty-six points to help the Bulls beat Detroit 119-78. Unfortunately, their win was followed up a few days later with a loss to Philadelphia 105-97.

Halfway through the season, they were still playing well and looking to get into the playoffs. TaSean missed the rematch against New Orleans for the birth of his son, who unexpectedly decided to show up earlier than he was due to arrive.

TaSean spent the next few days home with his girl and son, making sure the two of them were okay. He hired extra help around the house, including a cook, butler, and someone the two of them agreed would help Nina take care of TaSean Prince Jr. TaSean was back to work when the Bulls played against the Miami Heat.

Both TaSean and Anthony showed up for the game, with each of them scoring over forty points to help the Bulls beat the shit out of Miami 124–108.

TaSean was back in Chicago and heading home when his cell phone went off. He got it out and found out that he had two text messages from a Regina Wagner.

He opened the first message to see a photo of a baby that made his heart stop a brief moment, thinking it was his son. He then pulled over and was looking at the second picture, when his cell phone suddenly began ringing.

"Who the fuck is this?" TaSean barked into the phone after seeing the same Regina Wagner name across his screen.

"Hey, handsome!"

"Alexus?"

"Hey, baby! Did you get the pictures of your daughter?"

"My what?"

"I had her a few days ago, but I had to wait to get

the pictures to you since I was being released under house arrest probation. When are you coming to see your daughter and me?"

"Alexus, don't play with me! Whose child is that?"

"What, nigga?" Alexus yelled. "I know your ass did not just sit on this phone and ask me no shit like that with the way we was fucking!"

"You told me you was on the pill!"

"I may have forgotten a few times."

"Alexus, that's bull—!"

"When you coming to see us, TaSean?" she asked, again cutting him off. "Your daughter needs to see her daddy."

"This some bullshit!" TaSean said, unable to believe the games Alexus was playing. He sighed to try and calm himself down before he asked, "Where the hell are you at, Alexus?"

"Right now, I'm at a friend's house in New York, but your daughter and me need a place to stay so I can have my house arrest transferred."

"Ain't this a bitch!" TaSean stated with a

disbelief type of laugh.

"Yeah, but we're your bitches, Daddy!" Alexus told TaSean with a laugh of her own.

* * *

TaSean finally made it home, trying to block out the bullshit in his mind from Alexus. He found both Nina and his son in the media room laid out across the suede sofa with the flat-screen playing with the sound lowered. He stood staring down at the two of them for a few minutes, when Nina's eyes slowly opened and she looked up at him.

"Hey, baby!" Nina whispered, smiling at the sight of her baby. "You just getting home?"

"Yeah!" he answered as he bent down and kissed Nina's lips and then softly kissed his son on top of his small head.

"You okay, TaSean?" Nina asked, watching him as he took his son but also noticing the look on his face.

"We'll talk later!" TaSean told her as he took Nina's hand and the two of them walked their son to the nursery that was right across the hall from their bedroom.

The two of them put their son to bed and stood watching him a few moments until Nina took TaSean's hand and led him into their bedroom.

Nina climbed into their California king-sized bed and got under the thin blankets and lay watching her man as he undressed for bed. But she still noticed the mood he was in, especially considering it was after the great game that he had that night. She also noticed that it was already 2:00 a.m.

TaSean sighed as he climbed into bed and laid his head onto Nina's chest. He put his arm around her middle and then told his lady he loved her.

"I love you too, TaSean!" Nina replied. "But I still wanna know what's wrong with you."

She waited a few minutes for TaSean to answer her before she opened her mouth to question him again, when he finally spoke up.

"Alexus called me a little while ago while I was on my way home."

"What did she want now, TaSean?" Nina asked with a loud and deep sigh afterward.

"She's out of jail, and she's staying with a friend."

"Okay, what did she want?"

TaSean rolled over and grabbed his phone from the side table. He pulled up the pictures Alexus had sent him, and he handed the iPhone over to Nina.

"What's this?" Nina asked as she took the iPhone from TaSean. She looked down at the screen to see the picture of a baby on it. "TaSean, whose baby is this?"

"Alexus says that's our baby together, Nina!"

"Excuse me?" Nina stated, catching an instant attitude. "No! Hell no it ain't!" Nina went off. "This baby don't look nothing like you, TaSean. Look at those eyes on this baby. Whose eyes are brown like this baby's? Last time I checked, Alexus had greenish eyes, and your eyes are gray. This is not gonna work! This is not your baby!"

"Nina, I'm really not—!"

"You not what, TaSean?" Nina continued, cutting him off. "I know what your ass gonna do though. You about to get a blood test for this baby, because I'm not letting you take care of no baby but your son who's asleep in his room. You hear me?"

Nina heard TaSean Jr. begin to cry, so she got up and walked into the nursery, leaving TaSean by himself in the bed.

"This shit just keeps getting worse and worse!" TaSean stated, talking to himself as he rolled over onto his back and stared up at the ceiling.

* * *

TaSean talked with Nina early the next morning before he had to go to practice. They agreed that he would get a lawyer to handle the whole baby situation. TaSean then contacted his agent on the way to the arena to see if Brian could help him find a good attorney.

"Adams!" Brian answered the phone.

"Brian, it's TaSean."

"TaSean, how's it going?"

"I need ya help, Brian."

"What can I do for you, TaSean?"

TaSean then explained his problem he was having with Alexus and then got into what he needed his agent to do for him. TaSean hung up after Brian told him to give him a few minutes to contact a friend who was an attorney.

TaSean arrived at the arena a little while later. He parked his G-Wagen and was climbing out just as Tyrone Baily's Range Rover was turning into the parking lot as well.

"What up, Superman?" Tyrone joked as he climbed from his SUV.

Superman was the nickname the team has given to TaSean.

"What's good, Ty?" TaSean replied as he and the shooting guard dapped up with each other.

TaSean and Tyrone exited the parking lot, entered the arena, and bumped into Coach Reed, who stopped them and said he wanted to speak with TaSean about something.

"What's up, Coach?" TaSean asked as Tyrone walked off.

TaSean talked with the assistant coach about a small issue of him training with the backup point guard, Josh Allen, after practice. TaSean agreed and then headed to the locker room.

* * *

TaSean felt a little better after practice and training with Josh Allen, who he realized was a lot better of a player than he had realized. TaSean showered and dressed and was then kicking it with his cousin Samuel Forster and Tyrone Baily, when he heard his name called.

He looked up to see Coach Green waving him into his office. TaSean left the group and walked into the coach's office.

"You got a phone call, Prince!" Coach Green told him before stepping out of his office to give the young ballplayer some privacy.

TaSean picked up the receiver and spoke into the headset.

"Hello!"

"Mr. TaSean Prince?" a female voice asked.

"This is him! Who am I talking to?"

"Mr. Prince, my name is Erica Byron, and I was contacted by your agent, Brian Adams, concerning legal issues. I am an attorney."

* * *

TaSean spoke with the attorney and agreed to meet with her in person later in the afternoon. He left the arena a short time later after telling Anthony to hit him up on the cell phone later. He then stopped to get something to eat, and was just climbing back into his G-Wagen when his cell phone woke up.

"What's good, shorty?" TaSean answered the phone after seeing Nina calling.

"How you doing, papi?"

"I'm good. I spoke with a lawyer."

"What happened?"

"I'm supposed to meet up with her this afternoon a little after 2:00 p.m. today."

"It's a female attorney, huh?"

TaSean smirked when he caught the change in Nina's voice.

"Ma, relax! It's a lawyer, not some chick that's after me!"

"Whatever!" Nina stated. "I wanna be there for this meeting!"

TaSean could hear the seriousness in her voice,

so there was no need to ask her if she was really going to attend the meeting.

"Be there in fifteen minutes, Nina. I'm almost home now."

After hanging up with Nina, TaSean had to smile at his lady's protectiveness or jealousy. His phone began to ring again, and he picked it up.

"Yeah!"

"Hey, handsome!"

TaSean instantly lost his smile when he recognized Alexus's voice. He also heard what sounded like a baby in the background.

"What do you want now, Alexus?" he sighed.

"You already know what I want, TaSean. The question is when you gonna leave that bitch you playing house with and come be with your family?"

"Alexus, I really don't got time for this! Either tell me what you want, or we done talking, shorty."

"You need to tell me what you gonna do, TaSean! You either coming to New York to see me and your daughter, and help us get another place, or you're not! What you gonna do?"

"I'll send you the money to find a new place since I remember what you did for me, but I'm not coming to New York to see you or your daughter!"

"What?" Alexus yelled. "What the fuck you mean my daughter, nigga? This is our daughter, and you better get your ass to New York, TaSean, or I promise—!"

TaSean hung up the phone in the middle of what Alexus was saying. He was sick of all the bullshit that was flying out of her mouth. He ignored the phone when it rang back, knowing it was her calling back. He then pulled up to his mansion's front gate.

Chapter 19

Alexus was pissed the fuck off after leaving the courthouse and hearing that another court date was set for her to return to the fucking place. She left the courthouse with her girl Regina and her man, Kevin, inside his Navigator.

Alexus pulled out her phone and tried to call TaSean's number again. She was caught off guard when she heard the wireless number she was calling was out of service.

"Hell naw!" she said as she tried TaSean's cell phone number again, only to get the same message that the number she called was out of service.

"I know this muthafucker didn't!" Alexus went off, trying the number again and again, only to find out that TaSean had shut off his phone.

"What's wrong, Alexus?" Regina asked as she sat staring back at her friend.

"This muthafucker changed his phone or turned that shit off!" Alexus vented angrily as she stared at her cell phone.

"What are you gonna do now, girl?" Regina asked Alexus in concern.

"His ass don't know who the fuck he's fucking with! I got his ass!" Alexus shouted, thinking about how she was going to find out TaSean's new number and where he lived. She then told Regina she wanted to stop and pick up a few things for her daughter before they got back to the apartment.

Alexus was deep in thought after texting another friend that worked at the DMV, who was going to help her track down TaSean. Alexus felt the Navigator stop, which broke her out of her train of thought as she realized they were parking in front of a marketplace ten minutes from Brooklyn.

"I'ma be right back!" Alexus told her girl and Kevin as she climbed out of the SUV.

She started toward the front entrance to the store, when she suddenly heard a horn blow. She turned around toward the Navigator and saw Regina and her man talking. Alexus then heard her name being called out. She looked to the far right to see a 2018-model Lincoln Navigator, and she was very surprised to see two familiar faces climb out of it.

"Damn!" Alexus said under her breath when she recognized Derrick.

She also noticed how totally different his ass looked dressed like money with gold and ice on.

"Alexus, what's up, girl?" Derrick said, smiling as he walked up to her. He hugged her and then stepped back and looked over her now different body. "Girl, what happened to you? You gone and got thick as hell!"

"It's called having a baby, nigga!" she told him, seeing the look in his eyes as he lustfully looked her over. "What the hell are you doing in New York, boy?"

"Business!" he answered before he asked, "When the hell you have a baby?"

"The end of last month."

"So, you still fucking with that nigga TaSean Prince, then?"

"You must have given up all that basketball stuff, huh?" Alexus laughed at the question.

"Why you ask that?"

"Because if you didn't, you would have found out that TaSean is fucking with your ex-girlfriend, Nina Ortiz!"

Alexus smiled when she saw the instant anger that appeared on Derrick's face.

"Relax! It's gonna be over between those two real soon, once I put it out there that Superstar NBA player TaSean Prince has a baby with another woman!"

Derrick laughed lightly as he shook his head.

"I see you plotting on that clown. I'm just glad after we kicked it that one time that you ain't hate me the way you seem to hate this dude TaSean all of a sudden. Check me out though, Alexus. I gotta handle some business, so let me get ya number and maybe we can hook up sometime."

After exchanging numbers with Derrick, Alexus gave him another hug and felt when he gave her ass a squeeze before releasing her and walking off. She stood a moment and watched him until he got back up into his Navigator. She shook her head and smiled as she turned and entered the store.

* * *

Alexus arrived back at Regina's apartment and left her girl in the truck with her boyfriend. She then walked inside to hear her daughter Angel's happy baby talk while playing with Regina's younger sister, Jennifer. Alexus smiled when she saw her daughter smiling up at the young girl.

"Hey, Alexus, girl!" Jennifer said as she handed the baby over to her mother. "How'd everything go in court?"

"Another court date!" Alexus stated, smiling as she continued to play with her daughter.

"Yeah! You've got some mail that came for you," Jennifer told Alexus. "Where's Regina?"

"She's outside with Kevin!" Alexus told the young girl as she looked through the mail that was on the coffee table and found the letter addressed to her.

"Children and family?" Alexus read out loud on the envelope.

Alexus set Angel down in her baby chair in front of the cartoons that were playing on the television. She then opened the letter and began reading.

"What the fuck is this bullshit?" Alexus said out loud after she was finished reading.

"What's what, girl?" Regina asked as she was walking into the room and caught Alexus's statement.

"I can't believe this nigga's got the nerve to have me take some blood test for Angel, girl!" Alexus told Regina. "This muthafucker's really trying everything not to claim his daughter, all because of that bitch he's messing with now. This is some bullshit!" Alexus said out loud as she walked off.

She thought hard about TaSean and that bitch he was seeing, and they were really starting to get on her last nerve.

"I got something for this muthafucker!" Alexus said as she walked back into the front room to see Regina holding and playing with Angel.

"What you say, girl?" Regina asked Alexus as her friend sat down after grabbing her phone from the coffee table.

"Hold on, girl!" Alexus told Regina as she called up some old friends for a little help.

Chapter 20

TaSean received the information about the court date when he was set to appear in front of the judge concerning the blood test of infant Angel Kristen Prince. TaSean told Nina about the court date and showed her the notice, only to receive a look that he recognized. He simply left the issue alone and focused on the up-and-coming game against the Oklahoma Thunder.

TaSean let his agent and coaches know about the court date on the morning of practice before the team left for Oklahoma City. He couldn't help but wonder how things would play out if the baby Alexus was claiming was actually his baby. He had to admit to himself that he had his doubts about everything since she never showed him any flaws. However, he had to consider that she was mostly gone instead of with him, so there was no telling what went on when they weren't together.

TaSean was getting the cold shoulder from Nina on the night he was to leave for Oklahoma City. He barely got a kiss out of her before walking out the front door. He kept it simple and understood that she was feeling some type of way about the whole baby issue he was going through with Alexus.

Once he arrived at the United Center and saw his team already loading onto the bus to leave, TaSean parked next to Anthony's new SUV. Just as he was getting out of this G-Wagen, his cell phone began ringing.

"What the fuck!" TaSean stated after pulling out his cell phone and seeing Alexus's name and number.

"How the fuck you get this number, Alexus?" TaSean asked louder than he intended while standing in the middle of the parking lot.

"Hey, handsome! You miss me?"

"How the hell you get—?"

"That's not important, TaSean!" Alexus cut him off in the middle of what he was saying. "What's important is that you're wasting your time with this blood test mess you've allowed that bitch to talk you into having done! You know you was my only boyfriend and the only one I was fucking. Why are you doing this?"

"Alexus, we'll deal with this in two weeks when we get in front of the judge," he told her before hanging up the phone on her.

* * *

TaSean played his worst game since joining the Bulls and even the Knicks. He scored fourteen points the entire game. Although he shot badly, he ended up with eleven assists and five rebounds against the Oklahoma Thunder. The Bulls were still able to win 98–95, with Anthony finishing with twenty-nine points, two blocks, ten rebounds, and four assists, and he shot four for ten from the three.

"Cuz, what's up?" Anthony asked TaSean once the team was back on the bus and was headed back to the airport. "You been acting off ever since we left Chicago. What's really up?"

"Shit just crazy right now, Cuzo!" TaSean admitted.

He then began telling Anthony everything that was going on with him and Nina concerning Alexus and the baby she was claiming was his.

"What do you think?" Anthony asked his cousin as soon as TaSean finished explaining everything.

"Cuzo, I really don't know!" he answered truthfully while shaking his head.

* * *

TaSean scored twenty-two points in the home game the Bulls played against the Sacramento Kings. He was still feeling a little off even though the team won again.

The next morning, TaSean finally stood before the female judge on the date of the court hearing. He allowed his attorney to be his mouthpiece, and never said a word as the judge ordered a blood test to be taken. Depending on the outcome of the test, another court date would decide the outcome.

"TaSean!" Alexus called to him as they exited the courtroom.

Alexus grabbed his arm when he ignored her, and pulled him around to face her, only for his girlfriend, Nina, to decide that she wanted to act bad.

"You may wanna keep your hands off my man!"

Nina told the white trash, ready to punch a hole through her face.

Alexus laughed in Nina's face and looked right past the Puerto Rican bitch.

"So this is how you gonna do me, TaSean? What happened to you telling me that you loved me?"

"Bitch, that was then and I'm what's right now, so get over it!" Nina told Alexus, ready to fight.

"Nina!" TaSean said, grabbing her around the waist and then whispering in her ear, trying to get her to relax just a little.

He then looked back at Alexus.

"Alexus, look! I'll say this once and only once. Yeah, I loved you at one point before you led me to believe something that wasn't real, and that's what fucked it up between us; but I'm being truthful because I think you deserve that. There were always feelings between Nina and me, but because we agreed to just stay friends, that allowed you and I to become something."

"So you telling me I was just a backup plan?" Alexus asked him, starting to get upset.

"Look, Alexus! If Angel's mine, then I'll be there for her!" TaSean said with a sigh.

"So that's it then, huh?" Alexus asked, only for Nina to grab TaSean's hand and lead him away.

Alexus hard-stared hatefully at Nina as she and TaSean walked off. Alexus then looked over at Regina, who was holding her daughter.

"I hate that bitch!" Alexus said to her girl.

* * *

"TaSean, I'm telling you now!" Nina told him once the two of them were inside the Range Rover they rented when they arrived in New York City. "After this mess is over and that blood test proves what I've already told you about this baby not being yours, I do not want to see or hear from this bitch again, or I promise there's gonna be a real serious problem!"

"Not bothering with saying anything, TaSean just drove toward their hotel to lay down and get his mind right.

* * *

TaSean drove out to Brooklyn later in the night

while Nina was sleeping. He stopped at his mother's house and caught his step-sister, Tiffany, also pulling up.

"Boy, what you doing in New York?" Tiffany cried happily as she rushed to hug her step-brother. She released him after a moment, only to ask, "Where's my nephew and Nina at?"

"Nina's back at our hotel asleep, and lil' TaSean is still in Chicago with his godmother, Vanessa," TaSean told Tiffany as the two of them walked up to the front door to their parents' house.

Tiffany used her key that she still had and let herself and TaSean inside, only to find the front room television on and Yolanda asleep on the sofa.

"Hey, gorgeous!" TaSean whispered as he kissed his mother's cheek and awakened her from her sleep.

"Hi, baby!" Yolanda said, smiling at the sight of her son. "What are you doing here, TaSean? Where's my grandson at?"

"I asked him the same thing!" Tiffany said as she kissed her step-mother on the cheek.

"Lil TaSean's still in Chicago, Momma," he told

her as he sat down beside her after she sat up.

"Why is my grandbaby in Chicago and you're here, TaSean?" Yolanda asked him. "Didn't you think I would want to see my baby too?"

"I'm sitting right here!" he told his mother with a smile.

"TaSean Prince, do not play with me, boy," Yolanda told him. But she couldn't help but smile as he laid his head onto her chest. She wrapped her arms around her big baby. "So, where's Nina at?"

"He left her asleep at their hotel!" Tiffany spoke up. She then stuck her tongue out at TaSean.

"TaSean, why you leave that woman at the hotel by herself?" Yolanda asked. "You should be with her!"

"She really ain't talking to me right now!" TaSean told his mother. He then went straight into explaining what was going on between him and Nina as well as with Alexus and the issue concerning her daughter that she was claiming was his.

"Is that little girl yours, TaSean?" Yolanda asked her son with all traces of her earlier playfulness gone.

"Truthfully, Momma, I really don't know!" TaSean answered. "Alexus lies about too much sh—! I mean, she lies about a lot of stuff, Momma! I really don't know!"

Yolanda shook her head and saw the frustration on her son's face. She grabbed her son and wrapped her arms back around him, only for him to wrap his arms around her.

"We'll figure this all out, sweetheart! Just be strong for your family, TaSean!" Yolanda told her son, kissing the top of his head.

* * *

TaSean flew back to Chicago two days after taking the blood test. He had to prepare to play the Cleveland Cavaliers that night. TaSean scored ten points in the first quarter, seven points in the second, and seven in the third, and he finished with eighteen points in the fourth quarter. The Bulls went on to beat Cleveland 110-107.

After the game, TaSean was answering a few questions in an interview, when the reporter asked him what had changed since his performance in his previous three games.

"My fiancé and my son!" he simply answered.

TaSean was kicking it with the team back in the locker room after the game when he was called into the coach's office.

"What's up, Coach?" TaSean asked after walking into the office and standing in front of the coach's desk.

"I just wanted to speak with you for a moment, Prince!" Coach Green told the young ballplayer in a concerned tone of voice.

TaSean talked with the coach for longer than was planned. He explained the issue he was dealing with concerning an old girlfriend and her claim that he was the father of her child. He finally made it out of the arena and out to his truck.

He pulled out his cell phone while he was driving away. TaSean powered up the iPhone and instantly saw that he had eleven missed calls and ten voice messages.

He ignored them all and called Nina's number.

"Hello!"

TaSean heard Nina crying when she answered the phone after two rings. He smiled since he was sure she watched the game.

"You was on the phone, ma?"

"Yes!"

"Where's lil' TaSean at?"

"He's asleep in his room."

"You need me to bring you something home while I'm out?"

"TaSean, stop!" Nina cried out. "Why are you torturing me?"

TaSean laughed after hearing what she had just told him.

"I wasn't gonna say anything until later, but go into my dresser drawer where I keep my socks, and take out the pair of navy-blue Polo socks. Look inside there, and I'll see you when I get home."

Hanging up the phone after telling Nina where the 8.5-carat blue diamond engagement ring was, TaSean drove the rest of the way home with a smile on his face.

To be continued.

To order books, please fill out the order form below:
To order films please go to www.good2gofilms.com

Name: __ _____

Address:_____

City: _____ State: _____ Zip Code: _____

Phone:_____

Email:_____

Method of Payment: Check   VISA   MASTERCARD

Credit Card#:_ _____

Name as it appears on card: _____

Signature: _____

Item Name	Price	Qty	Amount
48 Hours to Die – Silk White	$14.99		
A Hustler's Dream - Ernest Morris	$14.99		
A Hustler's Dream 2 - Ernest Morris	$14.99		
A Thug's Devotion – J. L. Rose and J. M. McMillon	$14.99		
Black Reign – Ernest Morris	$14.99		
Bloody Mayhem Down South – Trayvon Jackson	$14.99		
Bloody Mayhem Down South 2 – Trayvon Jackson	$14.99		
Business Is Business – Silk White	$14.99		
Business Is Business 2 – Silk White	$14.99		
Business Is Business 3 – Silk White	$14.99		
Childhood Sweethearts – Jacob Spears	$14.99		
Childhood Sweethearts 2 – Jacob Spears	$14.99		
Childhood Sweethearts 3 - Jacob Spears	$14.99		
Childhood Sweethearts 4 - Jacob Spears	$14.99		
Connected To The Plug – Dwan Marquis Williams	$14.99		
Connected To The Plug 2 – Dwan Marquis Williams	$14.99		
Connected To The Plug 3 – Dwan Williams	$14.99		
Deadly Reunion – Ernest Morris	$14.99		
Dream's Life – Assa Raymond Baker	$14.99		
Flipping Numbers – Ernest Morris	$14.99		
Flipping Numbers 2 – Ernest Morris	$14.99		
He Loves Me, He Loves You Not - Mychea	$14.99		
He Loves Me, He Loves You Not 2 - Mychea	$14.99		
He Loves Me, He Loves You Not 3 - Mychea	$14.99		
He Loves Me, He Loves You Not 4 – Mychea	$14.99		

He Loves Me, He Loves You Not 5 – Mychea	$14.99		
Lord of My Land – Jay Morrison	$14.99		
Lost and Turned Out – Ernest Morris	$14.99		
Married To Da Streets – Silk White	$14.99		
M.E.R.C. - Make Every Rep Count Health and Fitness	$14.99		
Money Make Me Cum – Ernest Morris	$14.99		
My Besties – Asia Hill	$14.99		
My Besties 2 – Asia Hill	$14.99		
My Besties 3 – Asia Hill	$14.99		
My Besties 4 – Asia Hill	$14.99		
My Boyfriend's Wife - Mychea	$14.99		
My Boyfriend's Wife 2 – Mychea	$14.99		
My Brothers Envy – J. L. Rose	$14.99		
My Brothers Envy 2 – J. L. Rose	$14.99		
Naughty Housewives – Ernest Morris	$14.99		
Naughty Housewives 2 – Ernest Morris	$14.99		
Naughty Housewives 3 – Ernest Morris	$14.99		
Naughty Housewives 4 – Ernest Morris	$14.99		
Never Be The Same – Silk White	$14.99		
Shades of Revenge – Assa Raymond Baker	$14.99		
Slumped – Jason Brent	$14.99		
Someone's Gonna Get It – Mychea	$14.99		
Stranded – Silk White	$14.99		
Supreme & Justice – Ernest Morris	$14.99		
Supreme & Justice 2 – Ernest Morris	$14.99		
Supreme & Justice 3 – Ernest Morris	$14.99		
Tears of a Hustler - Silk White	$14.99		
Tears of a Hustler 2 - Silk White	$14.99		
Tears of a Hustler 3 - Silk White	$14.99		
Tears of a Hustler 4- Silk White	$14.99		
Tears of a Hustler 5 – Silk White	$14.99		
Tears of a Hustler 6 – Silk White	$14.99		
The Panty Ripper - Reality Way	$14.99		

The Panty Ripper 3 – Reality Way	$14.99		
The Solution – Jay Morrison	$14.99		
The Teflon Queen – Silk White	$14.99		
The Teflon Queen 2 – Silk White	$14.99		
The Teflon Queen 3 – Silk White	$14.99		
The Teflon Queen 4 – Silk White	$14.99		
The Teflon Queen 5 – Silk White	$14.99		
The Teflon Queen 6 - Silk White	$14.99		
The Vacation – Silk White	$14.99		
Tied To A Boss - J.L. Rose	$14.99		
Tied To A Boss 2 - J.L. Rose	$14.99		
Tied To A Boss 3 - J.L. Rose	$14.99		
Tied To A Boss 4 - J.L. Rose	$14.99		
Tied To A Boss 5 - J.L. Rose	$14.99		
Time Is Money - Silk White	$14.99		
Tomorrow's Not Promised – Robert Torres	$14.99		
Tomorrow's Not Promised 2 – Robert Torres	$14.99		
Two Mask One Heart – Jacob Spears and Trayvon Jackson	$14.99		
Two Mask One Heart 2 – Jacob Spears and Trayvon Jackson	$14.99		
Two Mask One Heart 3 – Jacob Spears and Trayvon Jackson	$14.99		
Wrong Place Wrong Time – Silk White	$14.99		
Young Goonz – Reality Way	$14.99		
Subtotal:			
Tax:			
Shipping (Free) U.S. Media Mail:			
Total:			

Make Checks Payable To:
Good2Go Publishing
7311 W Glass Lane,
Laveen, AZ 85339

SMITH WIGGLESWORTH

A Living Classic

A MAN WHO WALKED WITH GOD

BY
GEORGE STORMONT

Harrison House
Tulsa, Oklahoma

Cover photo courtesy of Flower Pentecostal Heritage Center

20 19 18 17   10 9 8 7 6 5 4

Smith Wigglesworth:
A Man Who Walked With God
ISBN 13: 978-1-57794-975-6
ISBN 10: 1-57794-975-7
(formerly ISBN 0-89274-595-9)
Copyright © 1989 by George Stormont
Duluth Gospel
1515 West Superior Street
Duluth, Minnesota 55806

Published by **Harrison House, LLC**
P. O. Box 35035
Tulsa, Oklahoma 74153
www.harrisonhouse.com

CONTENTS

Preface: From the Turnip Fields to the World v

1 I Meet "The Man Who Walked With God" 1

2 Rough Kindness 7

3 Natural Forthrightness Becomes Holy Boldness 11

4 A Heart of Compassion 21

5 Simplicity: A Defense Against Temptation 25

6 An Emphasis on Life 31

7 A Man of One Book 35

8 Faith: The Key to Wigglesworth's Ministry 43

9 New Testament Faith 51

10 Sanctification: Unbroken Communion With God 57

11 Standing on Holy Ground 69

12 To Hunger and thirst After Righteousness 75

13 His First Desire Was Witnessing 85

14 Six Ways He Reached the Lost 93

15 Wigglesworth's Healing Ministry 105

16 "Wholesale" and "Retail" Healings 115

Conclusion: Glimpses of the Future 121

Tribute to Smith Wigglesworth 123

Appendix: New Zealand Sermons 129

    "Sanctification of the Spirit" 129

    "Perfect Rest" 138

    "The Gifts of the Spirit: Prophecy and Tongues" 142

DEDICATION

To Ruth,
my wife of fifty-one years—God's love gift.

FROM THE TURNIP FIELDS TO THE WORLD

Smith Wigglesworth was born in 1859 in Menston, a small Yorkshire village in England, to John and Martha Wigglesworth, one of three sons and a daughter—a very poor family. Today, one hundred and thirty years after his birth, he is perhaps more well-known than he was in his lifetime. And, since his death forty-two years ago, his sermons and the books written about him have touched probably more people than he did during his life.

He began work at six years of age, pulling and cleaning turnips in the fields of a neighboring farmer. That was hard work, especially for a small boy, but even that was used by God. He learned discipline and developed an attitude toward work—and toward doing well what was entrusted to him—that stood him in good stead later in the work which God gave him to do.

From the turnip fields of Yorkshire to the mission fields of the world, Smith Wigglesworth always was a dependable and hard worker, who knew the meaning of responsibility and accountability for the tasks set before him.

This book is not intended to be a biography, nor a chrono-logical account. As one who knew him in the years of the fullness of his ministry, I have here set down my remembrances of him with the earnest hope that the ministry the Lord entrusted to him will challenge others to discover and fulfill their own ministries.

I have been more concerned with the spiritual significance of the characteristics he displayed than with the "story of his life." He is one of the few people I have known whom I believe truly to be *conformed to the image of Christ.*

Wigglesworth's parents were not saved, but his grandmother was. She took him to a Wesleyan Methodist Mission Hall when he was eight years old. Although he was so young, he said later that he had a hunger for God; and, in fact, he could not remember a time when he did not have such a hunger.

He knew even at eight that he was not saved. He listened intently to the preaching that evening and joined sincerely in the singing. They came then to a point in the service when those dear Wesleyan brothers and sisters began to dance around the old-fashioned coal stove as they sang a song about the Lamb of God and the precious blood of the cross.

Little boy Wigglesworth danced with them and later movingly described what happened.

"Suddenly I saw that Jesus had died for *me.* Suddenly I realized that He had borne *my* sins. I lifted my heart to Him, and I knew that I was born again."

I DON'T WANT THEM TO SEE *ME* ANYMORE— ONLY JESUS!

Then he could sing with as much abandon as any Wesleyan Methodist! There, in that little mission hall, he got a revelation of the simplicity of conversion. For the rest of his life, he used the words of his revelation, *only believe,* over and over in his witnessing and in his messages.

I MEET "THE MAN WHO WALKED WITH GOD"

Once when Smith Wigglesworth stayed in our home, he came down early one morning and told me, "God spoke to me on your bed."

"What did he say?" I asked.

"He said, 'Wigglesworth, I am going to burn you all up, until there is no more Wigglesworth, only Jesus.'"

Standing at the foot of our stairs, he raised his hands to heaven, and with tears running down his cheeks, he cried, "O, God, come and do it! I don't want them to see *me* anymore—only Jesus!"

If I had to sum up the man Smith Wigglesworth as I knew him, that one statement would be it. He lived so that people would only see Jesus.

I first met Smith Wigglesworth in 1941 as he traveled from Bradford, England, to London en route to meetings in my church, Elim Pentecostal Church, Leigh-on-Sea, Essex. We

WIGGLESWORTH WOULD HAVE BEEN DISTRESSED AT THE MANY BOOKS THAT HAVE BEEN WRITTEN ABOUT HIM, BUT HE WOULD HAVE REDEEMED THE SITUATION BY SAYING WITH PAUL, "BE YE FOLLOWERS OF ME, EVEN AS I ALSO AM OF CHRIST" (1 COR. 11:1).

were meeting in a hired building on the north shore of the River Thames estuary, about forty miles east of London, because our church had been destroyed by a German landmine.

I met Wigglesworth at a London railway terminus and escorted him across the city to another where we had an appointment with a man whose wife was dying of abdominal cancer. This man was seeking the Lord's help through Wigglesworth. Our train to Leigh-on-Sea was due to leave in a few minutes, so the man accompanied us for part of the journey.

As soon as the train started, Wigglesworth said out loud, "Jesus is up. Jesus is down. Jesus is up."

I was puzzled, and so was the man.

This man of God—who was so much an "original," so much an individual, that to some he seemed eccentric—continued:

"It says in John 3:13, 'No man hath ascended up to heaven, but he that came down from heaven, even the Son of man which is in heaven.'

"You see, my brother, Jesus is in heaven with all power. I reach out the hand of faith and touch Him. His power flows down through me. I stretch out the hand of compassion and faith and touch the sick and the needy. They are healed and begin to praise the Lord. The life of Jesus goes back to Him in worship. My brothers, that is the cycle of life in the Holy Spirit."

Then Wigglesworth turned to me saying, "Come on, Brother Stormont, let us pour life into this fellow."

Without regard for the other people in the railway carriage with us, he stood up—and I with him—and prayed in a firm voice, "Lord, pour Your life into this man."

Turning to the man, Wigglesworth said, "Go home and lay your hands on your wife's stomach, and she will be healed."

Months later, I met the man's pastor, who told me the woman's healing happened just as Wigglesworth had said it would.

Wigglesworth would have been distressed at the many books that have been written about him, but he would have redeemed the situation by saying with Paul, "Be ye followers of me, even as I also am of Christ" (1 Cor. 11:1).

He did not want people to copy him but many tried. He was totally himself, and he wanted other people to be themselves. Sometimes it was very amusing to see those who copied him. Some students at a San Francisco Bible institute noticed that when Wigglesworth was preaching, he would stroke his mustache. After he left, many of the students when preaching could be seen stroking "the substance of things hoped for the evidence of things not seen!"

What God's Word said of Moses is, in its own measure, true of Smith Wigglesworth: "There arose not a prophet since in Israel like unto Moses, whom the LORD knew face to face" (Deut. 34:10). That should have a challenge in it for every Christian. We cannot be Moses or Wigglesworth, yet we can press on to know God face to face.

While in our home and at my request, Wigglesworth usually led us in prayer before meals. He would start off most of the time by singing a chorus, then in confident belief, he would thank God for the food.

One day after the main course, as my wife served an apple pie, she apologized by saying, "I'm sorry, Brother Wigglesworth, this pie isn't up to standard."

Both my wife and I were taken aback by his response.

"Shut up, woman! No complaints. The blessing is on it! Once we have prayed over our food, it is sanctified, and we must never complain or apologize!"

He took the Word of God seriously: "For every creature of God is good, and nothing to be refused, if it be received with thanksgiving: for it is sanctified by the word of God and prayer" (1 Tim. 4:4–5).

Because of his unique personality, even his close friends tended to look at him with astonishment at times. At another meal with us, something occurred of which I soon became ashamed, but it reveals his attitude of walking in love so well that I will tell it.

He had made one of his extraordinary remarks, and I glanced at my wife and winked. He caught sight of my wink and simply said, "Brother, Proverbs 10, verse 10."

I had no need to read it, because I knew the verse said: "He that winketh with the eye causeth sorrow." Blushingly, I apologized, but I had learned my lesson! Another proverb came to my mind: "Faithful are the wounds of a friend" (Prov. 27:6).

At the end of a series of meetings he had with us, he told the congregation he would pray for each one as they left the building. He said, "Brother Stormont and I will stand by one of the exits, and you must all go out by that door."

He had chairs placed on each side of the aisle and stood on one while I stood on the other. We laid hands on each member of the happy, seeking, and believing congregation. One man among those people stood out to me at the time.

Later, he told me, "As hands were laid on me, I was filled with the power of God. My life was changed." Indeed it was. He went on into full-time service for God and served Him effectively until his homecall. The man, Cyril Lyndon, became a close friend of ours.

Another evening, my wife drove Wigglesworth to a meeting in another church, and on the way home, the car broke down. He was unperturbed. He just talked to "Father," and very soon help appeared in the form of a man who had been at the meeting. The man arranged for the car to be taken care of then brought Wigglesworth and my wife home.

Wigglesworth told us, "He is a very kind man, but there is something wrong with his life that must be put right if he is to have any blessing from God."

We knew his discernment was right, because we knew the man and his life. At the time, Wigglesworth was eighty years of age. An old man, tired after ministering the Word and praying for many people, still he was sensitive to God. He lived so close to God at all times that he perceived people's needs, and at the same time, he was part of "the cycle of life in the Holy Spirit" so that he could minister to those needs as people were ready to receive.

Chapter 2

ROUGH KINDNESS

Many times I am asked, "Did Wigglesworth really hit people when he prayed for them?" My answer is, "Yes, sometimes."

He also was very blunt in his speech at times. Once a man said to him, "You believe in divine healing. What are you doing wearing glasses?"

Sensing insincerity, Wigglesworth said, "And what are you doing with that bald head?"

He felt bluntness and roughness were necessary. He said you have to get people's attention before you can do anything for them. He certainly got their attention! Secondly, he knew when he was dealing with sin and sickness that he was in direct conflict with the devil. The vigor of his attack on the devil came out in his methods. One day I asked him why he hit people.

He said with a smile, "I don't hit them—I hit the devil!"

When I said I did not know you could hit the devil with your fist, he replied, "You're learning."

> YOU HAVE TO GET PEOPLE'S ATTENTION BEFORE YOU CAN DO ANYTHING FOR THEM.

Here are some examples of his "rough kindness."

- A Salvation Army lassie came forward for prayer wearing her regulation straw bonnet. She was crippled and walked with a cane. As he prayed for her, he shook her so vigorously that her bonnet fell off. She was totally unmindful of the fact for, as she was ministered to, the power of God seemed to shoot through every part of her body.

  She dropped her cane saying, "I shall not need that any more," and moving around the building, she demonstrated that she was completely healed.

- A farmer in Kent went up for prayer for a stomach problem. Wigglesworth said, "Stand there." He then hit the man amidships saying, "In the name of Jesus, be healed!" The man was healed instantly.

> SHE DROPPED HER CANE SAYING, "I SHALL NOT NEED THAT ANY MORE," AND MOVING AROUND THE BUILDING, SHE DEMONSTRATED THAT SHE WAS COMPLETELY HEALED.

- Justus du Plessis, brother of the late David du Plessis who became known as "Mr. Pentecost," interpreted for Smith Wigglesworth during his meetings throughout South Africa. Du Plessis was for many years general secretary of the Apostolic Faith Church of South Africa. He told of how in one meeting, a big Afrikaans woman came for prayer and Wigglesworth hit her as he prayed.

She said, "Oh, that's the way, is it?" and hit him back! But the next night she was back and asked for an opportunity to make a public apology for hitting the servant of the Lord. After she got home the night before, she had discovered that every trace of her illness was gone.

John Carter, former general secretary of the Assemblies of God of Great Britain and Ireland, once related to me an amazing account:

I was in Australia, one of two speakers at a Bible conference. The other speaker was the principal of the Commonwealth Bible College of Australia. This man said to me, "My father was a Methodist preacher. He developed cancer of the throat and wore bandages around his throat at all times to hide and protect painful cancerous sores. He believed in a general way in prayer for healing, but hearing of Wigglesworth and some of the claims made for his ministry, he decided to check him out.

"There was a meeting at Melbourne, and he went to see for himself. As he listened, he was convinced and went forward for prayer at the end of the service. Smith Wigglesworth asked him what was wrong, then slapped my father's neck hard. The astonishing thing was that my father could hardly stand even the bandages around his throat because his neck was so painful, but when Wigglesworth slapped him, he felt no pain at all. In fact, he didn't even notice the slap!

"Then Wigglesworth said to him, 'Go home. Take those bandages off in the morning, and you will find the growths have gone.' He returned home, went to bed and

9

> SOME PEOPLE INTERPRETED HIS BOLDNESS AS ARROGANCE.

slept, when previously severe pain had kept him awake for hours. The next morning, my father removed the bandages, and the growths had disappeared entirely. There was not even a scar or mark left."

Wigglesworth was not averse to using the same principle of rough kindness on himself that he did on others. I worked for eighteen months with John Nelson Parr at Bethshan Tabernacle, Manchester, who had Wigglesworth for services. He told me that one day the evangelist was in pain from a bad back and asked Parr to pray for him. Parr did, gently laying his hands on the afflicted part of the back.

"That's no good, John," said Wigglesworth. "You must 'thump' it out. Come on, pray properly!"

Parr did as he was instructed and prayed again, this time hitting Wigglesworth really hard where the pain was.

Wigglesworth shouted, "Hallelujah! That's it. It's gone!" He had taken his own medicine.

Often, he would refer to Matthew 11:12: "The kingdom of heaven suffereth violence, and the violent take it by force."

Adam Clarke described this principle as "the required violent earnestness," and Smith Wigglesworth certainly had that!

Chapter 3

NATURAL FORTHRIGHTNESS BECOMES HOLY BOLDNESS

Wigglesworth was born in Yorkshire, England, a few miles from the city of Bradford. Yorkshire people are noted for their plain speaking, and Wigglesworth was a true Yorkshireman! More importantly, his vital faith in God added power to his natural forthrightness, a boldness that can properly be called "holy boldness." He so feared God that he feared no man. He had the fearlessness that God commanded Jeremiah to have (Jer. 1:8) and an "Ezekiel forehead" (Ezek. 3:8,9).

Some people interpreted his boldness as arrogance. However, the truth is that behind a bold demeanor was a deep sense of humility that made him totally dependent on God. He carried a deep sense of his own inability apart from God.

When he was chairman of the great Easter Convention at Preston, Lancashire, he would make short comments between the other speakers on the agenda. There was a fullness of the Spirit as he spoke, and once a man in the balcony became so excited that he burst out loudly in other tongues.

Wigglesworth looked up to where the man was and clearly called out, "You there! Be quiet. When I'm talking, it is not the time for you to speak in tongues. I like speaking in tongues more than any of you, but when someone else is talking, you are out of order to interrupt." He believed in the liberty of the Spirit, while at the same time insisting that things be done decently and in order.

At that same convention, he was leading an afternoon meeting with hundreds present. Quite suddenly, he stopped his talk and then spoke these words: "God has shown me there are people in this meeting bound with a demon of impurity. Whoever you are and wherever you are, stand to your feet."

I could hardly believe he would issue such a challenge openly. He did not even ask us to bow our heads. I sat on the platform weeping as I saw people rise to their feet all over the building—young men and women, middle-aged men and women, even white-haired older people. Pointing to each one, he prayed for them one by one. A young man beneath the balcony, as he was prayed for, flung his arms in the air and shouted, "I'm free! I'm free! Praise God, I'm free!"

Physically, Wigglesworth was exceptionally strong with a stocky build, although he was of medium height. The Lord used his physical strength along with the holy boldness instilled in him to deal with a witchcraft situation one night.

Wigglesworth was conducting a meeting in a long and narrow meeting room. The main entrance was in the middle of a side wall. The people were seated on movable benches. He related this incident to me, saying that, as he began to preach, he found himself bound in spirit.

He said, "I shouted, but nothing happened. I took off my jacket, but nothing happened. I asked Father what was wrong, and He showed me a line of people on a bench opposite the door. They were holding hands, and I knew at once that they were spiritualists who had come to bind up the meeting.

"So I kept on preaching, but I walked off the platform and down the aisle, still preaching. When I got opposite them, I turned, took hold of the end of the bench, lifted it up, and said, 'Out, you devils!' They slid in a heap by the door, got up, and slunk out. They had not come for deliverance, so I didn't cast the devils out of them. I cast *them* out with the devils in them. We had no more problems that night."

Arne Dahl, a Norwegian preacher in America, told me of Wigglesworth's meetings in Norway. At one of them, a preacher who could not speak above a whisper came up for prayer.

After hearing the man's problem, Wigglesworth said, "Look here, man, if you were in business doing all you could to destroy that business, yet asked me to pray for God to prosper your business, I wouldn't do it. I would tell you to sort out your methods and get your business on a proper foundation, *then* I would pray.

"Now, what is the good of me praying that God will heal your voice when you are going to destroy it again by using it wrongly? If you will learn to use your voice properly, I will pray for you."

The preacher agreed. Wigglesworth prayed, the man was healed and went on to learn that he could use his voice without abusing it, Dahl said.

The testimony of Dr. Mildred Serjeant of Lakenheath, Suffolk, England, brings out another aspect of Wigglesworth's holy boldness. Here is the account in her own words, used by her permission:

About 1933, I was on a campaign on Mersea Island, Essex, with Smith Wigglesworth. The day before he finished his campaign, he said, "Now, tomorrow night, I will just speak. You take the rest of the meeting. Find the hymns, read the lesson, do everything, and I will just do the speaking."

I spent a lot of time selecting hymns and the Scripture portion to be read. I felt this was important, because he was a very great man. I was only twenty-three; he was seventy-four.

We got to the meeting the next night, which was Sunday—and up he jumped. He always had his glasses on the end of his nose and he sort of looked over the top.

He said, "We'll have a hymn," and we did. He said, "We'll pray," and he prayed. Then he said, "We'll have another hymn," and after that, he said, "We'll read a portion," and he took his New Testament out of his pocket.

I thought, *Oh, he has forgotten all about me leading the service and doing everything but the preaching. But I'm not going to remind him.*

Then he said, "We'll have another hymn." We did, and when we got to the last two lines of the last verse, he turned to me and said, "You've got to preach next."

My legs turned to jelly, and my mind went blank. To this day, I cannot tell you a word of what I said.

Afterwards, he said to me in a rather gruff voice, "I'm going to 'roll you out' before I've finished with you."

"Why?" I asked. "What have I done?"

"It isn't what you've done; it is what you haven't done."

> YOU KNOW, YOU CAN'T TREAT THE DEVIL LIGHTLY. YOU HAVE TO BE ROUGH WITH HIM. YOU HAVE TO MEAN BUSINESS.

When I asked what he meant, he said, "Well, you can't run away and get ready when an emergency arises. The child of God is always ready. When I'm traveling by train and people know I am on that train and it stops at a station even for five minutes, I'll go to the window and they will say, 'Have you got a word from the Lord?' Of course I've got a word from the Lord. The child of God always has a word from the Lord. You've got to be ready, my girl. You can't run away and *get* ready. You've got to always *be* ready."

Dr. Serjeant went on to tell me of what she felt was one of her failures, a time when she did not put into practice what she had learned from Wigglesworth. A lady brought to her a little boy who had never walked. As Dr. Serjeant prayed for him, she felt the Lord definitely touch him and said so to his mother, who agreed.

Then the little boy said, "Mummy, I want to walk," but the mother picked him up, murmuring, "You will, darling, you will."

Dr. Serjeant did not confront the mother and confessed that at the time, she had not the courage. She later realized that she was not as ready as she should have been. She should have taken authority, commanded the mother to put down the child and let him walk. She continued:

> Brother Wigglesworth used to say, "You know, you can't treat the devil lightly. You have to be rough with him. You have to mean business. You must tell him with authority to come out. It's no use telling him a second time, because if you do, he knows you didn't meant it the first time. You have to have enough authority in the name of Jesus to command him to come out. In that name, he *must* come out."

When Smith Wigglesworth went to the Middle East to preach, his guide in Jerusalem was Tom Kemp, a missionary. Kemp has related what Wigglesworth did once to his interpreter, a government official who spoke classical Arabic. The man apparently was in some sort of bondage which brought a stiffness into the service the evangelist could not endure, and he decided to deal with it. He began to tell of a paralyzed man who had come to him for prayer.

WIGGLESWORTH MAY HAVE BEEN ROUGH IN HIS SPEECH, BUT HE WAS A MAN OF HIS WORD.

As he spoke the words, "There was a man who was paralyzed, and

I took hold of him like this," he turned, grabbed the interpreter by the throat, and said, "And I said, 'Loose him, and let him go.'"

The Spirit of God came on the interpreter, and he was liberated. Wigglesworth said, "From then on, we had the freest meeting I have ever had in my life."

In the early days of the Pentecostal movement in Great Britain, there were not many well-educated preachers in the movement. They really knew God, but they did not know grammar!

This posed a problem for one couple who wanted to introduce an aristocratic friend to the wonderful truth of the fullness of the Spirit. However, they were afraid she would be distracted by uneducated speakers. Then a splendid opportunity presented itself. A convention was being held near their home and the announced speakers were two godly men with first-class educations. They decided to take their friend to the meeting.

She went with them and heard a good word, but to the distress of her hosts, Smith Wigglesworth was there and said he had a message from the Lord. He gave it in his homespun style.

On the way home, this couple were hesitant to ask their guest her opinion of the service, but finally one of them did, and her reply surprised them.

"My dears, I thought those first two speakers were boring. But that old man! He had something, and I want it."

The reality of the Holy Spirit anointing had rested on his message, regardless of his style of speech and lack of grammar.

THERE WAS NO PRETENSE ABOUT SMITH WIGGLESWORTH. HE WAS BOLDLY STRAIGHTFORWARD BECAUSE HE WANTED TO STRIP AWAY FROM THE CHURCH ALL THAT WAS A SHAM.

Wigglesworth may have been rough in his speech, but he was a man of his word. He promised one young man that he would come and help him if he ever needed help. Some time later, the young man wired that he did need help. Wigglesworth traveled at his own expense from the west coast of America to the east, from large crowds to a small, struggling group, because he had given his word.

He had asked God to help him never to exaggerate but to tell things as they really were. Those who knew him heard him repeat many incidents from his vast experience in illustration after illustration. They never heard his stories "grow." He never varied the facts.

It is said that a lady once came to the great evangelist Dwight L. Moody asking prayer to conquer exaggerating. Moody responded, "Don't call it exaggeration. Call it by its proper name—lying." And that is also how Wigglesworth regarded embroidering or coloring incidents to make good stories.

He was outspoken about church membership methods. He did not believe in adding names just to increase the roll.

Quoting Acts 2:47, he would say, "Notice that the Lord added to the Church daily. If the Lord adds them, they'll be a blessing. But if you take in any that the Lord hasn't added, they'll be a nuisance. I would rather have the Lord build the Church one by one than have half the town join it."

He had the same strong views regarding people holding office in a church. We were traveling home from a church once where he had held a meeting when suddenly, out of the blue, he said, "They'll never have a revival in that church while they have that woman at the piano."

The pianist was gifted but overbearing. She ruled the service from the piano stool. I later shared with the pastor what Wigglesworth had said, but he rejected it. That lady stayed at the piano for twenty-five years, and they never had even the slightest breath of revival.

There was no pretense about Smith Wigglesworth. He was boldly straightforward because he wanted to strip away from the Church all that was a sham. His heart was set on revival, and he knew that cleansing and obedience were vital to the manifestation of the presence and power of the Lord.

Chapter 4

A HEART OF
COMPASSION

Wigglesworth's rough methods and blunt speech hid a heart that was full of compassion. While staying in a missionary home in what was then Palestine, he met an "upper class" lady who argued the superiority of her class. Wigglesworth, on the other hand, was very much for the working man.

When the discussion got too warm, he would stop and say, "I want to pray." He did, with tears, and the lady told Tom Kemp, "When I saw his tears and felt his heart throb for the needy, I knew that he was a man of God. It changed my attitude toward him."

I had my office in my home in those days, and many times I would be interrupted by Brother Wigglesworth, asking me to come and help him pray over requests that had reached him by mail. When he read these to me before prayer, he would comment on the sad cases brought to his attention. When he prayed, it was often with strong crying—weeping over people he had never met.

I experienced this compassion personally when I was invited to be one of the speakers at the Preston Easter Convention one year. This was one of the largest Pentecostal conventions in

Great Britain. Some of the other speakers were of international renown, and at the time, I was a mere beginner on the convention circuit. These and other factors put me under considerable stress.

Wigglesworth discerned this in the ministers' room before the first meeting. When the other preachers had gone to take their places on the platform, he turned to me, and in such a gentle, gracious manner, said, "Brother, you'll be the first speaker after I—by and through the operation of the Holy Spirit—have opened the door as wide as possible." He laid his hand on my shoulder and prayed for me.

Within ten minutes, I was on my feet delivering my first message in the full liberty of the Spirit.

Esther Horton, wife of a pastor and a friend of ours, told us of the following incident:

> I took a friend crippled with rheumatoid arthritis to hear Brother Wigglesworth speak. After his message, he called the sick forward for prayer. Because of her crippled condition, my friend was still at the back of the hall when the others who had gone forward had reached the front.
>
> Wigglesworth looked up, saw my friend struggling, and called to her to stand still. He said, "Sister, the trial of your faith is as gold." Turning to the congregation, he said, "We

THE MAINSPRING OF HIS COMPASSION WAS TO FEEL AS CHRIST FELT.

don't even need to minister to our sister. She's receiving healing now."

His compassion overflowed in his voice. He wept as he prayed, and the healing virtue of Jesus ministered life to my friend. She didn't need to go to the front of the church for healing, but she ran forward to show that she was healed.

Another incident that, at first glance, seems far removed from compassion comes to my mind as I write. When Wigglesworth was chairman of a large meeting, one of the speakers had just returned from a visit to the mission field, and he became very intense. The longer he spoke, the more intense and emotional he became until the atmosphere was growing unbearable. The congregation got more and more uncomfortable by the minute.

Then Wigglesworth stood up, moved just behind the speaker, and quietly said, "Sit down, brother, you're killing yourself *and* us." Turning to the congregation, he said, "We'll sing a hymn, while our brother gets quiet."

When the song was finished, he told the preacher, "Go on now, and go quieter." The speaker was a very godly man with much grace, and he accepted the rebuke of his chairman. He learned a valuable lesson from this astonishing experience and came to see it as a revelation of the compassion as well as the strength of Brother Wigglesworth—compassion for the speaker as well as for the congregation!

The Lord does not pour compassion into us the way we pour gasoline into our cars. It is released in our spirits as we are filled with the Holy Spirit and dwell continually in the presence of

Jesus. That means being filled with God. Wigglesworth's frequent prayer was to be emptied of self and filled with God.

The mainspring of his compassion was to feel as Christ felt.

Chapter 5

SIMPLICITY: A DEFENSE AGAINST TEMPTATION

Wigglesworth was a simple man, but I do not mean simpleminded nor simplistic. He was far from that, having a very sharp, clear mind. However, he was uncomplicated. His faith was simple and strong. He considered nothing impossible because he simply believed God's Word. Apparently, he originated the often-repeated saying: "God says it; I believe it; and that settles it!"

He was free from distraction because he did not multiply possessions. He did not seek or need an affluent lifestyle but lived for Jesus. This was one of his strengths and a defense against every temptation. His simplicity was in his absolute obedience to God, his lack of ambiguity. Consequently, Satan in all his craftiness, could not take him by surprise.

It seems he was guided by two things in his relationship to God:

1. What endangers my relationship with Jesus?

"GOD SAYS IT; I BELIEVE IT; AND THAT SETTLES IT!"

2. What would the Lord have me do?

Other people could have hobbies, read books, and listen to music, but for him these were distracting things. If he was in the company of Christians who were engaged in any of these things, he passed no judgment on them. In a gracious and kindly way, he would just say, "If you don't mind, I'll go to my room and pray."

He sought earnestly to ascertain God's will, and when he found it, he unhesitatingly carried it out. Jesus really was his Lord. He retained his simplicity by a moment by moment walk with Jesus. He had eyes for Jesus only and saw others only through those eyes. When out walking, he would be worshipping. When he was being driven by car, frequently he would be heard murmuring, "Lovely Jesus."

For Wigglesworth, there were no "unnecessary necessities"—just faith and apostolic simplicity. He was totally open to God so that the life and energy of the Spirit flowed through him without hindrance.

His Generosity Was Based on Faith

Many thousands of pounds—when the English pound was worth $4 or $5—were given to Smith Wigglesworth. He could have been a very wealthy man; however, he kept only enough to minister to his simple needs. The rest he gave away to missions and to the needy.

Harold Womersley, later an outstanding missionary to Zaire, was a driver for Wigglesworth on some of his meetings in

England. One thing that impressed him greatly was that Wigglesworth always gave him, just a young candidate for the mission field and "chauffeur" for the well-known evangelist, half of whatever honorarium he received.

In America, Wigglesworth saw for the first time the practice of taking up "love offerings" to meet a visiting speaker's needs. This kind of offering was unknown in England at the time. Sometimes when he was conducting a long series of meetings, more than one such offering would be suggested. Usually, he declined—unless the folks were willing for him to give the extra offering to missions.

WHEN WIGGLESWORTH LEARNED TO GIVE, HE WAS RELEASED FROM BONDAGE. HE MOVED FROM THIS WORLD'S ECONOMY TO GOD'S ECONOMY.

His special joy at the time was to give to what was then called Congo Evangelistic Mission, founded in the heart of the African continent by his son-in-law, Jimmy Salter, and noted missionary Willie Burton. On one occasion, Wigglesworth received a large check, but hearing of the need of a couple longing to get back to their mission field, he endorsed the check and gave it to them.

As in all things, he was very practical in following the commands of Scripture. He lived by faith in Christ. Yet living by faith did not mean going around acting like a pauper. He bought good clothes, because they were more economical. He felt a Christian should honor the Lord in his appearance. He did not choose the cheapest way to travel because it was more physically draining, and he knew he had to be fit for a demanding ministry schedule. He said, "I'm not saving the Lord's money; I'm saving the Lord's servant." But he was careful not to carry this to the extreme.

So convinced was he of the Lord's sufficient supply that on one occasion he is reported to have said, "If the Lord doesn't look after me, it will be time to go back to plumbing."

At this time, there was a splendid generation of men and women who lived by faith, among them Wigglesworth, Burton, Salter, and their good friend Howard Carter.

Someone once said to Carter, "You must have had some hard times, living by faith."

"Hard times!" replied Carter. "My brother, that would not be *living* by faith; it would be *dying* by faith."

> IF CHRISTIAN PERFECTION IS PERFECT LOVE, AS JOHN WESLEY DEFINED IT, THEN THIS QUESTION OF TEMPER CAN BE THE ACID TEST OF OUR SPIRITUALITY.

When Wigglesworth learned to give, he was released from bondage. He moved from this world's economy to God's economy.

Victory After Severe Battles

Wigglesworth was a holy and righteous man in his later years, but he had not always been self-controlled. He had severe battles in the earlier days of his life and ministry, but he pressed through to

God for victory. At one time, he had a violent temper and sought earnestly to conquer it. John Carter sent me this report in Wigglesworth's own words, as he told it once in a meeting in Switzerland:

> I used to have a tremendous temper, even going white with passion. My whole nature was outside God that way. But God knew His child could never be of service to the world unless he was wholly sanctified.
>
> I was difficult to please at the table. My wife was a good cook, but there always was something wrong. After God sanctified me, I heard her testify in a meeting that from that time I was pleased with everything.
>
> She said, "I never saw such a change in a man."
>
> (Also) I had men working for me. I wanted to be a good testimony to them. After I was sanctified, one day they waited for me after work and said, "We would like the spirit you have."
>
> The Spirit of God can change our nature. His Word is creative, and as you believe, the creative power will change your whole nature. You cannot reach this attitude, except by faith. No man can keep himself. The God of almightiness spreads His covering over you, saying, "I am able to do all things. All things are possible to him that believeth" (Mark 9:23).

If Christian perfection is perfect love, as John Wesley defined it, then this question of temper can be the acid test of our spirituality. Not only temper in its outbursts, but temper in its touchiness. Smith Wigglesworth encourages us all by his experience of deliverance. There is victory over temper, moods, temperament, and every alien thing that would rob us of God's best in our lives.

The secret lies in allowing Jesus to reign in our hearts. For Wigglesworth, that meant ten days of earnest, determined seeking of God's face. It was then, he said, that God dealt with the "Wigglesworth nature" and worked in him the Jesus nature.

Chapter 6

AN EMPHASIS ON LIFE

One day I offered Wigglesworth a beautiful rosebud to wear. He declined it quite strongly. "No, thank you, Brother. As soon as that rose was cut from the bush, it began to die. I don't want any death on me."

Walking down the road one day, he remarked that in the south of England most houses had tiled roofs, while in the north slate was used. He called tiled roofs "dead." The life is baked out of them, he said, and he preferred slate roofs because they were living stone. His emphasis always was life!

Because he had to begin work in a woolen mill when he was seven years old, Wigglesworth had little formal education. He did not learn to read until after he married Mary Jane Featherstone, whom he and everyone else called "Polly." They were married in 1882 and had five

> "IT IS NOT THE POSSESSION OF EXTRAORDINARY GIFTS THAT MAKES EXTRAORDINARY USEFULNESS, BUT THE DEDICATION OF WHAT WE HAVE TO GOD."

children. For years, she was the minister and he helped while building a successful plumbing business.

Polly taught him to read, "But," said he, "she never taught me to spell!" He would no doubt have appreciated President Grover Cleveland's remark that it is a poor kind of mind that can think of only one way to spell a word.

Wigglesworth was ministering in our church once, speaking on Mark 11:23: "He shall have whatsoever he saith," when he asked the congregation, "Have you begun to 'saith' yet?"

For twenty minutes, he spoke about "saithing." At home after the service, I said, "You know, Brother Wigglesworth, you can't *saith*."

He replied, "If you can't *saith*, you don't know God!"

I persisted, "It is 'I say, you say, he saith.'"

"You've got it," said Wigglesworth, "hang onto it!"

But I pressed my point, "Your grammar is wrong."

Wigglesworth replied, "I don't know much about grammar, but if you can't *saith*, get down on your knees until you can."

When a young man challenged Dwight L. Moody saying, "I don't like your grammar, Mr. Moody," the great evangelist quickly replied, "Young man, I'm using all the grammar I have for God. What are you doing with yours?"

J. W. Robertson, an outstanding British preacher, said, "It is not the possession of extraordinary gifts that makes extraordinary usefulness, but the dedication of what we have to God."

That was Wigglesworth's secret. He was wholly yielded to God, and all there was of him could be used by God.

One sunny day in our peaceful garden, we were discussing a criticism both of us had seen about Christians who went forward frequently at the end of services. Some thought it indicated insecurity, which perhaps it did. Yet Wigglesworth saw something important in it, saying, "Every fresh revelation calls for a new dedication."

He perceived that while we have made, or should have made, once and for all a consecration of our lives to God, there will be all along the way further unveilings of the Lord, of His power, and of His purposes. As each fuller revelation comes into view, we commit ourselves afresh to God for its fulfillment in our lives (Rom. 12:1–2).

Chapter 7

A MAN OF ONE BOOK

To Wigglesworth, the Word of God was so precious, he carried it in his heart and he carried a copy of at least the New Testament everywhere he went. He even offered a reward to anyone who found him without a portion of the Scripture on his person.

You could not be with him long before you discovered two things. First, he had an overmastering love for the Word, and secondly, he had an absolute confidence in the God of the Word. Because he loved God's Word, he read it; because he read it, he had faith; because he had faith, he acted; and because he acted, his faith grew. For this reason, he was "a man of one book," a phrase coined by John Wesley.

Wesley was well-educated, one of the best-read men of his day. After reading widely, he came to see

> BECAUSE HE LOVED GOD'S WORD, HE READ IT; BECAUSE HE READ IT, HE HAD FAITH; BECAUSE HE HAD FAITH, HE ACTED; AND BECAUSE HE ACTED, HIS FAITH GREW.

> YOU WILL DO
> MORE WORK IN
> LESS TIME AND
> WITH LESS STRAIN
> IF YOU LISTEN TO
> FATHER FIRST.

the Bible as utterly unrivaled, the book above all other books, hence his longing and determination to major in the Bible and to be a "man of one book."

Wigglesworth, as I have mentioned before, had a very limited education. After he learned to read, he made a deliberate choice to limit his reading to the Bible. He told me that, because he learned to read so late, he felt he should keep that ability for the reading of the supreme book.

At one stage, Wigglesworth even advised young ministers to burn their libraries. Donald Gee, a widely traveled and honored Bible teacher, told me he had to go around comforting and counseling those who had taken Wigglesworth at his word—and later regretted it.

Frankly, I do not think he meant his words to be taken literally. By overemphasis, he was stressing the priority and indispensability of God's own Word for preachers. Some people criticized him for inconsistency because, while advising others not to read books, he authored two—*Ever Increasing Faith* and *Faith That Prevails*. He would reply with a smile, "I didn't write those books. Someone took down my sermons in shorthand and then published them."

One of the reasons for Wigglesworth's high esteem for the Word was its cleansing power. He believed deeply the need for being spiritually clean. He told his grandson, "Leslie, if I read the newspaper I come out dirtier than I went in. If I read my Bible, I come out cleaner than I went in, and I like being clean!"

You never needed a devotional book when Wigglesworth stayed with you. After every meal, he would say something like this, "Well, we've fed our bodies. Now we must feed our souls." Then out would come his Bible. He would read a portion, then comment on it, as God had spoken to him that very day. Then he would illustrate what he was saying with some vivid experience from his ministry. After every meal he shared with us, we rose from the table satisfied physically and also with a glow in our souls.

An American lady missionary ran a missionary home in Ramalah, Palestine (now Israel), and she was a strict disciplinarian. A missionary living there at the time Wigglesworth visited told me, "You went to bed at a certain time. You got up at a certain time. You sat down to breakfast on time. You finished on time. You rose from the table on time."

This did not suit Wigglesworth, and he told the lady, "Sister, this won't do. We must take time to listen to Father. You will do more work in less time and with less strain if you listen to Father first."

He insisted on reading the Word, then commenting on it, following that with prayer. Tom

> HE BELIEVED THAT BY PRAYER AND THE REVELATION OF THE HOLY SPIRIT, THE SIMPLEST BELIEVER COULD UNDERSTAND THE WORD OF GOD.

Kemp, who reported this, said this practice changed the atmosphere of the home.

"There was a sense of sweetness that persisted even after Wigglesworth had left," Kemp said. Wigglesworth had bestowed blessing through the Word.

One day, I tried an experiment, asking Wigglesworth if he would like me to read to him.

"What do you want to read?" he asked.

I suggested a sermon by the great 19th century preacher Charles H. Spurgeon, whose last years as pastor of London's Metropolitan Tabernacle spanned Wigglesworth's young manhood. Wigglesworth was not enthusiastic, but he allowed me to try. So I began to read Spurgeon's sermon on the crucifixion. He talked so tenderly about the cross that Wigglesworth began quietly to weep.

However, as I moved to Spurgeon's second main point, it was only a short while until Wigglesworth exclaimed, "Stop it! He's missed it"—and he had! That ended my attempts to read books to Wigglesworth. But he would listen untiringly if you read to him from the Bible.

He had a conviction that if you did not have a hunger for righteousness as revealed in God's Word, you were not in the place God wanted you to be. You needed an insatiable appetite for the Scripture of truth, he thought, otherwise you missed God's plan.

This was his belief:

If it is in the Bible, it is so. It's not even to be prayed about. It's to be received and acted upon. Inactivity is a robber which steals blessings. Increase comes by action, by using what we have and know. Your life must be one of going on from faith to faith.[1]

This belief he applied to everything—holiness, witnessing, baptism in water and in the Spirit, and divine healing. For example, if you asked him for a good book on divine healing, most likely he would reply, "What's wrong with the Bible?"

He believed that by prayer and the revelation of the Holy Spirit, the simplest believer could understand the Word of God. He had a saying, "Some people like to read their Bibles in the Hebrew; some like to read it in the Greek; I like to read it in the Holy Spirit." Consequently, he had some remarkable insights into the Scriptures.

One day he said to me, "Brother, God wants all He's got in you." When I asked him what he meant, he said, "You'll find it in James."

So I read the Epistle of James more than once, but found nothing like what Wigglesworth had said. Finally, I read James on my knees praying, "Lord, show me what Wigglesworth is trying to tell me." I came to a halt at James 4:5:

> Do ye think that the scripture saith in vain, The spirit that dwelleth in us lusteth to envy?

Even that did not seem to say what Wigglesworth had said.

THE WORD TRULY CAME ALIVE WHEN WIGGLESWORTH READ IT.

Prayerfully I began to study with the help of what Greek scholarship was within my reach. I discovered that this passage is saying that God has a passionate desire for a full response from the Spirit He has placed in us.

This was confirmed by other versions of the New Testament that were published long after Wigglesworth's death. God longs intensely for unhindered communication and total response between Him and the believer indwelt by the Spirit.

This is a profound explanation of a verse which, in the *King James Version*, is extremely difficult. How did Wigglesworth arrive at this interpretation, which later was confirmed by scholarly translators? He found it because he read his Bible in the Holy Spirit.

That does not mean we should despise scholarship. Far from it! We would not have the Bible in our own language without scholars. But it does mean that by prayer, meditation, and diligence—all under the anointing of the Holy Spirit—our renewed minds and spirits can discern the hidden truths of God's precious Word (Eph. 4:23, Col. 3:10).

The well-known 18th century preacher, Dr. G. Campbell Morgan, was a Bible scholar of the first order, but even his view of a Bible verse was surpassed by that of an old lady he was visiting. She was dying, and Dr. Morgan read to her Jesus' words in Matthew 28:20, "Lo, I am with you alway." Then he said, "Isn't that a wonderful promise?"

"Sir," replied the woman, "that isn't a promise—it's a fact!"

A deep reverence for God's Word is not "biblidolatry," but a recognition of the Divine Source and amounts to worship for the

Author. Our respect for the holy Scripture also should extend to the public reading of it. One preacher I heard called the people to stand to honor God's Word as he read, but then he garbled the reading so badly it was difficult to follow its meaning.

Another preacher rarely read the Bible publicly without interpolating the reading with his own comments. Preachers should concentrate on an unadulterated, uninterpreted, meaningful, Spirit-anointed public reading of the Scripture. Expounding on it can come later. The Bible then will come alive to their congregations.

I heard one lady say to a preacher, "I want to thank you for the way you read Romans 6 tonight. I had never understood it until I heard you read it."

The Word truly came alive when Wigglesworth read it. He *was* a "man of one book."

Chapter 8

FAITH: THE KEY TO WIGGLESWORTH'S MINISTRY

Smith Wigglesworth many times was called "the apostle of faith" because he believed God unequivocally.

Many today use the title "apostle" very freely and loosely, when it needs safeguarding. Even the Apostle Paul was careful in his use of the term. In Romans 1:1, he said he was *called* to be an apostle. In Second Corinthians 12:11, he said he was nothing behind the chiefest of apostles, and in First Corinthians 15:9, he said he was "least" of all the apostles and was not "meet" to be called an apostle.

Obviously he viewed the title differently at various times in his life, but the marks of an apostle—the reality that is more than a name—were ever present (2 Cor. 12:12).

> SEEING THE EVIDENCE OF HIS FAITH, WE ARE MOVED TO ASK, "IS SUCH A FAITH WITHIN MY REACH? CAN I POSSESS LIKE PRECIOUS FAITH?"

> EVERY BELIEVER CAN HAVE ENOUGH FAITH FOR THE FULFILLMENT OF GOD'S WILL IN HIS OR HER LIFE.

Wigglesworth also recognized that it is not the title you have, nor the gift you claim, but the manifestation of the power of God that counts (1 Cor. 1:31). The manifestation of the power of God was shown in his life through faith.

Seeing the evidence of his faith, we are moved to ask, "Is such a faith within my reach? Can I possess like precious faith?" I trust this chapter will help and encourage those true seekers after that kind of faith.

I have two important observations to make concerning such faith. First, Wigglesworth did not arrive at his degree of faith in one leap. He reached it by a process of failure and success. Whoever you are, whatever situation you are in, however weak your faith is at this moment, *your faith can grow.*

Secondly, Wigglesworth believed that *God has no favorites.* He believed *all* Christians have the potential to grow into strong faith. This matter of favorites was illustrated quite sweetly for us by a Swiss friend of my wife's named Martha.

In broken English, Martha said one day, "I was cross with Jesus because He had favorites, and I told Him so. He asked me why I said that, and I told Him, 'Because you let John lean on your bosom.' Do you know what Jesus said? He said, 'Martha, *all* the disciples could have leaned on My bosom. Only John wanted to.'"

Every believer can have enough faith for the fulfillment of God's will in his or her life. Wigglesworth had a noble concept of God's plan for him and was determined to seek God for the faith required to exercise his ministry.

Not all will have the same calling; not all will need the same dramatic faith. But all Christians have the potential for the gifts of the Spirit to operate through them, and all Christians can possess faith for the effective exercise of whatever gift He chooses to operate through them.

> FAITH THAT SAVES IS A FAITH THAT WORKS. FAITH THAT ACHIEVES IS A FAITH THAT ACTS.

William Hacking, a pastor in the north of England, had Wigglesworth in his church for meetings. One day some of the young men of his church, soul-winning young men, accompanied the evangelist on a walk.

He said, "Well, young men, you can ask me any question you like, and I'll answer it best as I can."

One of them asked the inevitable question, "Mr. Wigglesworth, how can we come to possess great faith?"

"Now, listen," said Wigglesworth, "here is the answer: 'First the blade, then the ear, after that the full corn in the ear.' Mark 4:28."

Wigglesworth saw three degrees of faith. The first degree is *saving* faith. All who receive Jesus as Savior have received that faith. This faith is seed that, nourished by hearing the Word of God, can grow:

> For by grace are ye saved through faith; and that not of
> yourselves: it is the gift of God.
>
> Ephesians 2:8

The second degree he saw was *the faith of the Lord Jesus.* In Galatians 2:20, Wigglesworth saw that it was the faith *of* the Lord Jesus being spoken of, not faith *in* the Son of God. It is Christ's own faith imparted to His children:

> I am crucified with Christ: nevertheless, I live; yet not I,
> but Christ liveth in me: and the life which I now live in the
> flesh I live by the faith *of* the Son of God, who loved me, and
> gave himself for me.

Thirdly, he said, there is the *gift of faith:*

> But the manifestation of the Spirit is given to every man to
> profit withal ... to another faith by the same Spirit.
>
> 1 Corinthians 12:7,9

There were those who quibbled over these distinctions, but Wigglesworth blithely ignored their quibbles and went on demonstrating he had a faith that glorified God in practical results. Faith that saves is a faith that works. Faith that achieves is a faith that acts (James 2:18-20).

For Wigglesworth, there was one thing more: He pressed through by faith in the Word of God to faith in the God of the Word. There is a distinction. Romans 4:3 says that Abraham believed *God.* The Apostle Paul did not write that Abraham believed *about* God nor even believed *in* God. Abraham believed God as a Person.

It follows inevitably that if you believe God as a Person, you will believe every word that He speaks. Faith in God Himself is direct contact with God. It is a confidence that inspires action.

For Smith Wigglesworth, Hebrews 12:2, "Looking unto Jesus the author and finisher of our faith," meant unbroken communion with Jesus, dwelling deeply in the presence of the Lord. As he gazed on Jesus, his faith grew, and

> HE BEGAN IN TREMBLING AND FEAR, BUT HE ACTED ON WHAT FAITH HE HAD, AND GOD HONORED HIS ACTING IN FAITH.

he was changed from glory to glory (2 Cor. 3:18). That same place of abiding, that same privilege of gazing on the Lord, is open to us!

Wigglesworth believed that faith means action. Once while preaching, he said, "If there is anything in your heart in the way of condemnation, you cannot pray the prayer of faith. Purity is vital to faith. How is faith received? It is received by your acting with what you now have. If you act with what you have, your faith will be increased. You can never increase faith but by acting."

Once a lady wrote a long letter to Wigglesworth telling about her problems and quoting a large number of scriptures.

He sent the letter back to her with these words written on it, "Believe your own letter." She did—and was healed. In other words, she *acted* on what she already had.

Praying for the Sick

FAITH BASED ON TOTAL TRUST IN JESUS IS THE FAITH THAT SUPPORTED THE EARLY CHRISTIANS, THE FAITH THAT WIGGLESWORTH HAD, AND THE FAITH WE NEED TODAY.

Wigglesworth told me of the first time he ever prayed for the sick. It was during the time he and Polly were operating a mission in Bradford, Yorkshire. Wigglesworth heard of a meeting in Leeds, nine miles away, where they prayed for the sick. Each week, he took people there from his mission to be prayed for, and miracles took place.

One day, the leader of the meeting said, "Brother Wigglesworth, I have to be away next week, so you must take the meeting."

"I can't!" said Wigglesworth, "I have never prayed for the sick."

The leader replied, "God has shown me that you are the one to take the meeting. You must do it."

When he arrived the next week, there was no one else to take charge, so he did his best. This is what he told me:

I don't know what I preached, but I do remember that when I called for the sick, about twelve people came forward for prayer. The first was a large-framed man leaning on two sticks. As soon as I touched that man, the power of God hit him. He dropped his sticks; he started to jump; then he started to run, and ran all around the place. The faith of the others—*and* mine—was so quickened that everyone I prayed for that day was healed.

Wigglesworth saw this as God's compassion, helping him in a time of need, and helping his faith to grow. He began in trembling and fear, but he acted on what faith he had, and God honored his acting in faith.

John Wesley taught his preachers, "Preach faith until you have it, and then because you have it, you will preach faith."

Faith is reciprocal—act in faith, and you will have greater faith. So many people, seeing Wigglesworth in his later ministry, forgot or most likely never knew of, his early struggles. He knew poverty and hard work, even as a youngster of six beginning to work in the turnip fields by 6 a.m. and staying at it for ten to twelve hours. But from a child, he was determined to know God, "precept upon precept; line upon line" (Is. 28:10).

He said, "Great faith is the product of great fights. Great testimonies are the outcome of great tests. Great triumphs can only come out of great trials."[2]

The tests he went through led him to a simple, basic faith, startling

"IT IS NOT FOR ME TO CLAIM THAT I HAVE A GIFT. IF I HAVE IT, THE MANIFESTATION OF IT WILL BE THE EVIDENCE THAT IT IS THERE. IT'S NOT WHAT I CLAIM, BUT WHAT GOD DOES."

in its simplicity. He had such confidence in God that he took him at His Word. Consequently, he was not moved by human opinion. He knew the danger spoken of by the Lord:

> How can ye believe, which receive honor one of another, and seek not the honor that cometh from God only?
>
> John 5:44

Wigglesworth knew that Hebrews 12:2 is true, Jesus is the "author and finisher of our faith"—and that is the basis of "New Testament faith," faith based on total trust in Jesus. That is the faith that supported the early Christians, the faith that Wigglesworth had, and the faith we need today.

Chapter 9

NEW TESTAMENT FAITH

Faith is not mental acquiescence, nor even the ability to count a thing done. It is the deep awareness imparted by Jesus that a certain thing *is* done.

Early in his ministry, Wigglesworth was called to pray for a young woman who obviously was demon-possessed. He went into the home and the woman's husband was there with the baby. When they tried to bring the baby to the woman to nurse, she flung herself away. Wigglesworth was moved deeply with compassion. He knew the situation was desperate and needed a desperate remedy.

He got on his face before God, and his faith was quickened. He began to penetrate the heavens. He saw in the presence of God the limitations of his own faith. As he tarried there, another faith came to him, a faith that could not be denied. He came back from that experience of the immediate presence of God a changed man.

With authority, he commanded the demons to come out of the woman. The young lady rolled over in bed and went to sleep for fourteen hours. Then she woke completely free. This "storming of heaven" (spiritual warfare) was vital in his view. By it, Wigglesworth pressed through into the presence of God against every satanic attempt to hinder.

He gazed on Jesus, and his faith grew strong. He had eyes for Jesus only. He communed with Him through the Word, through prayer, through speaking with other tongues. His faith was not a formula, but came of discipline, through pressing through (Heb. 4:11, 10:20).

The real issue is that, for Smith Wigglesworth, faith flowed out of a relationship with Jesus.

I once asked him if the Holy Spirit operated the "gift of faith" listed in First Corinthians 12:9 through him, and his reply was, "It is not for me to claim that I have a gift. If I have it, the manifestation of it will be the evidence that it is there. It's not what I claim, but what God does."

He saw danger in claiming a gift or a title. It could cause people to look to the person through whom the gift operates rather than at the true Giver of the gift to the Body, to look at the instrument rather than the One who is using the instrument. Then there may be the temptation to get into pride or to move into areas not of God's choosing. Furthermore, he saw that a man could lose touch with God and be left with an empty title.

Let me conclude this chapter with the account of some unusual demonstrations of faith.

Faith in Operation

The Rev. J. E. Stiles, an Assemblies of God minister and author, had a remarkable ministry of leading people into the baptism in the Holy Spirit. This ministry began when he saw and heard Wigglesworth minister in California at a large camp meeting.

To a large company of people gathered that night, Wigglesworth taught two lessons on faith. First, he asked all those who had not received the baptism in the Spirit to stand. Then he asked all those who had been baptized but had not spoken in tongues for at least six months to stand. Finally, he called all of the several hundred people standing to come forward and crowd around the pulpit.

"Now," said Wigglesworth, "I'm going to teach you the first lesson in faith. You will speak with tongues by faith. I want you to lift your hands and press forward."

When everyone did, he said, "I'm going to pray a simple prayer. When I've finished, I'll say, 'Go,' and you will all speak in tongues."

Stiles said to the man standing next to him, "This might work in Britain, but it will never work here."

The next thing he heard was Wigglesworth praying. Then he heard him say, "Go!" To his astonishment, the next sound was like that of many waters. Everyone was praising God in tongues, "And," said Stiles, "I myself was speaking louder than anyone else."

Presently, Wigglesworth cried, "Hold it!" in stentorian tones. Things quieted down, but a few people kept speaking in tongues. Again he said, "Hold it!" Finally all was quiet. Then he told them he was going to teach them the second lesson on faith, and that was how to sing in the Spirit by faith.

He commanded them to press forward again and raise their hands. They did.

He said, "I'm going to pray a simple prayer. When I've finished, I'll say, 'Go!' and you will all begin to sing in tongues by faith."

Again Stiles demurred, saying, "That cannot happen. The other did happen, but not this. He hasn't given us any tune. We don't know what to sing. It will be utter confusion."

But Stiles said that when the evangelist prayed then said, "Go! Sing!" the sound was like a vast glorious choir. The group sang in perfect harmony and at other times in unison. He said it seemed as if there were solos, sometimes groups, and sometimes a full choir, all under the baton of the greatest conductor. He had never heard anything like it.

Stiles said he learned a bigger lesson than speaking and singing in tongues by faith. He learned that the Holy Spirit operates on faith, and from that moment, he was launched on a ministry of faith which extended throughout the United States and Canada, a ministry that saw thousands baptized in the Spirit by faith.

One day Wigglesworth was being shown around a farm by the owner, a dear friend. Visiting one field, he commented on the beauty of it. But his friend said, "It's not what it looks. The whole field is ruined by blight."

Wigglesworth lifted his heart to God. Faith flowed in, and he stretched out his hand over the field in the name of Jesus. The field was completely cleansed of blight and the entire crop was saved. In fact, that was the best crop his friend had from any field!

A lady with advanced cancer asked Wigglesworth to pray for her. He went to her home with James Salter, his son-in-law, and they prayed. She was immediately and gloriously delivered.

Later, as she cleaned out a closet, she came across an old Bible that she had not seen in twelve years. Glancing through it, she saw that years before she had underlined part of Isaiah 58:8, "Thine health shall spring forth speedily." She realized that God had spoken to her all those years ago, but she had never actuated her faith. She could have been spared those years of suffering.

Bishop Ronald Coady and his wife were ministering in New South Wales, Australia, in 1950 where they met a Methodist deaconess called Sister Mary. She brought them large quantities of tracts to use in their crusades.

While there, they were reading Stanley Frodsham's book, *Smith Wigglesworth—Apostle of Faith*. The incident of his raising a young woman from the dead especially had gripped them, and when Sister Mary came in, they read it to her, adding, "How we should love to meet that lady!"

She said, "You know that lady."

They protested that they did not, but she persisted, "You've known her for some time. I am that lady."

The three of them laughed together with holy joy at God's "coincidences." She then told them of being paralyzed from the waist down in 1922 and of being seriously ill. Wigglesworth was holding meetings in her town, and her friends urged her to let them take her to a meeting for prayer. However, she did not believe in divine healing and did not wish to be prayed for.

She soon became worse and, in fact, was dying. Her friends asked if she would allow the evangelist to pray for her if they brought him to the house. She finally consented, but he was delayed. Before he arrived, she died.

Sister Mary Pople related that she went to Heaven and was allowed in the throne room. She saw the Lord Jesus sitting on His throne. She saw light such as she had never seen and heard music such as she had never heard. Her heart was filled with rapturous joy.

As she looked at the Lord, He pointed to the doorway by which she had entered, and she knew she had to go back even if she did not want to. When she went through that door, she heard a voice that later she knew was Smith Wigglesworth's. He was saying, "Death, I rebuke you in the name of Jesus." Then he commanded Mary to live.

Her eyes opened, and those who had been weeping around her bed began to rejoice. She arose and dressed, and there was a knock at the door. Some girls from her Bible study group had arrived, thinking she was dead. To their surprise and joy, Mary herself opened the door to them.

She continued in the Lord's service for many years. Not only was she raised from the dead, but she was totally healed of her sickness that had been unto death and of the paralysis that had bound her for years.

Without faith, it is impossible to please him.

Hebrews 11:6

Chapter 10

SANCTIFICATION: UNBROKEN COMMUNION WITH GOD

I heard American author-pastor-teacher Judson Cornwall say once concerning Smith Wigglesworth:

> I will never forget the sense of awe I felt at the authority that man had. It was an absolutely glorious, positive authority in God. He knew the voice of his God. He knew what God was about to do, and he was always there at the right time when God did it. He had the ability to speak it just as God did it; or, as he spoke it, God did it.

The secret lay, I believe, in the large degree to which Wigglesworth had entered into the inmost life of the Lord Jesus as revealed in John 5:19–20. Jesus said in those verses that He did nothing on earth that He had not seen the Father do in heaven. That is an increasing revelation.

HE KNEW WHAT GOD WAS ABOUT TO DO, AND HE WAS ALWAYS THERE AT THE RIGHT TIME WHEN GOD DID IT.

> WIGGLESWORTH
> ACHIEVED THE
> GOAL OF HOLINESS
> BECAUSE HE
> DETERMINED
> NOT TO SETTLE FOR
> ANYTHING LESS.

Perhaps the emphasis on the miraculous in Wigglesworth's life and ministry has obscured, to a large extent, his insistent call for holy living.

Kathleen Chambers, daughter of Oswald Chambers, heard a great deal about holiness in her home when she was a small girl. One day while playing with a rag doll, she tried to make it stand up. Its limp rag legs collapsed every time. In disgust, she exclaimed, "He ain't 'sankified' yet!"

That is sadly true of many oft-collapsing Christians! However, what joy there is in true holiness. The pure in heart see God. Samuel Chadwick said:

> Holiness brings the soul into fellowship with the redeeming Son of God. When believers rejoice in its possession, sinners are awakened and saved.[3]

The truth of the great prayer of the writer of Hebrews needs to be experienced by us all:

> Now the God of peace, that brought again from the dead our Lord Jesus, that great shepherd of the sheep, through the blood of the everlasting covenant,
>
> Make you perfect in every good work to do his will, working in you that which is well-pleasing in his sight, through Jesus Christ; to whom be glory forever and ever. Amen.
>
> Hebrews 13:20–21

There is a winsomeness in the Greek word *katartizo* translated "make you perfect":

In Matthew 21:16, it means to set in order as in music.

In Galatians 6:1, it is translated "restore" and carries the idea of putting back in place a dislocated limb.

In First Thessalonians 3:10, it means to supply what is "lacking."

In Hebrews 11:3, it is translated "framed" and implies setting in order as in a machine.

In Matthew 4:21, the translation is "mending." This carried a double idea: repairing what was broken and arranging for future use.

In Ephesians 4:11–12, the thought is of equipping for service.

Wigglesworth achieved the goal of holiness because he determined not to settle for anything less. He "prayed through." His experience of sanctification by faith was fundamental to his later life and ministry. Teachers in the holiness movement called it the baptism in the Spirit, and so did he at first.

Later, he came to see what the true baptism in the Spirit is, but he never denied his earlier experience. It was an essential part of God's plan. For the rest of his life, he associated holiness with power.

Wigglesworth lived so close to God in the last years of his ministry. He dwelt in the secret place of the Most High. *Unbroken communion* best describes his relationship with God. In that intimacy, he entered deeply into the experience of Jesus. He, too, saw what God did in heaven, then in Jesus' name, he did it on earth.

Comparatively few dwell where he dwelt. It is an "awe-full" place Isaiah describes so vividly in Isaiah 33:14:

> Who among us shall dwell with the devouring fire? Who among us shall dwell with everlasting burnings?

David asked the same question in Psalm 24:3,4.

Wigglesworth knew that without holiness, no man can see the Lord (Heb. 12:14), so with all his heart, he sought holiness. There was no "shilly-shallying," no playing games, no pretense— He meant to *see* God (Matt. 5:8). One of his great joys in the baptism of the Holy Spirit was the sense of cleansing. He had a vision of an empty cross and Jesus glorified. He cried out in ecstasy, "Clean, clean, clean."

His Life in the Spirit

"GOD WORKED THE OLD WIGGLESWORTH-NATURE OUT AND BEGAN TO WORK THE NEW JESUS-NATURE IN."

Wigglesworth's life in the Spirit began with the certainty of the new birth he experienced as a young boy. Yet he felt that was not all there was to a relationship with God. He was eager to grow spiritually. A few months after his fourteenth birthday, when he was confirmed in the Church of England with the bishop laying hands on him, he was filled with an overwhelming joy. Afterwards, he came to believe this was the

beginning of the work of the Holy Spirit in his life that culmi-
nated in the baptism of the Spirit nearly forty years later.

Yet even that was not enough. As he grew older, he came to
realize that he had to face up to temptation and defeat in his
Christian walk. Perhaps, as we have already seen, his greatest
weakness was his temper.

His temper was at times all-consuming. He would go pale and
shake with rage over sometimes trivial matters, almost losing control.

Also, there was a period in his life when he turned almost
completely from the mission ministry to business. A plumber by
trade, he became very busy and successful. He and his employ-
ees worked from early morning until late at night, and he began
to prosper greatly. As a result, his private devotions and church
attendance suffered.

His love for Jesus, prayer, the Word, and the fellowship of
believers lessened until he was gripped by materialism. In the
meantime, Polly increased in spiritual fervor as she continued in
the ministry. As he grew colder, she grew hotter. This irritated
him. One night, when she was very late returning from a service,
he said to her in a severe tone, "This must stop."

She said, "Smith, you're my husband, but Jesus is my Lord."

This angered Wigglesworth so much that he put her out the
front door and locked her out. But he had forgotten that the
back door was unlocked. She ran around the house and came in
the other door laughing. He could not resist her laughter and
joined in. That was the beginning of his restoration.

He said to himself, "This won't do in a child of God," and he
determined to meet God at every opportunity. Setting aside ten

days, he presented his body a living sacrifice (Rom. 12:1–2). He prayed, wept, soaked in the Word, and pleaded the promises. He faced up to the cross until he began to understand what Paul meant in Galatians 2:20.

This is how he described the experience to me: "God worked the old Wigglesworth-nature out and began to work the new Jesus–nature in."

The transformation was obvious to all who knew him. He became the calmest, purest man I ever knew. What he taught after that, he lived. His grandson, Leslie Wigglesworth, saw him in the relaxed environment of family life, and he bears witness that he never saw him moody or out of sorts.

Wigglesworth's failure at that point in his life was real. His sin was real, but it brought him to the end of himself and caused him to cry mightily unto God. He reached the place of brokenness. Such brokenness may well be the prerequisite of full spiritual development.

He faced the love of business and consequent love of money that took him away from God for a while. He faced his almost uncontrollable temper, surrendering it to Jesus until it was totally conquered.

The Baptism in the Spirit

Over the next few years, however, Wigglesworth realized there was still more for him in God. Holiness was vital, but God had promised power. Acts 1:8 kept returning to his mind, the passage where Jesus promised the disciples power *after* the Holy Spirit came upon them: "But ye shall receive power, after that the Holy Ghost is come upon you...."

Then he heard that the Holy Spirit had fallen upon people at All Saints Church, Sunderland. This was the spreading wave of Pentecostalism that followed the 1907 Azusa Street, California, revival. He attended the meetings in Sunderland, and here is the story in his own words, as he related it to John Carter:

When this Pentecostal outpouring began in England, I went to Sunderland. I was as certain as possible that I had (already) received the Holy Spirit and was absolutely rigid in this conviction. I met with people who had assembled for the purpose of receiving the Holy Spirit, and I was continually in those meetings causing disturbances, until the people wished I had never come. But I was hungry and thirsty for God and had gone to Sunderland because I had heard that God was pouring out His Spirit in a new way, and that God had visited His people and manifested His power, and that people were speaking in tongues as on the Day of Pentecost.

When I got there I said, "I cannot understand this meeting. I have left a meeting in Bradford all on fire for God. The fire fell last night, and we were all laid out under the power of God. I have come here for tongues, and I don't hear them."

"Oh," they said, "when you get baptized in the Holy Spirit, you will speak in tongues."

"Oh, that's it," said I. "When the presence of God came upon me, my tongue was loosed. When I went into the open air to preach, I felt I had a new tongue."

"No," they replied, "that's not it."

"What is it then?" I asked.

They said, "You'll know when you're baptized with the Holy Spirit."

"I am baptized," I interjected, "and there's no one here that can persuade me that I'm not baptized."

So I was up against them, and they were up against me. I remember a man saying, "I'd been here three weeks, then the Lord baptized me with the Holy Spirit, and I began to speak with tongues."

"Let's hear it," I said, "that's what I'm here for." But he would not talk in tongues.

As the days passed, I became more and more hungry. I had opposed the meetings so much, but the Lord was gracious. I shall ever remember the last day, the day I had to leave for home. God was with me so much as I went to the last meeting, but I could not rest. I went to the vicarage, and there in the library I said to the vicar's wife, Mrs. Boddy, "I can rest no longer. I must have these tongues."

She said, "It is not tongues. It is the baptism you need. If you will allow God to baptize you, the other will be all right."

"My dear sister," I said, "I know I am baptized. You know I have to leave shortly. Please lay your hands on me that I may receive tongues."

She rose up and laid her hands on me, and the fire fell. (Just then) she had to go out to answer a knock on the door. It was the best thing that could have happened. I was alone with God. Then He gave me a revelation. Oh, it was wonderful!

He showed me an empty cross and Jesus glorified. Then I saw that the Lord had purified me. It seemed that God gave me a new vision, and I saw a perfect being within me with mouth open, saying, "Clean, clean, clean." When I began to repeat it, I found myself speaking with other tongues. The joy was so great, I could not utter it in my own tongue, and I worshipped God in other tongues as the Spirit gave utterance. It was all as beautiful, as peaceful, as when Jesus said, "Peace, be still" (Mark 4:39). The tranquility of that moment and the joy surpassed anything I had ever known. What had I received? I had received the Bible evidence.

This was Wigglesworth's real baptism in the Holy Spirit that allowed him to become the man and minister that he was in late years. He constantly urged others to seek a similar experience for themselves, then to move on into a life of continuous receiving of more and more of the blessed Spirit of God.

However, both Smith and Polly recognized that the evidence of the baptism was *more* than tongues. A prayer language was the initial evidence, but Jesus had promised power. Polly showed her perception of this when—in response to his testimony about having received the baptism in the same way as the apostles—she said, "If you've got what they had, you can do what they did."

Wigglesworth, for his part, began to pray, "Lord, show me what you baptized me for."

One day, when he was still working as a plumber, he returned to his home to find an old man had been brought there who was in need of ministry. The man was crying out that he had committed the unpardonable sin. Immediately, Wigglesworth heard the Lord say in his heart, "This is what I baptized you for."

> "WHAT DO YOU
> WANT MOST, A
> STOMACH FULL OF
> FOOD OR A SOUL
> FULL OF GOD?"

With this confidence in his spirit, he went into the room where the old man lay, still crying, "I'm lost, lost! I've committed the unpardonable sin."

Wigglesworth went up to him, and in the name of Jesus commanded the tormenting, lying spirit to come out of the man. Immediately, the old man was delivered, and his peace and assurance returned. And Wigglesworth heard the echo in his heart, "This is what I baptized you for."

He was not content with the *blessing* of Pentecost, he wanted to know the *power* of Pentecost. Many years after his baptism, he was taken to a resort in New Zealand for a rest after a great campaign. One evening his host asked him the secret of his power and success.

In a broken voice, and with tears slowly trickling down his face, he replied:

I am sorry you asked me that question, but I will answer it.

I am a broken-hearted man. My wife, who meant everything to me, died eleven years ago (in 1913). After the funeral, I went back and lay on her grave. I wanted to die there. But God spoke to me and told me to rise up and come away. I told him if he would give me a double portion of the Spirit—my wife's and my own—I would go and preach the Gospel.

God was gracious to me and answered my request. But I sail the high seas alone. I am a lonely man, and many a time all I can do is to weep and weep.

Here was a secret indeed.

The sacrifices of God are a broken spirit: a broken and contrite heart, O God, thou wilt not despise.

Psalm 51:17

In this context, the full blessing of Pentecost was to him a costly enduement. If he went farther than others in seeking its outworking "in demonstration and power," it was because he did not want to have paid the price in vain.

For himself and others, he was utterly discontented with a baptism that did not fundamentally change a person and impart a power that had not been present before. Perhaps today we have seen too many "easy baptisms," baptisms lacking life-changing force. Wigglesworth prayed for and received a real baptism and went on to prove and demonstrate its mighty effects.

In one city, a man invited him to his home in order to be prayed for to receive the baptism. Wigglesworth arrived to find a beautiful meal had been prepared for him. The man and his wife suggested they eat first and pray afterwards. Wigglesworth bluntly asked, "What do you want most, a stomach full of food or a soul full of God?"

The man was shocked into the realization of his wrong priorities. Wigglesworth immediately began to share the Scripture, showed the man his need of cleansing and faith, then prayed for him. In no time at all, he was filled with the Spirit. The glory of the Lord filled the room, and the couple and Wigglesworth rejoiced together. The meal, so kindly prepared, was forgotten.

Wigglesworth's son-in-law, James Salter, later a powerful and outstanding missionary to Central Africa, told on one occasion of his experience of the need of cleansing as a prerequisite for the full baptism in the Holy Spirit. When he was in prayer seeking the fullness of the Spirit, it seemed there was only one thing he could think about—carrots.

The more he tried to pray, the louder "carrots" echoed in his mind. He realized that God was speaking to him about something that had to be dealt with. He rose up out of the prayer meeting and went to a green grocer's shop (in America, what would be called a produce or vegetable shop) kept by a friend's father.

He waited until the shop was clear of other customers, then the shopkeeper said, "Well, Jim, lad, what do you want?"

Salter told him that often when he had stopped by the shop to see his friend, he had stolen a carrot. He had come to confess and make restitution.

"Jim, lad, we all take a carrot from time to time. It doesn't bother me," the man said.

Salter replied, "But God is bothering me about it. I must put it right."

He did, then went to the prayer meeting, sought the Lord and, in a very short time, was filled with the Holy Spirit.

Chapter 11

STANDING ON HOLY GROUND

Wigglesworth was the purest man I have ever known, a man who lived daily in the immediate presence of God.

At one time Wigglesworth was ministering at Zion City in Illinois, founded by John Alexander Dowie. There, he called the ministers to a special prayer meeting and was already praying when they arrived. As he continued in prayer, sometimes in English and sometimes in tongues, the awesome presence of God filled the room.

One by one, the ministers were smitten by the power of God and fell prostrate on their faces. The reality of God's presence so gripped them that they were unable to move for at least an hour. Wigglesworth was the only one who remained standing as he continued in praise and prayer. A cloud, like a radiant mist, filled the room where the ministers were.

In 1922, Wigglesworth was in Wellington, the capital city of New

> THE REALITY OF GOD'S PRESENCE SO GRIPPED THEM THAT THEY WERE UNABLE TO MOVE FOR AT LEAST AN HOUR.

Zealand. One afternoon at a special meeting, eleven prominent Christians gathered for prayer at Wigglesworth's request. One after the other they prayed, until all had taken part except the visiting evangelist. He then began to pray for their city and country, and as he continued, the sense of God's presence and power so filled the room that one by one the others left, unable to continue in the blazing light of God's holiness.

One minister, hearing of this from one who had been there, greatly desired to be in a similar meeting—but with the determination that whoever else left, he would not. An opportunity soon came for him to attend such a meeting. Several people prayed, then Wigglesworth began to pray.

As he lifted up his voice, it seemed that God Himself invaded the place. Those present became deeply conscious that they were on holy ground. The power of God in its purity was like a heavy weight pressing on them. One by one, the people left until only the man remained who had set himself to stay.

He hung on and hung on until at last the pressure became a compulsion, and he could stay no longer. His own testimony was that, with the floodgates of his soul pouring out a stream of tears and with uncontrollable sobbing, he had to get out of the Presence or die. He added that Wigglesworth, a man who knew God as few men do, was left alone in an atmosphere in which few men could breathe.[4]

This closeness to God, seeing what God was doing and hearing what God was saying, then doing and saying the same on earth, is clearly seen in an incident related by William Davies when pastoring in Chesterfield, Derbyshire, England. Wigglesworth was conducting a crusade for Davies. One night in the healing line, there was a young man with a bandage around his throat.

When the evangelist asked him, "What's up?" he replied in a hoarse whisper, "Can God do anything for me?"

"Of course He can," answered Wigglesworth, "unless He has forgotten how to make voice boxes."

He placed his hands on the young man's throat, prayed in his usual way, then turned the young man around, saying, "Go home and eat a meal of meat and potatoes."

BEFORE THEIR VERY EYES, THE HOLE HEALED RIGHT UP. WHAT HE HAD SEEN GOD DO IN HEAVEN, HE HAD DONE ON EARTH.

The young man turned back, saying, "I can't, Sir! I feed myself through this," pointing to a tube in the side of his throat.

Wigglesworth turned him around again, gave him a gentle push, and said, "Go on your way. Do as you're told. Be not faithless, but believing."

The next night, the young man was again in the healing line. When he came forward, Wigglesworth said, "What are you doing here? I prayed for you last night!"

The young man answered in a normal voice, "I've come to tell you what God did for me last night!"

Turning him to face the audience, Wigglesworth said, "You don't need to tell me. Tell them." This was the young man's testimony:

"After receiving the preacher's stern rebuke (to do as I was told), I went home and asked my mother to cook me a solid meal. She argued with me, but I told her to please prepare it. I *was* going to eat it. She prepared the meal. I sat down and took the first mouthful, chewing it a long time, hesitating to swallow it. Finally with fear and trembling, I swallowed that first mouthful. It just slipped down my throat, no pain, no obstruction, no trouble at all. Since then, I've had more meals, and I'm looking forward to one after this meeting."

Wigglesworth asked, "Then what are you doing with a bandage around your throat?" The young fellow explained that it covered the tube through which he had been receiving food and that he was going to the hospital the next day to have it removed.

The evangelist quietly but confidently said, "What the Lord has begun, He can complete." Calling Pastor Davies and other helpers to come near, he said, "Now watch this, for you will never see the like of it again."

He removed the bandage, gently drew the tube out of the young man's neck, then placed his thumb and forefinger on each side of the hole. Those who were watching were astonished. Before their very eyes, the hole healed right up. What he had seen God do in heaven, he had done on earth.

Wigglesworth often said, "What I have, you can have." And we can! But there is the same price to pay. We must be holy. We must live very close to Jesus. We must dwell in the presence of God.

Beyond contradiction, Wigglesworth's emphasis on holiness was a major factor in the amazing results of his ministry. There was a sense of awe in his meetings. One businessman had his unsaved secretary attend those Wellington meetings with him to record what was said and what took place. Later, this was his testimony:

> During the address, the evangelist suddenly burst into tongues and then gave an interpretation. I said to my typist, "Take that down," and a few moments later, "Did you get that down?" She said, "I'm sorry, but everything went strange, and I couldn't lift my hand." A little later, another message was given, and I again made request, but the pencil had fallen from her hand, and she was trembling like an aspen leaf. At the end of the meeting, she responded to the evangelist's plea and accepted Christ as her Savior.[5]

Chapter 12

TO HUNGER AND THIRST AFTER RIGHTEOUSNESS

Moses Copeland, a British preacher, said that in his youth he was given this word by Smith Wigglesworth: "When the child of God ceases to hunger after righteousness and purity, then Satan gets in."

His own way of preventing so sad a development was to nourish his life by communion with God. Once he had heard a godly minister tell this story:

There was a time in my life when I sensed that God was calling me to come apart and seek his face. But I was busy, and I would go on with those things that were keeping me busy. God was gracious and persisted in calling me. Bit by bit, I began to respond, until I formed the habit of going aside at the slightest breath of the Spirit to spend time with God.

This impressed Wigglesworth, and he developed the same habit. At home with his family or even in

> "WHEN THE CHILD OF GOD CEASES TO HUNGER AFTER RIGHTEOUSNESS AND PURITY, THEN SATAN GETS IN."

> EVERYTHING
> HE DID WAS
> BATHED IN THAT
> COMMUNION
> WITH GOD.

other people's homes, if he sensed a prompting in his spirit, he would quietly withdraw from company, go to his room, and enjoy the Lord's presence.

Leslie, his grandson, told me that his grandfather would pray a while, then lie on the bed and open his Bible "to see what Father had to say." Then he would meditate and worship, often in other tongues. Then he would pray again and repeat the process until sometimes several hours would pass. He was following the advice of the psalmist David: "When thou saidst, Seek ye my face; my heart said with thee, Thy face, LORD, will I seek" (Ps. 27:8).

In his earlier years, Wigglesworth prayed for long periods. At times, he spent whole nights in prayer for souls. He told me in later years, "These days (when he was traveling long hours, staying in different homes, and holding meetings all over the world) I cannot pray for half an hour on end. But there is not a half-hour of my waking life that I am not in prayer some time."

Everything he did was bathed in that communion with God— conversation, letter writing, preparing for ministry, preaching, or bringing healing and deliverance to multitudes. His chairmanship of meetings was likewise saturated with God.

For long years, one of the largest Pentecostal conventions in England was at Preston, Lancashire—the Easter Convention I have referred to earlier in this book. The convention was four days long with three meetings scheduled each day. The local pastor, Dick Coates, was a precious brother but not gifted in leading large meetings.

He and the elders invited Wigglesworth to be chairman. And what a chairman! He imparted something of the Spirit from the moment he entered the building. Few people knew, however, that every year before the convention he went away for a week to a quiet place to seek God's face for His anointing on every meeting, every preacher, every song.

> HE KEPT FROM SPIRITUAL STAGNATION BY EAGERLY PURSUING THE LORD.

The consequence was that every meeting he conducted was in the Spirit from the opening moment. No almost endless singing of choruses to get the people in the "right mood" and no tiring standing for long periods so that the congregation was too weary to appreciate the ministry of the Word.

Often the first speaker was up and preaching ten minutes after the service began, preaching to a Spirit-quickened, fresh, and responsive audience. Often, after the first song, Wigglesworth would ask the congregation, "Who wants a blessing? Put one hand up." The congregation would respond. Then, "Who wants a double blessing? Put two hands up." Again, there would be a response. Finally, he would say, "If you want a blessing you can take home with you, everyone stand up. Now, pray out loud." There were congregations up to two thousand, and when they obeyed Wigglesworth's instructions, it was like the sound of many waters, and the glory of God filled the place.

A friend who had been a "high churchman" told me of being at one of the conventions and being so horrified at what he thought was irreverence that he left the building. He had not gone far when God spoke to him, "If you don't go back and enter into that prayer and praise, I will cease to bless you."

He hurried back and entered into the worship as God had commanded. His testimony to me was that the worship time at the convention became a powerful force for change in his life. And it flowed out of Wigglesworth's communion with God.

That communion was nourished by partaking of holy communion. He did this every day whether he was at home or not. If other believers were with him, he would share with them. If not, he would partake alone.

He kept from spiritual stagnation by eagerly pursuing the Lord. Following is his own testimony to the various ways he was led as he followed on to know the Lord. While this resulted in some measure of upheaval in his life, but he felt no price was too high to pay to live in ever-deepening communion with God.

When I was in the Methodist Church, I was sure I was saved and sure I was right. The Lord said to me, "Come out," and I came out. When I was with the people known as the Brethren, I was sure that *now* I was right. But the Lord said, "Come out," and I went into the Salvation Army. At that time (the founding days of the Army), it was full of life, and there were revivals everywhere; but the Salvation Army went into natural things, and the great revivals I had known in the early days ceased. The Lord said to me, "Come out," and I came out. I have had to "come out" three times since.

I believe this Pentecostal revival we are now in is the best thing the Lord has on earth today. Yet I believe that out of this, the Lord has something still better. God has no use for any man who is not hungering and thirsting for yet more of Himself and His righteousness. The Lord has told us to covet earnestly the best gifts, and we need to be covetous for those that will bring the most glory to God.

His eager pursuit after God led to an unbroken sense of the presence of God. He would tell us, "You have to live ready. If you have to stop to get ready, you are too late. The opportunity will have gone."

A good illustration of this is the time a sick man asked me to bring Wigglesworth to his home to pray for him. I did, and introduced them to each other.

After only a few minutes, Wigglesworth said, "God has told me not to pray for you till you repent of your sin, your backsliding, your pride, and your unbelief."

The man said, "I don't know what you are talking about." Wigglesworth said, "You do. The Holy Spirit is not a liar."

The man's wife pleaded with him, but he told her to keep out of it. Wigglesworth prayed, "Lord, give this man repentance," and walked out.

When we were outside, he began to weep and said, "Why did I have to say that?" I told him the man had been a deacon in our church, but he had left us and joined a liberal church where he was publishing literature against the baptism in the Spirit.

"Then why did you take me there?" he asked.

I replied, "Because he asked me, and I felt a fresh voice might help him back to God."

The next day, Wigglesworth sent me to see if the man was ready to be prayed for but his wife greeted me at the door saying, "I don't think you had better see my husband today. He's still angry at Wigglesworth and you."

I said, "I'd rather see your husband than go back and tell Smith Wigglesworth that I didn't see him!"

When I entered the sick room, the man said, "You don't agree with Wigglesworth, do you?"

I replied, "I know, and you know, that what he said is true, but I didn't have the courage to say it to you before."

"Get out, and don't come back!" he shouted. That was the last I saw of him. He died shortly afterwards. But that incident showed me that Wigglesworth was always ready to hear God and follow his instructions.

The Importance of Praise

"IF YOU DON'T MINISTER THE HOLY SPIRIT, YOU MINISTER DEATH."

It would be a serious omission if I did not tell of the importance of praise in Wigglesworth's life. A. L. Hoy, shortly after he was saved, had tea with Wigglesworth and asked him what he thought pleased God most.

Wigglesworth looked at him, his eyes shining, and instantly replied,

"Worship! No man enjoys more the riches of divine grace and performs the Lord's will to a higher degree than the man who walks with God in continuous worship."[6]

He had unique ways of bringing home this truth. Once as he came to the platform before a large congregation, he said, "How many of you came in properly tonight? I mean with both hands in the air, praising the Lord."

No one raised a hand.

He then said, "Go out, the lot of you, and come in properly. The Scripture says 'Enter into his gates with thanksgiving, and into his courts with praise' (Ps. 100:4)."

Out they all went and came back joyfully praising the Lord. They had a most wonderful meeting. More than forty years later, I told this story in one church and a lady came up excitedly to say that she had been in that meeting and that it happened just as I had reported it.

At Lullingstone, Kent, England, there is the excavation of a Roman villa, the foundation of which was laid in A.D. 90. As the work proceeded, they found a chapel and on the wall of the chapel, a plaster painting. It depicted a man and woman standing with hands in the air, obviously singing. The work dates back to 320 A.D., and the archaeologist gave it the title, "Early Christians at Worship." From earliest times, Spirit-filled people have been a praising people.

Ministering the Spirit

One of Wigglesworth's joys in his experience of the consciousness of God's presence was that it enabled him to minister the Holy Spirit. On more than one occasion, he said to me, "If you don't minister the Holy Spirit, you minister death."

When Jack West was a young Canadian evangelist, he called to see Brother Wigglesworth at his home in Bradford, Yorkshire, England. Wigglesworth was away, but Jack was invited to stay overnight. He slept in the evangelist's bed and declared, "I verily felt the power of God in that bedroom."

The next day, Wigglesworth arrived home and prayed for West, "Lord, don't let this man be ordinary. Make him extraordinary." Jack said that he remained under the power of God for many days and began a ministry that God confirmed with signs following because God's servant had ministered the Holy Spirit.

Pastor George Miles, who lived for many years only a short distance from Wigglesworth, often visited him. This is his witness: "Mr. Wigglesworth was so filled with God that his little home in Bradford seemed to be holy ground, and like Moses of old, I wanted to remove the shoes from my feet in an act of reverence."

The best way I can clarify what he meant by ministering the Spirit is to say that he "believed into" what he spoke, whether in conversation, preaching, prayer, or prophecy. With him, there were no idle words. He, by faith, actively associated the Holy Spirit with his ministry. He believed God was with him and was anointing what he was saying and doing, even as he was in the act of ministering. His faith communicated this fact to many of his hearers.

In one church, he said, "I'll go out, and come back in. Everyone who touches me will be healed." Sad to say, only one woman touched him, but she was healed.

Wigglesworth believed it was possible, and often necessary, to begin in the natural and by faith rise to the spiritual. His total acceptance of Second Timothy 1:6 that talks of "stirring up the gift in you," led to his sometimes criticized statement, "If the Holy Spirit doesn't move me, I move the Holy Spirit."

Anyone with the slightest knowledge of Smith Wigglesworth could never imagine there was the least bit of flippancy or irreverence in that remark. His deep sense of the awesomeness of God's presence would preclude that. But he knew there were times when, without a conscious awareness of being moved by God, he had to step out in faith. He knew that as he moved toward God in faith, God would move toward him in power. In this sense only, would he say that he "moved" the Holy Spirit.

Chapter 13

HIS FIRST DESIRE WAS WITNESSING

Smith Wigglesworth's primary goal in ministry was soulwinning, and winning souls was not a "program" he felt was his duty to carry out, nor did soulwinning become "works." The best way to describe his success in getting people born again is that soulwinning was the spontaneous result of his relationship with the Lord.

In a sense, he no more tried to get people saved than an apple tree "tries" to grow apples or a vine "tries" to produce grapes. He truly was grafted into Christ, and his branch was abiding (John 15). His leaves were open to heaven. He made sure of the daily, continuous flow of the sap—the life of the Spirit. For him, there was a cycle of the life in the Holy Spirit, and he lived in that cycle.

SMITH WIGGLESWORTH'S PRIMARY GOAL IN MINISTRY WAS SOULWINNING, AND WINNING SOULS WAS NOT A "PROGRAM" HE FELT WAS HIS DUTY TO CARRY OUT, NOR DID SOULWINNING BECOME "WORKS."

> ### SUCH AN ANOINTING RESTED ON HIM THAT SEVERAL WERE WON FOR THE LORD.

A second aspect of his soulwinning ability is the baptism in the Spirit. From the day of his conversion, he was a soulwinner. In fact, the first person he got saved was his mother—and later he led his father to the Lord! But he was much more a soulwinner after he was baptized in the Holy Spirit. The baptism gave him a keen sense of the value of a soul.

He was saddened by those who enjoyed the baptism for the pleasure it gave them and did not press on to its primary purpose as declared by Jesus in Acts 1:8: "Ye shall receive power after that the Holy Ghost is come upon you: and ye shall be *witnesses* unto me."

He once said:

> Now, beloved, I am out for men. It is my business to be out for men. It is my business to make everybody hungry, dissatisfied. It is my business to make people either glad or mad. I have a message from heaven that will not leave people as I find them.[7]

When he stayed in our home in England, we lived in a lovely resort, Leigh-on-Sea. From pleasant gardens on the Marine Parade ("boardwalk" in America), you could look over the broad estuary of the River Thames to Kent. From the Marine Parade, one hundred and fifty steps led down to the railway station. People who came home by train had to climb those steps.

At the top of the steps was a bench, and day after day Wigglesworth would sit there enjoying the sun. He would take out his New Testament to "see what Father has to say." Then he would meditate and pray. But always he was alert for opportunities to reach people for God.

In the spirit of what he felt was his "business" not to leave people as he found them, he would speak to people passing the bench on which he was sitting.

As he saw older people struggling up the last of those steps, he would bluntly ask, "Are you ready to die?" A shock approach indeed—and hardly "textbook evangelism"! Yet so real was his concern and so deep his compassion that few took offense. Such an anointing rested on him that several were won for the Lord.

One young couple approached him, climbing the steps and walking as far apart on the six-foot-wide steps as they could get. He called them to him and asked in a kindly voice, "What's wrong? Quarreled?"

Indeed they had and decided that their marriage was finished. He invited them to sit, one on each side of him, and with a fatherly arm around each, he led them to Jesus. Arm in arm and with shining eyes, they went on their way, their souls saved and their marriage healed.

His passion for souls began when he was saved and lasted all of his life. As a boy, he frequently witnessed to his school fellows, not always wisely or tactfully, but always earnestly.

When he was in the Salvation Army, he would spend Saturday nights in prayer claiming fifty to a hundred souls each week. When he told of this later, he would add, "and we knew that we would get them." He could not understand what he called "modern indifference to soulwinning and modern-day occupation with trivialities."

For a time before his marriage, he lived in Liverpool, England, and at the weekend, he gathered together poor children. He spent his wages to provide for their physical needs as far as he could, then told them about Jesus. There was never a Sunday during that period but what at least fifty children were born again.

George Miles tells of an interesting and challenging situation. Here it is in his own words:

> Many years ago, after an American visitor had ministered in our Bridge Street Church, it was my privilege on the Monday following, to escort the preacher to the home of that great man of God, Smith Wigglesworth. I shall never forget that visit and the deep impression it made on my life when I was but a young (assistant) pastor longing for the deeper things of God. Mr. Wigglesworth was so filled with God that his little home in Bradford seemed to be holy ground, and like Moses of old, I wanted to remove the shoes from my feet in an act of reverence.
>
> Five times during our short stay in the Victor Road house, Mr. Wigglesworth interrupted the conversation, taking a well-worn New Testament from his pocket, saying, "Now, Brethren, let us pause a moment to hear what Father has to say." (Each time) he read a few verses, gave a brief exhortation, then offered an earnest prayer which made us realize we were very near to God.

Afterwards as I reflected on those precious moments of communion, I felt this must be what the Apostle Paul meant when he spoke of "living in the Spirit," or what our Lord inferred when He made mention of His Word abiding in us. I was profoundly aware that God was in that place.

Even during dinner, we heard again "what Father has to say." When the meal came to an end, Mr. Wigglesworth looked at me and said, "Young man, have you got any petrol (gasoline) in your car?" The query about petrol was understandable; we were living in World War II days and petrol was strictly rationed for essential purposes. When Mr. Wigglesworth discovered I had a supply of petrol, he said, "Good, we will go for a short outing." I felt a few qualms about using petrol for this purpose, but the man of God seemed to be so completely in control that I felt nothing could go wrong under such authority.

Mr. Wigglesworth asked our visitor to sit in the rear of the car, while he himself would sit next to the driver to direct the way. I remember it all so vividly. As soon as Mr. Wigglesworth got in the car, he lifted his hands heavenward and prayed so earnestly— and yet so naturally—"Lord, bless this young man. Bless this car." And then he added, "Lord, bless these tires."

Now, I must explain. I said a fervent "amen" to this last request, for in those days, we

RIGHT THROUGH TO OLD AGE, WIGGLESWORTH SOUGHT THE LOST.

were compelled to use synthetic car tires, and quite unknown to Mr. Wigglesworth, there was a nasty gaping split in one of my rear tires through which the inner tube was clearly visible. What a good thing it was that the man of faith included the tires in his report!

After traveling for some distance, we arrived at the foot of Ilkley Moor, a Yorkshire beauty spot. Immediately before us was a narrow, unpaved flinty road leading up the moor. To my astonishment, my guide said, "Ah, yes. This is the road we want. Go straight ahead, young man."

My heart sank. I thought, *I'll never get up here without a puncture.* But we did, you know. What would have happened had not Mr. Wigglesworth prayed, "Lord, bless these tires"?

Arriving safely on the top of the moors on that lovely June day, we sat for a while on a convenient seat while that remarkable man captivated us with some of his amazing experiences. Then the American preacher and I went for a short stroll on those glorious hills, leaving Mr. Wigglesworth to enjoy a few quiet minutes basking in the sunshine.

When we returned, we found our brother and another man kneeling at the bench, both of them engrossed in fervent prayer.

As we stood waiting for the prayers to finish, I sensed again the sacred atmosphere which I had breathed in his home. As the two men got up from their knees, Mr.

Wigglesworth introduced us to the stranger with whom he had been praying.

He said to me, "Now, young man, this brother has to go into the hospital tomorrow for a major operation. He used to be a servant of God, but had backslidden and got right away from the Savior. But today, he has come back home to God and now, whatever happens in the hospital, his soul is right with God."

The man, with a radiant face, happy in God's restoring grace, gladly gave testimony to what the Lord had done for him. Then Mr. Wigglesworth said, "I knew I had to come up here today. Father sent me. Now our task is fulfilled, we will give glory to God as we return home."

I drove my car all the way down that flinty road back to Bradford, then home to Leeds. The inner tube was still to be seen through the split in my tire, but I never had any trouble. Furthermore, I felt quite sure the precious rationed petrol had been used for an essential purpose.

Right through to old age, Wigglesworth sought the lost. There was a park near his home, and few people who frequented it were missed in his witnessing. He shared Christ with almost all he met, whether walking or riding.

Chapter 14

SIX WAYS HE REACHED THE LOST

Wigglesworth sought and won the lost through personal evangelism, inquiry room work; open-air preaching (in America, this is called "street preaching"); house-to-house visitation; evangelistic preaching, and missions.

An example of his always-ready personal evangelism concerns a railway journey he once made and later told me about. When the train stopped at one station, two ladies boarded. He saw the worried look on their faces and said bluntly, but compassionately, "You look miserable, what's wrong?"

They told him that one of them was going into the hospital to have her leg amputated. Wigglesworth spoke to them about Jesus and tenderly led them to the Savior. Then he went on to show them that the One Who saves also is able to heal. He prayed for the sick woman, and her leg was healed. When she arrived at the hospital, doctors could find nothing wrong with her leg.

In 1985, I was preaching in Edmonton, Alberta, Canada. A retired pastor came to tell me there had been a lady in the church he formerly pastored who, as a teenager, had worked as a servant in a home where Wigglesworth was entertained. The employer of this girl had introduced her to his distinguished guest.

GOD CAN SO USE ALL OF US.

Her first name was Grace, and Wigglesworth immediately said, "Oh, I found your name in the Bible." Then he read Ephesians 2:8 to her: "By grace are ye saved through faith; and that not of yourselves: it is the gift of God." He led her to Jesus.

That pastor declared that although the girl had been brought to Jesus in such a simple, almost simplistic, way, she was for fifty years afterwards one of the finest members of his church.

One day, God spoke to Wigglesworth telling him to go to a certain spot by the side of a street in Bradford and wait for a man he would send. He went and waited half an hour, then he waited an hour. After waiting an hour and a half, he was on the point of leaving when he saw approaching him a man driving a horse and carriage. "This is the man," prompted the Holy Spirit.

Wigglesworth jumped up and sat on the seat by the side of the driver. He was ordered off but stayed put. Lovingly, earnestly, patiently, God's servant spoke to the driver about his need of Jesus. Before they arrived at his destination, the man yielded to the Savior's claim. Very shortly after that, news came that the man suddenly had been taken ill and died, and with the news came a message that he had died trusting in the Lord.

God can so use all of us. One day in England, I was driving past a gypsy encampment. Only the day before, I had visited a fine Christian gypsy named Ken there, but I felt a strong urge to stop and visit him again. I got out of my car and began to walk across the field toward the shack he called home. Coming toward me was Ken's brother, Gilbert.

He looked at me in astonishment, saying, "Thank God, you've come.

"Why?" I asked.

"The old man (their father) is dying, and he's calling for you," Ken said.

I went into a lean-to attached to Ken's shack and found "Old Man" Buckley, as he was called, very sick. He was lying on old clothes and blankets on a dirt floor. He had been a wicked man. Every one of his sons had been in jail, and he had avoided jail only by his cunning.

I knelt by the side of his bed, and said, "Mr. Buckley, I'm here. What can I do for you?"

"Oh, Pastor," he said, "I want to find God, and I don't know how."

It was a joy to point him to Jesus. A few days later; he died.

Ken, the Christian son, told me, "The old man had been such a wicked sinner I had always been afraid he would have a dreadful death. But Jesus saved him, and he had a peaceful end. He died happy in Jesus. Wonderful Jesus!"

Wigglesworth knew the excitement of great crusade meetings where he saw thousands come to

"POLLY PUT DOWN THE NET. I LANDED THE FISH."

the altar for salvation. But he never lost sight of the value of one soul. To the very last day of his life, he sought to win souls.

Inquiry Room Work

Today, the "inquiry room" is called the "counseling room." The earlier name for the room meant something, however. People were not just there to discuss their problems. They were there to "inquire" how their sins could be forgiven.

In the earlier days of Wigglesworth's soulwinning work, both in the Salvation Army and at the Bowland Street Mission, his wife was the preacher. He worked at the altar or in the inquiry room. He used to say, "Polly put down the net. I landed the fish."

He wanted to make as sure as possible that the inquirers received a real salvation. He believed that strong births make healthy babies.

All Christians can, and should, prepare so that they are able to lead people to Jesus. My own soulwinning ministry began effectively in 1930 when, in a time of revival, souls were being won to Christ in my home church in Birmingham, England. But like many Christians, I began in embarrassment.

My pastor asked me to take charge of the inquiry room work. Ten to twenty people were responding to the gospel in every service, seven nights a week. They needed direction. I had to decline, because even though I had been saved many years, I did not know how to lead anyone to saving faith in Jesus.

This so convicted me that I went home determined to learn how to answer any inquiry about the Lord. I studied the Word and soul-winning books and prayed. After a month, I went back and asked my pastor if the job was still open. Happily for me, it was, and for some years—until I moved into full-time ministry—I had the joyous privilege of dealing with hundreds of souls in crisis.

> ALTHOUGH HE WITNESSED FREELY, HE DID NOT WITNESS INDISCRIMINATELY.

Open Air Preaching

Open air preaching is not so much in style today in our modern civilization, but in Wigglesworth's time, it was a major way of effectively reaching out with the gospel. He used it extensively because he believed in getting out where the sinners were.

He was never a polished preacher. His homiletics were non-existent, but his dynamics were mighty! His deep love for Jesus, his passion for souls, and his earnestness secured an entrance for his message. He won many souls who confessed Christ publicly through this kind of ministry.

His son-in-law wrote after his death, "He grew in grace and zeal for God, and his highest happiness was found in pointing others to the Lord Jesus. He tramped the country roads with that one purpose. To his dying day, he lived for this one thing, rarely coming home—morning, afternoon, or night—but what he had led someone to the Lord or ministered healing to a needy person."

House-to-House Visitation

Before visiting door to door was popular in England, Wigglesworth did it. He did not wait for his church to develop a visitation program. He *was* the program! With burning heart and unflagging zeal, he sought out people in their homes. He had what has been called "20/20 spiritual vision" (Acts 20:20).

Always he prepared for this visitation evangelism with much prayer. Although he witnessed freely, he did not witness indiscriminately, which is a very important point! *He waited on God for direction as well as power.*

An example of this occurred when he stayed at Roker in Sunderland with Pastor Fred Johnson. There was an elevator to the beach, and some men were working on it. At their invitation, he rode down with them and back up. Pastor Johnson remained at the top, but he was sure Wigglesworth would witness to the men.

When he returned, Johnson asked, "Did you give them a word?"

Wigglesworth replied, "No, I wasn't to pray for them. I wasn't to do anything at all. I was one with them in a way. But I left something behind for them—that was the presence of God. It was more real than a tract."

Because he carried this "sweet savor" of Christ and was so compassionate and earnest, Wigglesworth rarely was refused admission to the homes at which he called. He prayed in every home, and in so many, he did vital work for Jesus. Eternity alone will reveal how many were born again at their own firesides or in their own kitchens though the dedicated visitation ministry of God's servant, Smith Wigglesworth.

Evangelistic Preaching

When he joined the Salvation Army as a young man, the young lady who later became his beloved Polly was the lieutenant in charge of the local corps, and in the beginning of their marriage, she did the preaching. After his return from Sunderland, claiming to have received the baptism in the Spirit "as on the Day of Pentecost," Polly insisted that he preach.

Previously, he had not been able to say more than a few words before breaking down weeping, but this time, he preached with fire and a torrent of words. All Polly could do was say, "That's not *my* Smith! That's not *my* Smith! What's happened to the man?" From that day on, he preached without training, but he never preached without fire. God was able to love people through Smith Wigglesworth. With that love pouring through him, and the powerful anointing of God's Spirit resting on him, he made Christ fully known to his hearers.

He preached in Bowland Street Mission, in churches all over the world, in factories, quarries, and in tents. He preached in his homeland and around the world. While most seem to remember him for his ministry of the miraculous, his greatest ministry was in the winning of the lost. Here are some of his comments in New Zealand in the 1922 series of meetings:

"Healing of the body is not the main thing."

"I would sooner have one soul saved than ten thousand healed. I preach and practice healing to attract people just as our Lord did."

"My main aim is to win men for Christ."

Multiplied thousands came to a saving knowledge of Jesus as Lord under his ministry. In Ceylon, sometimes thousands of people at a time cried to God for salvation. In Norway, on one occasion when the Town Hall was full and hundreds were outside unable to get in, the Lord spoke to him as he preached and said, "If you ask Me, I will give you every soul in this place."

For a moment, he hesitated, then asked. He told later with awe how the power of God swept the place, and how people cried out for mercy all over the building. He would add, "I verily believe that God *gave* me every soul."

In South Africa, so great were the evangelistic results of his ministry that the results reached far beyond his meetings. Justus du Plessis, his interpreter there, gave his considered opinion that the whole of the country was affected. It was the same everywhere, even when he traveled on shipboard.

The story of his "concert" on one ship has often been told, but here it is in his own words as told to John Carter, who gave to me just as it was given to him:

When the ship began to move, I said to the people, "I'm going to preach on this ship on Sunday. Will you come and hear me?"

"No," they said. Later they came around and said, "We're going to have an entertainment, and we would like you to be in it."

I said, "Come back in a quarter of an hour."

They came around again and said, "Are you ready?" "Yes," I told them.

"What can you do?"

"I can sing," was my reply. They asked what position I wanted on the program, and I asked what would be on the program.

They said, "Songs, recitations, instrument(als), many things."

"What do you finish up with?" I asked.

"A dance."

Then I said, "Put me down just before the dance."

I went to the entertainment, and when I saw the people, it turned me to prayer. Every hour had been bathed in prayer. When I had heard all their pieces, my turn came. When I showed the pianist the music, she said she couldn't play it.

I said, "Be at peace, young lady, I have the music and words inside." So I sang, "If I could only tell Him as I know Him, my Redeemer Who has brightened all my way."

God took it up, and from the least to the greatest, they were weeping. They never had a dance, but they had a prayer meeting. And six young men were saved by the power of God in my cabin. Every day God was saving people on that ship.

Missions

Wigglesworth was never a missionary in the literal meaning of the word, but he had a passion for overseas missions. You needed only to see him at missionary conventions to realize his enthusiasm for missions. He would lead the missionary giving, pray for the missionary candidates, encourage the missionaries on furlough, and call for volunteers. He freely gave his own daughter, Alice, to the work, first in Angola, then in South America, and later in the Congo.

His delight in the wide sales of his sermon book, *Ever Increasing Faith*, was not only in the spreading of the message God had given him, but also in the fact that the profit went entirely to missions. When he gave a copy to his young friend, Willie Hacking, he said, "Now, Brother Hacking, don't lend this book. It's not for lending. If this book is lent, folks won't buy it, and we want them to buy it. This book has made twenty thousand pounds for missions." (At that time, that amount was about a hundred times a working man's wages for a year!)

His great zeal for missions was displayed when his grandson, Leslie Wigglesworth, sailed for the Congo from Tilbury, Essex, England, in 1934. Leslie was accompanied by Alfred Brown, Jim Fowler, and Fred and Isobel Ramsbottom and their baby, Alan.

Wigglesworth went to the dock to see them off and bid them "Godspeed." As the boat pulled away, he shouted across the widening gap, "Hallelujah!" And the young missionaries responded, "Praise the Lord!" Smith Wigglesworth, with his remarkably clear voice, continued to shout until he could not be seen. The incident conveyed to Leslie a strong sense that the spiritual link with him and a godly grandfather was unbroken. Said one of the others, "It imparted spiritual life to a group of young missionaries."

When on crusades, Wigglesworth would sometimes ask that in place of a love offering for himself, a missionary offering should be taken

THE CHURCH TODAY HAS THE GREATEST EVANGELISTIC OPPORTUNITY IT EVER HAS HAD.

He said on one occasion, "Today many are not laying themselves out for soulwinning but for fleshly manifestations."

Ian MacPherson, a Scottish Pentecostal preacher, put it succinctly, "We are in danger of becoming little groups of Pentecostal specialists feeling each other's pulses."

One day in Jerusalem, Wigglesworth said to a young missionary concerning a backslider, "It's killing me, the thought of anyone turning back." This deep sense of the lostness of people apart from Christ, this sharing of the compassion of the Savior Himself, could only come from "the love of God shed abroad in our hearts by the Holy Ghost which is given unto us" (Rom. 5:5).

As an ambassador for Christ, Wigglesworth continually besought men, "Be ye reconciled to God" (2 Cor. 5:20). The Church today has the greatest evangelistic opportunity it ever has had. More souls are being won, and there are more souls to win than ever before in history. Let us arise to the task, inspired afresh by what God did through Smith Wigglesworth!

Chapter 15

WIGGLESWORTH'S HEALING MINISTRY

Wigglesworth experienced the healing power of God in his own body. Early in his ministry, he suffered greatly from hemorrhoids and used natural means for relief. His wife challenged him on preaching one thing and practicing another, and he realized he was acting inconsistently with his professed belief. He repented, looked to God, and was healed. From that day, he was committed to God as his only Healer.

He had many physical trials, the greatest of which no doubt was his battle with kidney stones. He suffered much pain until, finally, at his family's urging, he went to a doctor who diagnosed his condition and said surgery was essential.

Wigglesworth thanked him and said he would trust God to do the surgery. What a test that was! He believed God would break the stones, and He did. But cleansing his system of all the broken pieces was a long and agonizing process. All of the time, he continued preaching, sometimes getting up from bed to preach and minister, then returning straight to bed.

In one service, he said, "I do not understand the ways of God! Here He is healing under my ministry, and yet, as I am preaching to you, I am suffering excruciating pains from kidney stones coming down from my body."

He never cared about "preserving his image" and was not ashamed to confess that he was suffering. There were for him mysteries about God's dealings in sickness. More than once he declared, "Whoso can explain divine healing can explain God."

But he persisted in faith, and the final day of deliverance came. For years afterward, he carried with him a small bottle containing the broken stones God had removed.

The last time I saw him was at Bloomsbury Chapel, London, where he had been speaking. He was over eighty-six and had been so ill that his loved ones thought he had died. Yet here he was ministering again in power.

In a later letter, written to me in his own hand, he describe the heart of his experience. These are his exact words and spelling:

God is fulfilling His Word, Romans 8 ch verces 11 & 12, 13 the same Spirit that rose up Jesus from the grave quickened His mortal body as also quickened my mortal body.

Not good grammar, but good Holy Spirit reality!

His Ministry to Others

Here is an instance of healing given in Wigglesworth's own words:

In Sydney, Australia, a man with a stick passed a friend and me. He had to get down and twist over, and the tortures on his face made a deep impression on my soul.

I asked myself, "Is it right to pass this man?" So I said to my friend, "There is a man in awful distress, and I cannot go further I must speak to him."

I went over to that man and said, "You seem in great trouble."

"Yes," he said, "I am no good, and never will be."

I said, "You see that hotel. Be in front of that door in five minutes and I will pray for you and you shall be as straight as any man in this place."

I came back after paying a bill, and he was there. I will never forget him wondering if he was going to be trapped, or what was up that a man should stop him in the street and tell him he was going to be straight. But I had said it, so it must be! If you say anything, you must turn with God to make it so. Never say anything for bravado, without you have the right to say it. Always be sure of your ground and that you are honoring God. Your whole ministry will have to be on the line of grace and blessing.

We helped him up the two steps and through the lobby to the elevator and took him up to my floor. It was difficult to get him from the elevator to my room as though Satan was making a last strike for his life. But we got him there. Then in five minutes, this man walked out of that room as straight as any man in this place. Oh, brother, it is ministration, it is operation, it is manifestation. Those are the three leading principles of the baptism with the Holy Ghost, and we must see to it that God is producing these three through us.

GOD DIDN'T SEND ME HERE FOR NOTHING.

Here is another example from Wigglesworth:

In a place in England, I was dealing on the lines of faith and what would take place if we believed God. Many things happened. One man, who worked in a colliery, heard me. He was in trouble with a stiff knee.

He said to his wife, "I cannot help but think every day that that message of Wigglesworth's was to stir us to do something. I cannot get away from it. All the men in the pit know that I walk with a stiff knee and how you wrap it round with yards of flannel. Well, I'm going to act. You have to be the congregation."

He got his wife in front of him, saying, "I'm going to act and do just like Wigglesworth." He got hold of his leg unmercifully, saying, "Come out, you devils, come out!" Then he cried out, "Wife, they're gone! This is too good to keep to myself. I'm going to act now!"

He went to his place of worship, and many miners were there. It was a prayer meeting, and he told them what had happened. They were delighted. Then one said, "Jack, come over here and help me." And Jack went. As soon as he was through in one home, he was invited to another, loosing people from their many pains.

If you do it outside of Jesus, you do it for yourself; if you do it because you want to be someone, it will be a failure. We shall only be able to do well, if we do it in the name of Jesus. Live in the Spirit, walk in the Spirit, walk in communion with the Spirit, talk with God. All the leadings of the first order are for you.

When he was in the plumbing business, Wigglesworth received urgent calls for prayer and sometimes could not wait to wash before he went to pray. He said, "With my hands all black, I would preach to those sick ones with my heart aglow with love. You have to get right to the bottom of cancer with a divine compassion, and then you will see the gifts of the Spirit in operation."

He was called at 10 p.m. once to pray for a young woman dying of consumption. The doctor gave no hope at all. When Wigglesworth arrived, he saw how things were and told the mother, as well as the rest of the family, to go to bed.

When they refused, he put on his overcoat and said, "Goodbye, I'm off." Then they changed their minds and went to bed. He knew God would move nothing in an atmosphere of unbelief and natural sympathy. He stayed.

He later said, "That was a time I surely came face to face with death and the devil." What a fight he had, praying from 11 p.m. to 3:30 a.m. He saw her pass away.

He said, "The devil told me, 'Now you are done for. The girl has died on your hands.'"

> HE MINISTERED HEALING BECAUSE HE BELIEVED HEALING WAS GOD'S PURPOSE.

He replied, "It can't be. God didn't send me here for nothing."

Wigglesworth knew it was time, as he put it, "to change strength." He knew that the God who could divide the Red Sea was just the same.

The devil said, "No" but Wigglesworth said, "Yes." Here is what he said happened:

I looked at the window, and at that moment, the face of Jesus appeared. It seemed as if a million rays of light were coming from His face. He looked at the young woman who had just passed away. As He did so, the color came back into her face. She rolled over and fell asleep. Then I had a glorious time!

In the morning, the young lady woke early, put on her robe, and walked to the piano. She started to play and sing a wonderful song. Her mother and family came down to listen. The Lord had undertaken, and a miracle had occurred.

His Motivation

He ministered healing because he believed healing was God's purpose. The Word of Jesus was to Wigglesworth the final authority.

He told me personally that he often was asked for a good tract on divine healing, but would always say, "What's wrong with Matthew, Mark, Luke, and John? They are the best tracts on divine healing. They are full of cases that show the marvelous power of Jesus. They will never fail to bring God's work to pass if only people will believe them."

Another important motivator for him was compassion, as I have talked about earlier in this book. I have written of how he would weep as he saw or heard of, the desperate conditions of many of those who asked him for prayer. Sometimes his compassionate sobs were so deep that an entire congregation would weep with him.

Repeatedly in the Gospels, we are told of Jesus' compassion. Because Wigglesworth was filled with the Spirit of Christ, he, too, ministered that same Spirit. Compassion is born of love, and faith works by love (Gal. 5:6).

A third motivation was his passionate desire to glorify God. He was always careful to attribute every miracle of salvation, healing, or deliverance to the grace and power of God. He did not care who got the credit as long as God got the glory.

His Methods

First, Wigglesworth anointed with oil on the basis of Mark 6:13 and James 5:14. He had a vivid realization that the oil symbolized the Holy Spirit. As he obeyed the promise and used the symbol, he expect to see God work in healing power through the Holy Spirit.

His introduction to this method was perhaps typical. Someone pointed out to him that Scripture commands us to anoint with oil when praying for the sick. Instantly, he decided to obey God's Word. He had no idea how much oil to use, so when he was next called to pray for someone—a dying woman—he poured a whole bottle of olive oil over her. Wonderful to relate, there was granted immediately a vision of Jesus. The woman was healed.

> WIGGLESWORTH NEITHER PRAYED FOR HIM NOR LAID HANDS ON HIM BUT SIMPLY SAID, "GO HOME, YOU'RE HEALED."

So committed was he to anointing that he used his practical skill to develop a leak-proof bottle so that he and other preachers could have oil always on hand. In those days, we did not feel properly dressed for our job if we did not have our "Wigglesworth oil bottle" with us!

At other times, he would simply lay hands on the sick as commanded in Mark 16:18. Sometimes his laying on of hands was over-vigorous, but God honored the man's heart sincerity and faith, not the method.

He also used handkerchiefs as points of contact, having in mind Acts 19:12. Almost every mail brought handkerchiefs with requests for prayer. He always responded in faith. Following is a letter he received from Calgary, Alberta, Canada:

Dear Brother Wigglesworth:

I praise and thank the Lord Jesus Christ. It was in March 1932 that I received the handkerchief I had sent to you to anoint with oil and pray for me. I had many forms of rheumatism, arthritis, synovitis, and sciatica for twenty years from 1912-1932. I was in constant misery. During that time, I took fifty thousand aspirins besides everything the doctors could give me. Only the Lord could have kept my stomach from the effects of what I swallowed.

When I got the handkerchief from you, all my pains left that same afternoon, and all the swelling in my arms and legs was gone three days later. From that day to this, I have had no rheumatism and have not been crippled in any way. I have not taken a single aspirin!

At the Preston Convention, one year they received a handkerchief from America for a mentally retarded boy. He was about thirteen with the mental age of four or five. This was the first year Wigglesworth had not been at the convention. He had been called home to the presence of God. So a group of us stood around and prayed, asking God to send His healing power as this handkerchief was laid on the boy as a token of His power.

I did not hear anything for several years, but about five years later, a lady came up to me when I was preaching in Preston and said, "Do you remember when we prayed over handkerchief for the American retarded boy?"

I said, "Yes, I do," and she continued, "I've just had a letter from my friend in America. The boy has just graduated from high school at 18 years of age, having been successful in all examinations." His healing had nothing to do with us. It was God Who did it, and He can use one method as well as another.

For example, often Wigglesworth ministered healing without specific prayer, just as Jesus and the disciples sometimes did (Matt. 10:8; Acts 3:6). A man from my first pastorate in Coulsdon, Surrey, England, went to hear Wigglesworth when he was preaching nearby. The man was suffering from diabetes and went out for prayer at the end of the afternoon meeting.

Wigglesworth neither prayed for him nor laid hands on him but simply said, "Go home, you're healed."

The man stayed on for the evening service, and as he had felt nothing when the evangelist spoke to him in the afternoon, he went forward again when the sick were called.

Wigglesworth looked at him severely and said, "I told you to go home. You are healed." The young man did go home, and he was healed.

A lady in New York went to Wigglesworth suffering from an ingrown toenail, and he simply said, "In the name of Jesus, stamp your foot!" It took courage because of the pain she felt, but she did it, and the toe was healed.

Another lady, from Raleigh, Essex, England, went for prayer for an ulcerated leg. Wigglesworth said, "Be healed!" Then he said, "Now, run!" She burst out laughing, because she had known his methods and had made up her mind not to do anything spectacular.

He repeated, "I said run, woman, run!"

Laughing all the way, she ran and was instantly healed. I was there at the time and enjoyed the whole scene.

Chapter 16

"WHOLESALE" AND "RETAIL" HEALINGS

During Wigglesworth's first series of meetings in Sweden in 1920, he was permitted to hold a service on the strict condition that he not lay hands on the sick. The authorities thought that would create crowd scenes they did not have enough police available to handle.

When he saw the needs of the people present in the open-air meeting, he was deeply moved and sought God's direction on what to do, since he was not allowed to lay hands on them. The Lord made clear to him that he was to get all the sick people to stand to their feet where they were.

Wigglesworth then said, "I'm not going to touch any of you." At the Lord's direction, he turned his attention to a lady standing on a rock and told her to place her hands on her body where the sickness was. She did, and he prayed. She cried out, "I'm healed." He then had all the others lay hands on themselves, and he prayed for their healings.

GOD SHOWED WIGGLESWORTH THAT IT WAS HIS POWER AND NOT ANY PARTICULAR METHOD THAT BROUGHT HEALING.

God showed Wigglesworth that it was His power and not any particular method that brought healing. He playfully called this "wholesale healing." Praying individually for people was "retail healing." If the crowds seeking healing were very large, he would use "wholesale healing" after that. But if it was possible, he would use "retail healing".

Add Patience to Faith

One day, while I was preaching at Preston and Wigglesworth was my chairman, I really got the people's attention by starting my message out this way: "Brother Wigglesworth is wrong, you know. He says, 'Only believe;' but that's not all." By this time, I had Wigglesworth's attention as well as theirs!

I continued, "In Hebrews 6:12, it says we are to be followers of them who through faith *and* patience inherit the promises. We need to add patience to faith."

Wigglesworth relaxed and called out, "You're right, brother, you're right. Preach it!"

A young lady living at Southsea, on the English south coast, was paralyzed from the waist down. A devoted Christian, she came across James 5:14-16 about the elders of the church anointing the sick with oil. When her pastor visited her, she showed it to him and asked him to anoint her with oil and pray for her but he did not believe that promise was for today and declined.

Later, the assistant pastor visited her, and she asked him. Without hesitation, he agreed. Her mother found a bottle of oil, and the young minister anointed the girl and prayed for her.

Nothing happened, but the girl told everyone who visited her, "Look what I have found in the Bible, and I've had this done to me."

There was no immediate change. Weeks passed into months, and after six months, she suddenly experienced great pain. Her legs crossed, and she was in worse condition than before. However, she said often through her tears, "Look what I've found in the Bible, and I've had this done to me."

Another three months went by. One night, in extreme pain, she asked her mother not to touch her to prepare her for sleep. Her mother left the room weeping. The girl lay quietly praying. Suddenly the room was alight with the presence of Jesus, and she heard His voice, "Arise in this thy strength."

Her legs instantly uncrossed. Miraculously, her muscles were strengthened. She rose from bed, went to the door of her room, and called, "Mummy, Mummy, come and see what Jesus has done for me." Her mother fainted!

That young lady later became a member of the church of Pastor F. R. Barnes, for many years a member of the executive council of the Assemblies of God of Great Britain and Ireland. He himself recounted this incident to me, assuring me of its authenticity. Through faith and patience, that young lady inherited the promise.

Whatever the situation, Wigglesworth focused on Christ. He had unquestionable confidence in Him. He saw sickness and oppression as the works of the devil (1 John 3:8), and in Christ's name, moved against Satan with holy violence. He even faced and overcame death in some instances.

However, there were other instances when he had no freedom to pray for certain people. One of the deacons of our church brought a sick neighbor for prayer. God's servant just took one look at him and said, "You ought to be in your coffin." He challenged the man to be ready, and a timely challenge it was—within two weeks the man was dead.

Usually it was not so dramatic as that. On one occasion he was asked to pray for a wealthy lady. He discerned pride and materialism in her and said, "You're not ready for me yet." She was angry at first, but later broke down before the Lord. Wigglesworth prayed for her, and she was healed.

One day, I introduced Wigglesworth to a young minister. After the man left us, Wigglesworth asked me, "What's wrong with that man?"

I told him the man's wife had died six months earlier, and he began to weep, saying no man who has not been through such a loss can begin to understand what it means. He then told that when his wife died, he had called her back from the dead but God spoke to him: "Leave her, Smith, she is mine." He said it was the greatest and costliest test of obedience.

To John Carter, Smith Wigglesworth said, "We need to wake up and be on stretch to believe God. Before God could bring me to this place, He has broken me a thousand times. I have wept. I have travailed many a night till God broke me. It seems that until God has mowed you down, you never can have this longsuffering for others."

The Final Call

Wigglesworth's homecall was as unusual as his life. In 1947 at almost eighty-eight years of age, he was attending the funeral of his dear friend, Pastor Wilfred Richardson, and entered Glad Tidings Hall in Wakefield, Yorkshire, praising the Lord.

He was taken to the vestry, the small room used for the ministers, where he greeted several colleagues and inquired after the health of the daughter of one of them. The news was not good. Wigglesworth sighed, stumbled, and his spirit departed.

His grandson, Leslie, said, "He sighed, and he died."

His earthly life was over. But, now, more than forty years later, his ministry is touching more lives than ever. If it has been true of any human being, it is true of Wigglesworth: "He being dead yet speaketh" (Heb. 11:4).

GLIMPSES OF THE FUTURE

When in New Zealand in 1922, a young preacher remarked to Wigglesworth, "One is tempted to envy you for the great success you have had."

He replied, "Young man, it is the other way around. I feel like envying you. I have had three visions—three only. The first two already have come to pass, but the third is yet to be fulfilled. I will most likely pass on to my reward, but you are a young man, and you most likely will be in what I saw."

He paused, then burst out, "Oh, it was amazing! Amazing!"

"What was amazing?" the young man asked.

"Oh," said Wigglesworth, "I cannot tell God's secrets, but you will remember what I saw—this

> "I CANNOT TELL GOD'S SECRETS, BUT YOU WILL REMEMBER WHAT I SAW—THIS REVIVAL WE HAVE HAD (THE PENTECOSTAL REVIVAL) IS NOTHING TO WHAT GOD IS YET GOING TO DO."

revival we have had (the Pentecostal revival) is nothing to what God is yet going to do."

In recounting this, the young preacher went on to say, "This was clearly prophetic and spoken with much power. It was evident that the evangelist had a special vision granted to him of the coming outpouring of the Spirit in an unprecedented effusion in the days just before our Lord comes to snatch away the Church."[8]

The story often has been told of Wigglesworth's prophecy over the late David du Plessis. He was conducting a crusade in David's church in South Africa. Early one morning, he walked into David's office and, without greeting, declared to him that in the last days before Jesus returned, there would be a move of the Holy Spirit, surpassing all previous moves. It would overrun all boundaries, national and denominational. David du Plessis, he declared would be a principal instrument in God's hand to bring this to pass.

In 1942, Wigglesworth talked to me about this prophecy, saying that he would not live to see this glorious revival. He died in 1947, the year that David du Plessis arrived from South Africa at the World Pentecostal Conference in Zurich, Switzerland. From that point, his ministry and influence spread.

Du Plessis carried the full message of Pentecost into areas no one thought it would ever go and prepared the way for the Charismatic Renewal, which developed in an astonishing way during the 1960s and 1970s. He became known as "Mr. Pentecost," and met with heads of otherwise liberal denominations and with the Pope in Rome.

A week before his death, Wigglesworth prophesied again during a week-long crusade. This time, he foretold a second move of the Spirit. The first move would bring the restoration of the gifts of the Spirit; the second would bring a revival of emphasis on the Word of God.

He said, "When these two moves of the Spirit combine, we shall see the greatest move the Church of Jesus Christ has ever seen."

Already there are signs that this is beginning to develop.

TRIBUTE TO SMITH WIGGLESWORTH

HE WAS NOT ... GOD TOOK HIM THE HOME CALL OF SMITH WIGGLESWORTH

by James Salter

*The following tribute was written immediately after the death of Smith Wigglesworth by his son-in-law, James Salter. Wigglesworth called his daughter and her husband, "our Alice" and "my son, Salter." He lived with them, and they were intimately acquainted with his lift and ministry for very many years. This tribute first was published on March 28, 1947, two weeks after the homecall of Brother Wigglesworth, in **Redemption Tidings,** official magazine of the Assemblies of God of*

Great Britain and Ireland and is used by kind permission of the editor.

On March 12, in the vestry of Glad Tidings Hall, Wakefield, Mr. Smith Wigglesworth discarded his earthly house of this tabernacle. He had gone there to attend the funeral service of Mr. Wilfred Richardson, a lifelong friend, and while waiting for the meeting to commence, he suddenly collapsed and without any pain or recovering consciousness, he went to be with Christ, dying the death of the righteous.

He would have attained his 88th birthday on June 10th and had had a saving knowledge of the Lord Jesus for nearly eighty years. Although so young at the time, his spiritual awakening must have been very impressive for, as he so often told us, he knelt to kiss the daisies growing in the field and sang with the birds in the lanes of his native village.

Beginning to work in a mill about that time, his childish trust sustained him in his daylight-to-dark employment. He used to take pride in pointing to the mill where he worked and telling us how he was often very tired and how to his boyish question, "How much longer?" his father would reply, "Night always comes to those who work, my lad!"

He grew in grace and zeal for God, and his highest happiness was found in pointing others to the Lord Jesus, and he tramped the country roads with that one purpose.

"Have you been talking to a man about his soul?" his mother asked him one day.

"Mother, you know I am always doing that," he replied. "But why do you ask?"

"Because," she answered, "Mr. So-and-So has had an accident and is dying, and he wishes me to tell you he decided for Christ the last time you spoke to him."

To his dying day, he lived for this one thing, rarely coming home morning, afternoon, or night but what he had led someone to the Lord or ministered healing to a needy person.

HE WAS THE MODERN "APOSTLE OF FAITH," BUT HIS FAITH WAS NOT THE DORMANT KIND.

When he commenced his healing ministry, he was officially and publicly derided by many of his old friends, but as the years went by, he was able to heap coals of fire on their heads by ministering to their needy bodies. Many who had scorned and scoffed publicly, later sought him privately and at nighttime for the blessing of the effectual and fervent prayers of the righteous man.

Lacking the advantage of a normal early education, he never read books. This shut him off from many things and left him not conversant with general topics. After the death of his wife thirty-four years before, he was naturally a lonely man. These things drove him to God and His Word, and he never considered himself fully dressed unless he had a copy of the Scriptures in his pocket. In that way, he came to know God to a degree attained by very few folks.

He was intimate with God before 1914, but in that year, God sent him to America for the first time, as he used to say, "to teach me geography." Having recently lost his wife, the one who had done much to make him thus far, he went abroad in an abandonment to God that found a continent-wide fruition in all the United States and Mexico. From that time, his gifts made room for him, and continents and countries opened wide to the plumber-preacher.

New Zealand was swept, Colombo in Ceylon shaken, Sweden roused, Switzerland stormed, Norway inflamed, and California stirred to its depth, as God confirmed His Word through this "mantled man." The permanence of these works is visible to this day in that souls were saved, bodies were healed, lives changed and delivered, and assemblies of believers were established.

Every mail brings testimonies from those who have read his book, *Ever-Increasing Faith*, telling of blessings to soul and body received through its ministry. Every kind of disease has succumbed to the healing power of God, as readers have found and exercised faith in the Living God, and in every country, its simple and sufficient message "only believe" has linked tens of thousands of people to the living, saving, healing, victorious Lord Jesus.

"IT BEHOOVES US ALL TO TAKE UP THE TORCH WHICH HE HAS LAID ASIDE AND BURN AND BLAZE FOR GOD."

His preaching was purely inspirational, and at times his words and their meanings were not easy to follow, but that "indefinable something which makes all the difference" rarely was lacking from his ministry, and under it, his hearers took spiritual strides and made godly progress.

He was the modern "apostle of faith," but his faith was not the dormant kind. One of his slogans was "Faith is an act," and said he, "the acts of the apostles is called the Acts of the Apostles because the apostles acted."

He probably was much misunderstood in his ministry to the sick, and he suffered considerably because of personal remarks, and so forth, although he triumphed in his spirit over such things. As one who shared his work over many years and in many countries, I am convinced he enjoyed a holy insight at such times, and he saw and heard things unspeakable, as frequently "two pierced hands" shared with him the "laying on of hands" in the destroying of the works of the devil.

His creed was not a big one, but it was the "most surely believed" type. He was valiant for the truth and absolutely uncompromising even in the matter of details. The Fellowship of Pentecostal folk owes much to him for his unswerving adherence to the peculiar aspect of their testimony.

His body, waiting interment, lies a few feet from me as I write, and piled high in front of me are letters, telegrams, and cables. "$300 ready to bring you by plane to...," reads one. Another, arriving only a few hours after he died, reads: "Planes are very comfortable these days. We want you in New York for our fortieth anniversary meetings in May. Be sure to come."

Some others received since his death say of him:

"A beautiful and lovely character; one of God's sweet men."

"That humble, yet great, master of victorious faith."

"A great loss to the whole church which owes much to his inspiring ministry and steadfast example in the things which we stand for."

"He has winged his way to be with Christ in a sudden and triumphant translation."

"May his mantle of faith, zeal, and power fall upon the generations following to glorify their fathers' God."

"Triumphant faith; whose faith follow."

"It behooves us all to take up the torch which he has laid aside and burn and blaze for God."

"Smith Wigglesworth walked with God, and he was not, for God took him."

In concluding, is it too much to hope that what he has sown during the past sixty years may bear an abundant harvest and result in a world-changing revival of soul-saving, Spirit-filling, body-healing, and delivering which will usher in the return of the Lord Jesus and the rapture of His waiting people?

NEW ZEALAND SERMONS

(The following messages were preached by Smith Wigglesworth in Wellington, New Zealand, in May 1922. They were transcribed by the Rev. Harry V. Roberts and are published by the kind permission of his grandson, the Rev. Ian Bilby, president of the Elim Church of New Zealand.}

Sanctification of the Spirit

I want to read to you a few verses from First Peter 1. I believe that God wants to speak to us to strengthen our position in faith and grace.

Beloved, I want you to understand that you will get more than you came for. There is not a person who hears me who will get what he came for. God gives you more. No man gets his answers to his prayers. He never does, for God answer his prayers abundantly above what he asks or thinks.

Don't say, "I got nothing." You'll get as much as you came for and more. But if your minds are not willing to be yielded and your heart not sufficiently consecrated, you will find that you're limited on that line, because the heart is the place reception. God wants you to have receptive hearts to take in the mind of God. These wonderful Scriptures are full of life-giving power. Let us read the first and second verses. There are some words there I ought to lay emphasis on.

Peter, an apostle of Jesus Christ, to the strangers scattered throughout Pontus, Galatia, Cappadocia, Asia and Bithynia,

Elect according to the foreknowledge of God the Father, through sanctification of the Spirit, unto obedience and sprinkling of the blood of Jesus Christ: Grace to you, and peace be multiplied.

1 Peter 1:1–2

I want you to notice that in all times, in all histories of the world, whenever there has been a divine rising or revelation of God coming forth with new dispensational orders of the Spirit— you will find that there have been persecutions. You take the case of the three Hebrew young men, or Daniel, or Jeremiah. With any person in the old dispensation as much as in the new, when the Spirit of the Lord has been moving mightily, there has arisen trouble and difficulty. What for? Because of three things very much against revelations of God and the Spirit of God.

First, humanity—flesh—natural things are against divine things. Evil powers work upon this position of the human life, and especially when the will is unyielded to God, then the powers of darkness arise up against the powers of divine order, but they never defeat them. Divine order is very often in a minority, yet always in majority. Did I say that right? Yes, and I meant it also. You have no need to fear, truth stands eternal. Wickedness may increase and abound, but when the Lord raises His flag over the saint, it is victory; though it is in minority it always triumphs.

I want you to notice the first verse because it says *scattered*, meaning to say they did not get much of the liberty of meeting together. They were driven from place to place. Even in the days of John Knox, the people who served God had to be in close quarters because they were persecuted, hauled before judges, and destroyed in all sorts of ways. They were in minority but swept through in victory. So may God bring us into perfect order that we may understand these days that we may be in Wellington in minority, yet in majority.

The Holy Ghost wants us to understand our privileges, elect, according to the foreknowledge of God through sanctification of the Spirit. Now this word "sanctification of the Spirit" is not on the lines of sin cleansing. It is a higher order than redemption work. The blood of Jesus is rich unto all, powerful and cleansing. It takes away other powers and transforms us by the power of God. But when sin is gone, yes, when we are clean and know we have the Word of God right in us and the power of the Spirit is bringing us to a place where we triumph, then comes revelation by the power of the Spirit lifting us to higher ground, into the fullness of God, unveiling Christ in such a way. It is called sanctification of the Spirit.

Sanctification of the Spirit, elect, according to the foreknowledge of God. I don't want you to stumble at the word *elect*, it is a blessed word. You might say you are all elect; everyone in this place could say you are elected. God has designed that all men should be saved—this is election. Whether you accept and come into your election, whether you prove yourself worthy of your election, whether you have done this, I don't know. But this is your election, your sanctification, to be seated at the right hand of God.

The word *election* is a very precious word. To be foreordained, predestinated—these are words that God has designed before the world was to bring us into triumph and victory in Christ.

Some people play around and make it a goal. They say, "Oh, well, you see, we are elected. We are all right." They say they are elected to be saved, and I believe these people are very diplomatic (because) they believe others can be elected to be damned. It is not true! Everybody is elected to be saved but whether they come into it or not is another thing.

Many don't come into salvation because the god of this world has blinded their eyes lest the light of the glorious Gospel should shine unto them. What does it mean? It means this, that Satan has got mastery over their minds, and they have an ear to listen to corruptible things.

Beloved, I want you to see this election I am speaking about, to catch a glimpse of heaven with our heart always on the wing, where you grasp everything spiritual, when everything divine makes you hungry, everything seasonable in spiritual fidelity will make you long after it.

If I came here in a year's time I should see this kind of election going right forward, always full, never having a bad report, where you see Christ, and every day growing in the knowledge of God.

It is through sanctification of the Spirit, unto obedience and sprinkling of the blood of Jesus Christ. There is no sanctification, if it is not sanctification unto obedience. There would be no trouble with any of us if we would come definitely to a place where we understood the Word that Jesus said: "For their sakes I sanctify myself, that they also might be sanctified through the truth" (John 17:19).

No child of God ever questions the Word of God. What do I mean? The Word of God is clear on the breaking of bread, the Word of God is clear on water baptism, and things like that. No person who is going on to the obedience and sanctification of the

Spirit by election will pray over that Word. The Word is to be swallowed, not prayed over!

If you ever pray over the Word of God, there is some disobedience; *there is some disobedience*; you are not willing to obey. If you come into obedience on the Word of God, and it says anything about water baptism, you will obey; if it says anything about speaking in tongues, you will obey; if it says anything about the breaking of bread and assembling of yourselves together, you will obey. If you come into the election of the sanctification of the Spirit, you will be obedient in everything concerning that Word. In the measure you are not obedient, you have not come into the sanctification of the Spirit.

A little thing spoils many good things. You hear people say, "He's very good, but…," "Mrs. X is excellent, but…." There are no "buts" in the sanctification of the Spirit. *But* and *if* are gone, and it is "I shall," "I will," all the way through.

Beloved, don't have any "buts," for if you do there is something not yielded to the Spirit. I do pray God the Holy Ghost that we may be willing to yield ourselves to the sanctification of the Spirit, that we may be in the mind of God in the election, that we may have the mind of God in the possession of it.

Perhaps to encourage you people, it would be helpful to prove to you what election is. I am speaking to believers. If you had to search your heart (as to) why you have been attending these meetings, you would not say "because of Wigglesworth." It would be a mistake. But if you felt in you a holy calling, or strange inward longing for more of God, you could say it was sanctification of the Spirit that was drawing you. Only He who elected you could do that!

There are people of all ages here in this place, and if I were to say to you, "Stand up all who never remembered the time when the Spirit did not strive with you," it would be marvellous how many would stand. What do you call it? It is God moving upon you, bringing you in.

When I think of my own case, on my mother's side and on my father's side there was no desire for God. Yet in my earliest infancy I was strangely moved upon by the Spirit. At eight years, I was definitely saved. At nine years, the Spirit came upon me (and it was) just the same when I spoke with tongues—elect according to the foreknowledge of God. There are people in this place who have the same experience.

It is a most blessed thought that we have a God of love, compassion, and grace Who wills not the death of one sinner. God makes it possible for all men to be saved. He gave Jesus, His well-beloved Son, to die for the sins of the people. It is true He took our sins. It is true He paid the price for the whole world. It is true He gave Himself a ransom for many. It is true, beloved! For whom? For "whosoever will."

What about the others? It would have to be a direct refusal of the blood of Jesus, a refusal to have Christ reign over them. Whosoever will, and whosoever won't! And there are people that won't. I say again, the god of this world has blinded their minds lest the light of the Gospel shine unto them.

Through sanctification of the Spirit, you will find out that you get to a place where you are not disturbed. There is a peace in sanctification of the Spirit, because it has a place of revelation, taking you into heavenly places. It has a place where God speaks and makes Himself known to you. When you are face to face with God, you get a peace which passes all understanding, lifting you from state to state of inexpressible wonderment. It is really wonderful!

> *O, this is like heaven to me,*
> *Yes, this is like heaven to me;*
> *I've crossed over Jordan to Canaan's fair land,*
> *And this is like heaven to me.*

Now look at verse three:

> Blessed be the God and Father of our Lord Jesus Christ, which according to his abundant mercy hath begotten us again unto a lively hope by the resurrection of Jesus Christ from the dead.
>
> 1 Peter 1:3

Lively hope! We cannot pass that, because this sanctification of the Spirit brought us into this definite line with this wonderful position of the glory of God. I want to keep before us the glory of it, the joy of it, a "lively hope." Now a lively hope is exactly opposite to dead!

Lively hope is movement.

Lively hope is looking into.

Lively hope is pressing into.

Lively hope is leaving everything behind you.

Lively hope is keeping the vision.

Lively hope sees Him coming!

Lively hope, you live in it! You are not trying to make yourself feel that you are believing. The lively hope is ready, waiting, filled with the joy of expectation of the King. Praise the Lord!

I want you to know that God has this in mind for you. If you possess it, you will love others towards God. They will see the real joy of expectation that will come forth with manifestation, then realization. Pray God, the Holy Ghost, that He will move you that way.

Come now, beloved, I want to raise your hopes into such activity, into such joyful experience, that when you go away from this meeting you will have such joy that you will only walk if you cannot run!

Now I trust that you will be so reconciled to God that there is not one thing that would interfere with you having this lively hope. If you have any love for the world, you cannot have it, because Jesus is not coming for the world. He is coming to the heavenlies, and all the heavenlies are going to Him. There is nothing but joy there! The pride of life is contrary to the lively hope, because of the greatness of the multi-magnitudinous glories of eternity, which are placed before Him with exceeding joy.

[Interpretation of Tongues: "The joy of the Lord is everything. The soul lifteth up like the golden grain ready to be ingathered for the great sheaf. All are ready, waiting, rejoicing, longing for Him, till they cry, 'Lord Jesus, we cannot wait longer.'"]

What a wonderful expression of the Holy Ghost to the soul is in interpretation! How He loves us, hovers over us, rejoices in us. Our cup is full and running over. The joy of the Lord is your strength. You have a right to be in these glorious places. It is the purpose of God for your soul.

> To an inheritance incorruptible, and undefiled, and that fadeth not away, reserved in heaven for you.
>
> 1 Peter 1:4

First, incorruptible. Second, undefiled. Third, fadeth not away. Fourth, reserved in heaven for you. Glory to God! I tell you it is great, very great. May the Lord help you to thirst after this glorious life of Jesus. Oh, brother, it is more than new wine. The Holy Ghost is the manifestation of the glories of the new creation. *An inheritance incorruptible.*

Incorruptible is one of those delightful words God wants all the saints to grasp—everything corruptible, everything seen, fades away. Incorruptible is that which is eternal, everlasting, divine, and therefore spiritual. It brings us to a place where God is really in the midst. This is one part of our inheritance in the Spirit, one part only. Oh, how beautiful, perfected for ever! No spot, no wrinkle, holy, absolutely pure, all traces of sin withered.

Beloved, God means it for us this morning. Every soul in this place must reach out to this ideal. God has ten thousand more thoughts for you than you have for yourself. The grace of God is going to move us on to an inheritance incorruptible, that fadeth not away.

Fadeth not away! What a heaven of bliss, what a joy of delight, what a foretaste of heaven on earth. Cheerfully go to the work you have to do, because of tomorrow (when you) will be in the presence of the King, with the Lord forever, an inheritance that fadeth not away.

Perfect Rest

I would like you to read Second Corinthians 10:4–5:

> For the weapons of our warfare are not carnal, but mighty through God to the pulling down of strong holds;
>
> Casting down imaginations, and every high thing that exalteth itself against the knowledge of God, and bringing into captivity every thought to the obedience of Christ.

Now the Holy Ghost will take the Word, making it powerful in you till every evil thing that presents itself against the obedience and fullness of Christ would absolutely wither away. I want to show you this morning the need of the baptism of the Holy Ghost, by which you know there is perfect rest when you are filled with the Holy Ghost. I want you to see perfect rest in this place.

I want you to see Jesus. He was filled with the Holy Ghost. The storm began so terribly. The ship filled with water. He lay asleep. Perfect rest. When the disciples cried, "Master, we perish," Jesus rose, filled with the Holy Ghost, and rebuked the wind and spoke His peace.

Come a little nearer. I want you to see that this Holy Ghost, this divine Person, has to get so deep into us that He has to destroy every evil thing. Quick, powerful, sharper than any two-edged sword, piercing even to the dividing asunder of soul and spirit, and of the joints and marrow (Heb. 4:12).

Some people get pain in their life after being saved because of soulishness. Any amount of saved people are soulish. They're in Romans 7. They want to do good but find evil. They continue to do the thing they hate to do. What is up?

They need the baptism of the Holy Ghost, for then the Holy Ghost will so reveal the Word that it will be like a sword. It will cut between the soul and the spirit, till a man can no more long for indulgence in things contrary to the mind of God and the will of God. Don't you want rest? How long are you going to be before you enter into that rest? God wants you to enter that rest.

> For he that is entered into his rest, he also hath ceased from his own works, as God did from his.
>
> Let us labour therefore to enter into that rest, lest any man fall after the same example of unbelief.
>
> Hebrews 4:10–11

Enter into rest, get filled with the Holy Ghost, and unbelief will depart. When they entered in they were safe from unbelief, and unbelief is sin. It is the greatest sin because it hinders you from all blessings.

There is another word that would be helpful this morning, and I want you to take notice of it because it is important. It is verse 12 of Hebrews 4:

> For the word of God is quick, and powerful, and sharper than any two-edged sword, piercing even to the dividing asunder of soul and spirit, and of the joints and marrow, and is a discerner of the thoughts and intents of the heart.

How we need the Holy Ghost! Now probably when You go outside you will say, "He preached more about the Holy Ghost than anything." It is not so. My heart is so full of this truth that Jesus is the Word. It takes the Holy Ghost to make the Word active. Jesus is the Word that is mighty by the power of the Spirit to the pulling down of strongholds, moving upon us so that the power of God is seen upon us.

[Interpretation of Tongues: "God hath designed the fullness of the Gospel in its perfection and entirety that where the Breath of Heaven breathes upon it, the Gospel which is the power of God unto salvation makes everything form in perfect union with divine power, till the whole man becomes a lovely hope—filled with life, filled with fidelity."])

Remember that Jesus is all fullness. Remember Jesus was the fullness of the Godhead. The Holy Ghost makes Him so precious that: "It's all right now, it's all right now, For Jesus is my Saviour, and it's all right now."

I want you all to have a share! Oh, for the Holy Ghost to come with freshness upon us, then you all could sing, "It's all right now!" Let me encourage you. God is a God of encouragement. Now turn to Hebrews 4:13:

> Neither is there any creature that is not manifest in his sight: but all things are naked and opened unto the eyes of him with whom we have to do.

No creature is hid from His sight, all are naked before Him. When God speaks of nakedness, He does not mean that He looks at flesh without clothing. He looks at our spiritual lack and desires that we are clothed with Christ within. He sees your weakness, your sorrow of heart. He is looking right into you now. Oh, what does He see?

Seeing then that we have a great high priest, that is passed into the heavens, Jesus the Son of God, let us hold fast our profession.

Hebrews 4:14

What is our profession? I have heard so many people testifying about their profession. Some said, "Thank God, He has baptized me with the Holy Ghost." That is my profession, is it yours? That is the profession of the Bible, and God wants to make it your profession. You have a whole Christ, a full redemption. You have to be filled with the Holy Ghost, a channel for Him to flow through. Oh, the glorious liberty of the gospel of God's power!

Heaven has begun with me,

I am happy now, and free

Since the Comforter has come,

Since the Comforter has come.

It's all there. I know that God has designed this fullness, this rest, this perfect rest. He has designed it, and there ought not to be a wrinkle, a spot, a blemish. The Word of God says "blameless." Praise the Lord for such a wonderful, glorious inheritance, through Him that loved us. Hallelujah!

Beloved, you must come in, every one of you. This morning's meeting is to open the door of your heart so that God can move in so that if you were to go away to live in some solitary place, you would be full there the same as in the Wellington Assembly. It would make no difference. The authorities tried to destroy John and sent him to the Isle of Patmos, but on a desert island he was "in the Spirit." It is possible to be in the Spirit wherever you are, in all circumstances.

> For we have not an high priest which cannot be touched with the feeling of our infirmities; but was in all points tempted like as we are, yet without sin.
>
> Hebrews 4:15

There He is! There is the pattern! There is the Lord! You say, "Tell me something wonderful about Him." I will tell you this, He loved us to the end. He had faith in us right to the end.

"There remaineth therefore a rest to the people of God" (Heb. 4:9). Some say, "O, yes, it is a rest up there." No! No! No! *This* rest is here, where we cease from our own works, this day!

I came to this meeting this morning entirely shut in with God, and if ever God spoke in a meeting, He has spoken this morning.

I may have been straight and plain on some lines, but I had such a vision of Wellington. I saw clearly people were resisting the Holy Ghost, as much as when Stephen said, "Ye stiffnecked and uncircumcised in heart and ears, ye do always resist the Holy Ghost: as your fathers did, so do ye" (Acts 7:51).

Oh, if you won't resist the Holy Ghost the power of God will melt you down. The Holy Ghost will so take charge of you that you will be filled to the uttermost with the overflowing of His grace.

The Gifts of the Spirit: Prophecy and Tongues

It is necessary that we have a great desire for spiritual gifts. God must bring us into a place where we thirst after them. They are necessary. They are important. May we, by the grace of God see their importance, so that we may be used for God's glory.

First, *Prophecy.* If you are saved here this morning, it is because of some person (who) was inspired and loved upon by the Spirit of Jesus to let the light of this glorious gospel come to you. Sometimes I think we miss what God has for us in the Gospels. I want you to see a word God has for us. It is pure gospel truth.

> Who hath saved us, and called us with an holy calling, not according to our works, but according to his own purpose and grace, which was given us in Christ Jesus before the world began,
>
> But is now made manifest by the appearing of our Saviour Jesus Christ, who hath abolished death, and hath brought life and immortality to light through the gospel.
>
> 2 Timothy 1:9–10

The Lord help us to see that above all, whatever we do, we seek the gift of prophecy. Now there are three classes of prophecy I want to speak about.

Bubbling Up: There is a prophetic utterance which you will find very often when I am speaking. So often when I am speaking, the Holy Ghost speaks through me in a flow of language. This is prophetic utterance which every Spirit-baptized believer ought to have. Holy Ghost ministry, Holy Ghost language, and Holy Ghost thought. Standing there clothed upon with prophetic utterances, always coinciding with God's will.

Another kind of prophecy is *testimony.* If you people in this Town Hall will come to meetings filled with the Holy Ghost and there is a chance to give your testimony, let it be a Holy Ghost utterance. Then people will feel that it is from the Holy Ghost. It will be different from any human testimony. In yourself, you can give your testimony until it is barren! "For the testimony of Jesus is the spirit of prophecy" (Rev. 19:10). Jesus said His words are spirit and life.

The last kind of prophecy is *the prophetic utterance in the assembly,* when everyone knows it is from the Lord.

> But he that prophesieth speaketh unto men to edification, and exhortation, and comfort.
>
> 1 Corinthians 14:3

Prophecy will not be denunciation. God wants you to have this prophecy, so that you rise up as if you had risen up out of death into life. You would be uttering divine revelation and consolation. It might be on the line of the coming of the Lord, or the atoning blood, or about the moving of the Spirit in our midst; but it will be to comfort, console and edify.

> For he that speaketh in an unknown tongue speaketh not unto men, but unto God: for no man understandeth him; howbeit in the spirit he speaketh mysteries.
>
> 1 Corinthians 14:2

This is a wonderful verse for anyone who has had a weary day, or is going through hard trials. You get before the Lord with such an utterance, and you will find that God by His Spirit will lift you, move you. It has not to be interpreted, it is spoken to God by the Spirit.

Laughter in the Holy Ghost: It may seem to some people very strange, but I have seen people come into a meeting down and out, exhausted. The power of God has come on them with laughter. Laughter in the Holy Ghost brings you out of everything! It is a thing you cannot create. The Holy Ghost laughs through you. You laugh from the inside. The whole body is so full of the Spirit of life from above that you are altogether new. For God to come into a needy soul and create laughter within is very wonderful.

Praying in the Spirit: Now we come to another wonderful word which is important. We must understand this morning that we are at the footstool of grace, and God the Holy Ghost is our Teacher. We must listen to see what God has to say to us at this time.

Some people think there is only one kind of prayer that brings down blessing, but you will find when God the Holy Ghost takes you, He can, through one pure heart, bring revival in spite of every power in the world. This verse we have been looking at is an unknown Scripture except to those who have received the Holy Ghost. Who is speaking? The Holy Spirit. To whom? To God. Where shall we find a verse to give us clear revelation on this? In Romans 8:26–27:

> Likewise the Spirit also helpeth our infirmities: for we know not what we should pray for as we ought: but the Spirit itself maketh intercession for us with groanings that cannot be uttered.
>
> And he that searcheth the hearts knoweth what is the mind of the Spirit, because he maketh intercession for the saints according to the will of God.

It is not you, remember! It is the Spirit that is in you, that is, the Holy Ghost.

Jesus is the Advocate.

The Father is the Answerer.

The Holy Spirit is the Pray-er.

The Spirit searches the hearts. Right in the heart, God is searching by the light of His Spirit. When God is moving in the heart, the Spirit begins to pray that God will be satisfied. The Holy Spirit prays through you and brings down the blessing!

[Tongues with interpretation: "The Lord Himself, it is He which hath opened into our heart His great fullness and now through the power of Himself is bringing out the great cry of the soul, mingled with the Spirit's cry, till heaven bends down and grants."]

I believe it would be helpful for me to tell you about Willie Burton, a missionary leader in Central Africa. He is a man with a big heart, doing a great work for God, a mighty man of God. He took fever and went down into death.

The people said, "He has preached his last. What shall we do?" All their hopes were blighted. They stood there broken-hearted. They left him for dead.

In a moment, without any signal, he stood in the midst of them. They could not understand it. He told them that he came to himself feeling a warmth through his body, right through. He rose, perfectly healed. It was a mystery, until he came to London. (There) he told the people (in a meeting) how he had been left for dead, and how he was raised up.

A lady came to him afterwards and asked, "Do you keep a diary?" When he said he did, she told him this:

"One day I went to pray, and as soon as I knelt down, you came to my mind. The Spirit of the Lord took hold of me and prayed through me in an unknown tongue. A vision came and I saw you laid out helpless. I cried out in the tongue till I saw you risen up, and go out of that room."

He turned to his diary and found it was exactly the date he had been raised up.

I want you to see that being filled with the Holy Ghost gives you great capabilities, even in your own room! Or anywhere! The Holy Ghost can give you liberty. He is wisdom; He is the Spirit of prophecy; He is the Spirit of revelation. Remember God wants you to be filled with the Holy Ghost. Everything about you will be changed by the dynamite of heaven!

There is one very important thing to be dealt with this morning. I want you to see in the first place that he who speaks in an unknown tongue edifies himself. We must be edified before we can edify the Church. The Holy Ghost has full charge of wisdom, so He comes to us on wisdom lines. Now in what revelation or capability or capacity will the Holy Ghost edify us if we are ready?

Language? None! Inability—full of it! I am here before you this morning as one of the biggest conundrums in the world. All the things about my life are entirely against the likelihood of me standing on this platform before you. There never was a weaker man on a platform. All things about my life are exactly opposite to the likelihood of me standing here, but the Holy Ghost came and brought edification.

I had been reading this Word all my life as well as I could, then the Holy Ghost came and took hold of it. The Holy Ghost is the breath of it and quickened it to me to edify me, so that I might edify the Church. He gave me language that I cannot speak fast enough. It is there because God has given it.

When the Comforter has come, He teaches you all things. First John 2:20,27 says:

But ye have an unction from the Holy One, and ye know all things.

But the anointing which ye have received of him abideth in you, and ye need not that any man teach you: but as the same anointing teacheth you of all things, and is truth, and is no lie, and even as it hath taught you, ye shall abide in him.

I am not leaving out the people who are not baptized in the Holy Ghost, but am putting you all as one. Because I believe God wants you all baptized. I believe you will go on until you are.

After you are baptized you may say, "I seem so dry. I don't know where I am."

The Word says you have an unction. Thank God, you have an anointing. The Holy Ghost is wisdom, language, and revelation, and He will teach you all things because of the anointing that abides, because of the Holy One that is in you. These are great and definite positions for us. In the Psalms, you often read "Selah." That means "Stop and think." I want you to think this over.

If the Holy Ghost wants to do anything it is to stir up your faith this morning to believe that this word is God's truth. If you allow yourself to rise up in spirit today, you will edify yourself.

Lord, lift me up and let me stand,
By faith on heaven's table-land;
Where love, and joy, and light abound,
Lord, plant my feet on higher ground.

ENDNOTES

1. Frodsham, Stanley. *Smith Wigglesworth—Apostle of Faith* (Springfield: Gospel Publishing House, 1948), p. 111.

2. *Apostle of Faith*, p. 135.

3. Chadwick, Samuel. *The Call of Christian Perfection*, (London: Epworth Press, 1936), p. 90.

4. Roberts, Harry V. *New Zealand, Greatest Revival*, (Auckland: Pelorus Press Ltd., 1951).

5. New Zealand's Greatest Revival, p. 11.

6. *Elim Evangel* 3.676.

7. Faith That Prevails, p. 51.

8. *New Zealand's Greatest Revival*, p. 29.

PRAYER OF SALVATION

God loves you—no matter who you are, no matter what your past. God loves you so much that He gave His one and only begotten Son for you. The Bible tells us that "...whoever believes in him shall not perish but have eternal life" (John 3:16 NIV). Jesus laid down His life and rose again so that we could spend eternity with Him in heaven and experience His absolute best on earth. If you would like to receive Jesus into your life, say the following prayer out loud and mean it from your heart.

Heavenly Father, I come to You admitting that I am a sinner. Right now, I choose to turn away from sin, and I ask You to cleanse me of all unrighteousness. I believe that Your Son, Jesus, died on the cross to take away my sins. I also believe that He rose again from the dead so that I might be forgiven of my sins and made righteous through faith in Him. I call upon the name of Jesus Christ to be the Savior and Lord of my life. Jesus, I choose to follow You and ask that You fill me with the power of the Holy Spirit. I declare that right now I am a child of God. I am free from sin and full of the righteousness of God. I am saved in Jesus' name. Amen.

If you prayed this prayer to receive Jesus Christ as your Savior for the first time, please contact us on the web at **www.harrisonhouse.com** to receive a free book.

Or you may write to us at

Harrison House
P.O. Box 35035
Tulsa, Oklahoma 74153

ABOUT THE AUTHOR

George Stormont of Duluth, Minnesota, was born in 1909 in Birmingham, England, and knew Smith Wigglesworth personally as a friend and a colleague for many years. Born again in June, 1918, he has served the Lord faithfully as school teacher, Bible college teacher, pastor, and evangelist.

He entered the full-time ministry in 1933. In addition to pastoring five churches in England, he pastored Duluth Gospel Tabernacle in Duluth, Minnesota, for five years. He served as superintendent of Elim Pentecostal Churches, England, for a quarter *of* a century, and for many years, he was a member of the Elim Church Inc.'s executive presbytery.

In addition, he served as national secretary of the British Pentecostal Fellowship and member of the following missionary councils: Elim Missionary Council, The Pentecostal Jewish Mission, Congo (now Zaire) Evangelistic Mission, and Russian and Eastern European Mission.

In 1963, he was invited to pastor Bethshan Tabernacle, Manchester, at the time the largest Assembly of God church in Great Britain. He transferred his membership then to the Assemblies of God, and in 1974, was elected chairman of the Conference of Assemblies of God.

In addition to pioneering new churches, Stormont conducted evangelistic and teaching crusades all over the world.

He was married to Ruth Kingston in 1938, and they had two children, Andrew and Deryn.

SMITH WIGGLESWORTH: THE SECRET OF HIS POWER

Albert Hibbert, friend and confidant of the world-renown 20th century minister Smith Wigglesworth, relates his personal accounts of this remarkable man of God.

"In the recorded history of mankind, few people have accomplished more in the realm of the supernatural than Smith Wigglesworth."

—Albert Hibbert

Discover the secret of Smith Wigglesworth's amazing relationship with God and relive the undeniable miracles performed under his ministry.

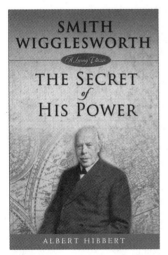

Smith Wigglesworth: The Secret of His Power

ISBN: 978-1-57794-977-0

SMITH WIGGLESWORTH: A LIFE ABLAZE WITH THE POWER OF GOD

Author W. Hacking, son-in-law to Smith Wigglesworth, reveals personal insights into the life of this 20th century apostle. Uncover Smith's intimate relationship with God, how he flowed in God's supernatural power, and his personal commitment and dedication to God's Holy Word.

Smith Wigglesworth:
A Life Ablaze With the Power of God

ISBN: 978-1-57794-976-3

OTHER LIVING CLASSIC BOOKS FROM HARRISON HOUSE

John G. Lake: Diary of God's General

Questions and Answers on Spiritual Gifts—Howard Carter

His Healing Power—Lilian B. Yeomans

Healing the Sick—T. L. Osborn

Available from your local bookstore

or from **www.harrisonhouse.com**.